A Divided Command

DAVID DONACHIE

Allison & Busby Limited
12 Fitzroy Mews
London W1T 6DW
www.allisonandbusby.com

First published in Great Britain by Allison & Busby in 2013.
This paperback edition published by Allison & Busby in 2014.

A CIP catalogue record for this book is available from
the British Library.

10 9 8 7 6 5 4 3 2 1

ISBN 978-0-7490-1677-7

Typeset in 10.5/16 pt Adobe Garamond Pro by
Allison & Busby Ltd.

The paper used for this Allison & Busby publication
has been produced from trees that have been legally sourced
from well-managed and credibly certified forests.

Printed and bound by
CPI Group (UK) Ltd, Croydon, CR0 4YY

To Laura and Olly who, if not related,
feel very like family.

All the best for your coming wedding
and for the arrival of your firstborn child, Sol

CHAPTER ONE

Sleep was fitful at best; there had been little wind for days and even inside the solid stone walls of the fortress of Calvi the high summer heat was oppressive, made more so by the number of men who now shared the limited space. To begin with Midshipman Toby Burns had occupied the cell on his own but in the weeks since his own capture the numbers of prisoners had grown. Officers of the three services, two navy, the rest army, as well as one marine, victims of many failed assaults on the formidable walls, had fallen into enemy hands, till they now numbered two dozen souls. At least as officers they were above ground, not a fate gifted to the common soldiers who shared their captivity; they were in a foetid dungeon.

Added to the stifling humidity were the other things that disturbed them, apart from merely being crowded into too small a space: the active vermin that shared each lumpy straw palliasse as well as the floor on which they were laid, these added to the number of flying and biting insects that seemed determined to feed on any exposed skin. Finally there were the rats, wary in daylight when the cell occupants were awake, bolder in the darkness of the night when the scrabbling of their tiny paws gave a fearful alert to their close presence.

For Toby Burns, when sleep was finally brought on by exhaustion, there was little respite, that being when he was exposed to the terror of his too vivid dreams. The things of which the youngster was frightened were legion and seemed to come to him in a tumbling panorama: shot and shell, naturally, to which he had been exposed too many times in his short naval career; the fear of drowning too, even if that had only nearly occurred once – yet still the memory haunted him. He would be struggling in the lashing waters that pounded the rocky shores of Brittany, sure he was about to die, until a strong adult hand grabbed him and hauled him on to the shore.

Then there would appear the disappointed faces of his parents, siblings and the people of his hometown, eager to castigate him for being less than an admirable representative of both their civic and family honour. How had they discovered he was not their acclaimed and much feted hero, but a liar and a coward?

Worst of all were the remembered faces of those he knew were out to get him maimed, killed or permanently locked up in prison. Admiral Hotham was very much of the former and allied to him was Toby's uncle by marriage, Captain Ralph Barclay. Even his Aunt Emily, who had married Barclay and was kind in the flesh, became a termagant and an accuser in his heated nocturnal imaginings.

Worst of all was John Pearce, a man with nothing but malice in his heart for a youth who had acted against him, not out of the same emotion but from the pressure applied to him by adults who hated a fellow they feared might be their nemesis.

At times they were naught but voices, soft in their reproval of his actions, but as the sweat ran off his body to soak the straw and his visions became more troubled, these chimeras would begin to shout, turning often into slavering beasts that seemed to want to tear at his naked flesh.

Flight was impossible; try as he might to escape, his legs would not obey the instructions of his mind and soon his whole body would feel as if it was trapped in some huge web of tangled ropes, unable to get away, while those who sought to devour him came ever closer, their voices of contempt rising to a crescendo.

'For the love of God, Burns, will you stop that damned caterwauling?'

It was not the sound of the complaint that brought Toby back to soaked wakefulness but the boot that kicked him, with scant gentility, in the ribs. Eyes open he had no initial idea where he was; the beamed ceiling could have been his attic bedroom or his old school dormitory, body blows being nothing unusual in the latter. Just then the boom of a cannon came through the barred slit in the wall, which brought him back fully to reality and, with a turn of his head, the glaring face of the naval lieutenant who had so rudely awakened him.

'Leave the poor lad alone.'

The response to that remonstrance was the harsh growl of an angry man and a dry throat. 'I cannot abide the noise, damn it.'

'Yet I do not hear you curse our fellows on the high ground for setting off their cannon.'

Sitting upright, the grey light of dawn was enough to show Toby the two men in dispute, one a naval lieutenant called Watson, the other, the fellow defending him, a major of infantry. This knowledge of identity and rank came from previous contact, for neither man was wearing uniform; indeed, the marine was without even a shirt, his bare and hairy torso gleaming with sweat. The navy man was clothed in his long shirt, a piece of linen that no longer showed the least trace of the white it had once been, so stained was it with perspiration and accumulated filth.

The lieutenant was unrepentant. 'Gunfire hints at salvation from this hellhole, sir, but the moans and screams of this fellow seem as portents of hell. I felt I was trying to sleep in Bedlam.'

'Forgive me, sir,' Toby croaked, 'for if I do disturb you, I am not aware of my doing so.'

'Thank the Lord I do not have to share a berth with you, Burns. I feel pity for your fellow mids if you behave in a similar manner aboard ship.'

The infantry major, a Scotsman who went by the name of Buchanan, was not listening; he had stepped over the still recumbent Toby to look out of a slot in the stonework that had once facilitated the firing of arrows, talking over his shoulder.

'Are you so fixated on your annoyance, sir, that you cannot register the fact that our French friends have not responded – in short, they have not returned fire as they normally do?'

'Perhaps,' Watson spat, 'they are allowed a better level of rest than that which is afforded to us – in short, they are still asleep.'

The next sound was not of a single cannon, but a salvo coming from a whole multitude of muzzles, as the whole of the besieging batteries opened up as one. That was followed by the combined whistles of their flight, then the various sounds as they struck home; sharp cracks on immoveable stone, dull repeated thuds if they bounced along the hard ground, the breaking of timbers and tiles if something less solid than fortress walls stood in their path, that whole cacophony followed by silence, which brought forth a whisper from Major Buchanan.

'And still the French are idle.' He turned to look at Toby, a wide smile on an unshaved face made bright red by heat. 'It would seem to me we are approaching a crisis in the action, young sir. Happen it will not be long before you do get to test your dreams again in that ship's berth.'

The rattle of keys brought all the occupants of the cell, Toby included, to their feet as the door swung open to reveal a sergeant bearing a pail. If the food they were about to receive was of poor quality, it was still sustenance and there was no other, even if payment was proffered. Yet more welcome was the fellow who came next with the water bucket and ladle, who cursed away in French as he sought to get the prisoners to form an orderly queue for a much needed drink.

There was another bucket in the room, the one that was used throughout the day, as well as the hours of darkness, for the prisoners to relieve themselves, and given their numbers it was near to overflowing with piss, while several turds floated alarmingly close to the lip. The French sergeant, once he had dished out his gruel, looked at it meaningfully, for that which was needed did not constitute a duty that fell to a gaoler.

'When you are done eating, Burns, empty the slops,' Watson ordered.

Buchanan raised his head from the wooden plate from which he was trying to scrape the last morsels of too little food. 'Have I not suggested it should be a duty shared? It is not the turn of Mr Burns, who was obliged, I recall, to carry it out yesterday.'

'He's the lowest in rank, sir, and so it should fall to him by right. This is not some Jacobin Republic.'

As Toby Burns made to move and obey his naval superior, Buchanan snapped at him to stay still.

'I do believe I have the seniority here and if I cannot get my way by agreement then I must insist on an imposition of authority. We are all equally prisoners and thus we will all take turns at emptying the slops.' He looked directly at Watson. 'And you, sir, will take the duty this day.'

There was a moment when Watson looked set to challenge the instruction, for no naval officer took readily to being ordered about by a bullock, whatever his rank. Making sure his reluctance was obvious, Watson picked up the slops bucket, and to drive home that his servility was not misconstrued, he made sure, as he passed Buchanan, that a small amount of the yellow liquid spilt onto the major's scuffed shoes.

'Splendid,' Buchanan cried, his broad face now alight; he was obviously determined not to be put out by such a deliberate and calculated insult. 'The Romans used piss for the purpose of cleaning, so how can I object to being obliged to employ the same when I have no boot black to hand! No doubt it is as much a naval tradition to wallow in piss as it was to the ancients.'

What followed Watson out of the cell door was laughter, not the silent approval he had clearly hoped for from a group of mainly redcoats, he and Toby Burns being the only sailors.

'Do you really think we are approaching a crisis, sir?' asked Toby.

'The French still do not respond, young fellow, which leads me to suspect they are short of both powder and shot. If they are low on that, it is safe, I think, to assume they will be short on other essentials, food especially, for they have the population of the town to feed as well as the garrison. If that is the case, then they have no choice but to parley for an honourable conclusion or face starvation.'

'I do so hope you are correct, sir, for I have spent more time cooped up here than anyone.'

'True,' Buchanan replied; he had only arrived two days previously, having become isolated following an assault that had carried one of the major French outworks. 'And I have to say I have found your nocturnal screams a bore, making me wonder what it is that so troubles you when you close your eyes?'

That had Toby floundering; he could hardly allude to his fear of death or mutilation in battle, that would never do, and nor did he want to mention anyone from his own family as the stuff of his nightmares. To allude to Admiral Hotham or even his Uncle Ralph, a full post captain well above three years in seniority, was to open a tub of worms best left sealed. So the name he mumbled was the only one that he could safely think to use.

'There is a fellow called John Pearce, sir, he comes to me in the night and never fails to induce terror.'

'He must be something of a monster, lad, to affect you so?'

'Oh, he is that, sir,' Toby replied with real venom, quite overlooking the fact that Pearce owned the hand that had once saved him from drowning. 'A true Gorgon.'

The vessels of the Mediterranean Fleet stood at single anchor in the Bay of San Fiorenzo, proof of the sound nature of the sheltered haven as well as the depth of water beneath and surrounding their keels; they could swing 360 degrees on the tide without fear of grounding. From first rates to frigates they were well lit by the blazing sunshine and, after a sudden downpour that had left the air clean and dropped the temperature several degrees, they provided, at a distance, a stirring and impressive sight, even to one as jaundiced about such things as Lieutenant John Pearce.

That impression faded somewhat the closer he came to a proper view, for proximity showed that the loose sails now flapping and drying in the wind were far from the pristine canvas they had once been, no longer a smooth cream in colour, instead a dun and much stained brown, more than one showing evidence of repair, so that even to his untrained eye the wear caused by endless exposure to the elements was obvious.

The myriad miles of ropes and cables necessary to make up the rigging, despite the layers of tar used to protect them, would be likewise degraded, and closer still the scantlings of the warships showed where endless layers of black paint had been applied, only to crack and split from the effect of sun, wind and rain, leaving a pattern on their chequered hulls that reminded Pearce of the bark of a diseased tree. It was impossible not to wonder at what that paint, badly in need of being scraped off, was hiding.

'I don't think I ever realised, Mr Dorling, what people meant when they bemoaned the lack of a proper dockyard.'

The sailing master of *HMS Larcher*, for all he was young, managed to reply with all the mordant gloom of those of his elders who saw no joy anywhere when rating the state for sailing of any vessel in King George's Navy: in doing so he replicated his captain's ruminations.

'What you can see won't be the half of it, Capt'n. Don't take much to imagine that there's a rate of rotten timber in them scantlings and the hulls will be in a bad way too, after a year in

14

the Med, copper-bottomed or no. Stands to reason, weed in warm water is a mite more apt to grow than it does close to home shores.'

'Flag's made our pennant, Your Honour,' came the cry from the masthead. 'Captain to repair aboard.'

That made the recipient smile: had Pearce observed the same message, run up on the halyards of *HMS Victory*, he would have, just to be sure there was no mistake and aware of the gaps in his own nautical knowledge, consulted the signal book. Not so the able seaman aloft, who was certainly no more advanced in years than he. No doubt the fellow had been at sea since he was a boy and that was a flag message he had observed fluttering too many times to have any doubts.

'Acknowledge and prepare the signal gun, if you please.'

Addressed to no one in particular these instructions were obeyed without fuss or noise. These men knew their duties and had been a well-worked-up crew long before John Pearce took temporary command of the ship. If the lieutenant he replaced had imposed his will by a form of low-level brutality that made him disliked, he had commanded better seamen than he knew.

John Pearce, with his more benign manner, albeit he would not be played upon, was certain he had brought out the best in men who were willing and very capable, which was just as well, given he was a commander who often had to think hard before issuing any orders. It was moot how many times their skill had silently mitigated his ignorance, a subject about which the dignity of his position forbade him to enquire.

'Anchor astern of the flag, Capt'n?' Dorling asked.

'Make it so,' Pearce replied. 'But come to it by sailing alongside – the quarterdeck will want to cast an eye over the state of our decks and the orderliness of our rigging and no doubt scoff.'

'Admiral might be lookin' hisself, sir,' Dorling replied, though there was a rasp in his tone that dared anyone to say a bad word about an armed cutter for which he had, as did the whole crew, a very proprietorial feeling.

Pearce nodded, yet he doubted that such an elevated person as Lord Hood, even if he were placed to observe, would spare such a minnow of a ship so much as a passing glance.

'Old Sam goes by the name of a tartar, I am told, sir.'

The temptation to reply as he wished had to be suppressed. Admiral Lord Hood, the C-in-C Mediterranean was, to John Pearce, a crusty despot as well as a devious and untrustworthy old bugger, who had no scruples whatsoever when it came to the abuse of his inferiors, which made it doubly galling that Old Sam, as he was affectionately known throughout the fleet, was much loved by the lower decks as well as a goodly number of his officers.

The notion that all did not share such warmth had Pearce looking towards *HMS Britannia*, rocking gently on the swell not far off, another first rate of 100 guns and home to Hood's second in command, Admiral Sir William Hotham. There was no affection for Old Sam there; the pair loathed each other at a distance and it was far from cordial even in public, while those captains who saw Hotham as their patron took the side of the man they looked to for advancement. That their feelings were exacerbated by the way Hood favoured his own client officers when it came to profitable cruising only rubbed salt into an already open wound.

Behind him Dorling was quietly issuing the orders that would bring *HMS Larcher* to the required station, this interspersed with the ritual, which Pearce saw as wasteful nonsense in terms of time and powder – not to mention the act of supplication itself – of firing off the small brass cannon that acted as a signal gun, the requisite number of times that were needed to remind a commanding vice admiral of that which was his due.

As soon as the armed cutter backed its topsails and the way came off the ship, the boat that would take John Pearce aboard the flagship hit the water, the men needed to row it, wearing their best rig, swift to take their stations, each oar set upright at a perfect angle once they were seated.

So close to the C-in-C and such a famous ship of the line, his crew were determined to display their smartness and efficiency. It was sad to reflect that, even if Hood was looking their way and even if they did make a good impression, it would be shattered as soon as the admiral saw who was in command; he and John Pearce were not and never had been on easy terms.

For all the sea state was good, there was still a swell of the kind that sent up a goodly quantity of spray and there had been rain, to guard against which he was presented, despite the warmth of the day, with his boat cloak, this so that his fine broadcloth coat, put on in anticipation of the summons like his best cocked hat, would not be streaked with salt.

The man who proffered this was his good friend and 'servant', Michael O'Hagan: friend because of many shared vicissitudes, servant for the very simple reason that the provision of one embarrassed the man being catered to; so much better to have someone see to his needs who was not in the least bit servile.

'Sure, it's the lion's den once more, John-boy,' Michael whispered, his mouth close to Pearce's ear, as he placed the garment over his shoulders.

'At least the early Christians only had to suffer it once.'

'And were martyred for their pains,' O'Hagan responded.

The voice, with its strong Irish accent, had taken on a sepulchral tone, for Michael O'Hagan was strong in his Roman faith and much given to crossing himself if he felt threatened. Not that such a thing happened too frequently: he was a veritable giant and a very handy fellow with his ham-like fists, so any fears tended towards the superstitious, not the human.

'Perhaps there is a pantheon somewhere, Michael, for non-believers.'

'There is John-boy. It's called Hell.'

With that O'Hagan stepped away, his manner immediately becoming respectful, which he was always careful to do when others could overhear his words. 'Will Your Honour be after requiring your sword, which I fetched from the cabin?'

'Best not, Michael,' Pearce replied grimly, as he was handed an oilskin pouch containing the letters he had brought from London. 'The temptation to employ it on Old Sam would be too difficult to resist.'

Before going over the side, Pearce cast an eye over the remaining crew, busy working to secure the vessel for anchoring, which would happen once the captain of the fleet, or the lesser being to whom he delegated the task, had allotted them a spot in the deep and wide bay. If he had become caring of the whole crew of *HMS Larcher*, none could match the affection he felt for the men he had so recently rescued, by a clever exchange, from the grip and the ship of Captain Ralph Barclay, a man they all hated.

Charlie Taverner and Rufus Dommet, along with him and Michael O'Hagan, went collectively by the soubriquet taken from the tavern, the Pelican, out of which they had at one time been illegally pressed. With Pearce they enjoyed a shared history that surpassed that of the rest of the crew and his glance was rewarded as both men looked up from their labours to throw him a warm smile and a short wave of the kind that on some ships, and under their previous captain, might have seen them stapled to the deck or even flogged.

As was custom the pipe blew as he went over the side, which was merely a single step down, to where he took up his place in the thwarts, *HMS Larcher*'s cutter being cast off smartly and with what Pearce could only reckon as display, so well-timed was the strike of the oars. His men were showing the away to the whole fleet, full – to their minds – of jumped-up jackanapes who would struggle to control a bumboat.

CHAPTER TWO

More whistling greeted his arrival aboard *HMS Victory*, commencing as he made his way up the set of steps that led to the entry port. Coming from strong sunlight into darkness meant he could not at first see who was there to greet him, and it came as a surprise to find out it was a fellow called Furness, who, when they had previously met, had been no higher in the hierarchy of the flagship than sixth lieutenant.

That made Pearce bristle, for it implied a deliberate insult; ranked as a master and commander, he being in command of an unrated vessel, he was yet the captain of a King's ship and deserved to be greeted by someone of higher standing than a sixth. Even if he was not prickly by nature, John Pearce had been the subject of much condescension from other naval officers in his time in the service and was wont to react badly if such a trait seemed to be on display.

Furness laid that to rest immediately: he now named himself

and with some pride as the premier, which was more than fitting. He had been told who was approaching by the officer of the watch, Pearce being no stranger on a ship he had been obliged to board more times than he was happy to recall.

Yet the ceremony was not yet complete: a party of half a dozen marines stamped to attention, which obliged Pearce to rate their smartness and issue a compliment to the lieutenant in command, before Furness took him aside for a less formal greeting, which allowed Pearce, with some relief, to divest himself of his heavy cloak.

The premier was keen that he should dine in the wardroom if no other duty interfered, for this particular officer, if he was something of a thorn to the admiral, as well as a lieutenant of dubious provenance, was also a fellow with tales to tell of successful naval actions, this in a circle where the reprising of gallant deeds was the very stuff of conversation.

Then there was his luck, which was seen by many as boundless and enviable, for no man could prosper in the King's Navy without opportunity. By both accident and design Pearce had been given a great deal of both; the members of the wardroom would wish for some of that lustre to rub off on them.

Pearce was sure there would be others in that same body that resented him, perhaps even some who harboured both emotions simultaneously, given the way he had come about his rank and the favour he had enjoyed since. Yet such was the level of good manners in a naval mess, necessary for men who spent months and sometimes years at sea in each other's company, he would not be made aware of it.

Furness brought Pearce up to date on the progress of the campaign in the Mediterranean since the debacle at Toulon, filling in with more detail than Pearce already knew the successful subjugation of Bastia, including the fact, delivered with something of a sneer, that it had been a naval expedition; the army had been dead against it, only turning up when it was obvious Corsica's main commercial port was about to fall.

Lord Hood had accepted the surrender before returning north, where, off the coast of Provence, he had encountered and chased the French fleet, forcing the enemy capital ships to seek safety in a Languedoc bay called Golfe Juan. There they relied on the narrow access created by a promontory and a set of offshore islands to prevent an attack.

Not so easily deterred and seeing them at single anchor, which meant deep water on their beam, Hood had attempted to sail in and get behind them on their landward side. This ploy had failed due to an alert French admiral, who had spotted the risk and moved his ships into shallower water where there was no channel at either end of his line for an enemy to sail through. They were still there, under the watchful eye of a couple of British frigates; should they emerge, Hood would immediately up anchor and seek to intercept them as they made for their home port of Toulon.

'What of Calvi?' Pearce enquired, for he had been told at Gibraltar of that operation.

'Still under siege, Mr Pearce. Captain Nelson is in command of artillery, which has been provided and manned by tars. They have, I am told, loosed off some twenty thousand balls into the fortress and town. When they make a breach, General Stuart sends forward the assault troops, though Nelson makes sure his officers have the chance to take part in any endeavours.'

'And, no doubt, he is to the fore himself.'

'You know Nelson?'

'Well enough to be sure that if there be shot and shell flying, that is where you will find him.'

The man's voice, as he agreed to that opinion, failed to hide his own gloom of being at a distance from the action: every officer in the navy craved a chance to excel in battle – and if that was on land it mattered not – this to gain the kind of glory that enhanced their chances of advancement. Even for a man so well placed for eventual good fortune as Furness – flagship officers got the fastest promotion and he must be in line for the next unrated ship – it was no different.

If it was a pleasant interlude, Pearce could not linger and he made his way to the tiny office set outside the great cabin, home to Lord Hood's senior clerk. There was no doubting the manner in which he was viewed in that quarter; as supercilious as every admiral's factotum tended to be, the clerk treated him with a level of disdain which no doubt reflected that of his master, swift to report that His Lordship was busy and it might be some time before he was called into the magisterial presence.

'You may not have observed it, fellow,' Pearce snapped, in a tone that got him a glare for this diminutive form of address, 'but someone else will. I am sailing under an Admiralty pennant, which means the despatches I am carrying are of a superior importance to that which is normal, and, I would add, they come from William Pitt himself.'

A momentary pause was taken to allow that name to sink in.

'If Lord Hood would not keep the King's First Minister waiting, it would ill behove him to do that to his chosen messenger. So, if Sam Almighty does not know who is here, please be so good as to tell him and also to pass on what I carry and from whom.'

Personal feelings of dignity required a decent pause before the injunction was acceded to, just to show that it was a considered response, not a reaction to an instruction. 'I will tell His Lordship you are waiting.'

'Thank you, my man,' Pearce replied, happy to see that the words and the haughty way they were imparted made the clerk actually wince.

'What damned sewer is it, Pearce, that throws you up with such regularity? I cannot but believe a bad penny would be disgraced in your presence.'

'As I recall it, Milord, the sewer you mention is the one much troubled by rats festooned in gold braid.'

Rear-Admiral Sir William Parker, the captain of the fleet and Hood's executive officer, standing at his superior's seated shoulder, had been brought to a grin at Lord Hood's welcoming words. The response Pearce gave soon wiped that away and he countered with a bark.

'I see that absence has not taught you respect!'

'I think I have pointed out, Admiral Parker, in this cabin and more than once, that respect is not something I am inclined to grant automatically merely to ingratiate myself with someone of rank.'

'Pearce,' Hood sighed, 'you have no idea how I long for the powers of an ancient tyrant, for it would give me great pleasure to still that loose tongue of yours by dragging it from your mouth with hot pincers.'

A hand came out to take the oilskin pouch, one with prominent bones and several large brown spots on the back. 'Now, what is it you have for me, given I long to see your back?'

'It is a letter I am instructed to say is for your eyes only.'

That made Hood visibly stiffen: it took no genius to work out that if it was not a normal set of instructions and was highly personal it was unlikely to be welcome in its contents. Hood stood and took the pouch over to the line of casements that made up the rear of his cabin, where the light was strongest. Still with his back to both Pearce and Parker he extracted Pitt's letter and broke the seal, speaking as he did so.

'You will oblige me, Lieutenant, by passing on to your crew, most particularly those who handled your cutter, my appreciation of their conduct. The vessel was anchored in fine style and the rowers were smart and efficient. I can only assume you have aboard your vessel someone who knows how to train a crew and sail a ship.'

'I would not claim to take credit for their level of ability,' Pearce replied, seeking to keep the surprise out of his voice; had the old sod really been watching and rating the men he led?

The fact that Hood was reading imposed silence by the mere act and looking at him, silhouetted against the sunlight streaming through the casements, Pearce was aware that he seemed somewhat shrunken from the man he recalled, or was it just that he had stooped to read, whereas he was normally studiously erect?

Still reading Hood turned and made his way slowly to the table from which he had risen, to resume his seat, and that allowed Pearce to look at him closely without being observed, which led him to conclude Old Sam was far from well. There was no doubt that his facial features, always sharp and with such a prominent nose and penetrating eyes, naturally commanding, were less fleshy than he recalled.

The cheeks were hollow now instead of full, and even his bushy eyebrows, another outstanding feature, seemed straggly, yet given his responsibilities that should not come as a surprise. Even if he had never spent an extended time at sea, it was no mystery to Pearce that commanding a fleet on a distant station had to be a debilitating experience, quite apart from the sheer exhaustion of being constantly aboard ship.

Sam Hood had been afloat for more than year without the respite of going ashore for more than one day at a time. His old legs had been obliged to cope throughout with a floor that was never still and sometimes, even on such a leviathan as *HMS Victory*, might rise and fall through twenty or more feet in stormy conditions, and that took no account of the permanent cant in the deck. Added to the sheer physical burden of such a life on a man of his seventy years, there were the responsibilities he bore to wear him down even further.

An admiral on station lived on a knife-edge of employment, where one move seen as false could engineer a swift downfall; that Pearce found Hood something of a bully did not in any way detract from the fact that he had a sneaking admiration for Old Sam's manifest abilities as a commander, he being a man who had a deft touch when it came to handling allies, as well as the various potentates that had to be dealt with and kept neutral.

To all extents and purposes the C-in-C Mediterranean was the British Government in the inland sea. There was no time, when decisions had to be made, to refer back to his political masters; events had to be dealt with by the man on the spot, well aware that whatever he did could so easily be seen as folly by London. Even his present moves might be questioned and seen as far from correct by the politicians who rarely, if ever, had any real knowledge of conditions in the fighting arena.

Pearce was aware from previous contact with Old Sam that his actions in Corsica had been engendered by two pressing demands: the first being for a safe anchorage from which he could intercept the French Fleet should it emerge from Toulon – a worth already proven – the second to secure for King George possession of an island that had voluntarily sought the protection of the British Crown. Hence, since the Corsicans held the interior, the need to take the two most important and garrisoned coastal towns.

The latest assault had lasted for a month now, yet there had been little surprise, given the memory he had of the place, that Calvi was taking time to subdue. The town was set in a yawning and inviting inlet he had once, under the command of a less than adroit captain, sailed into, their sloop very nearly coming a cropper from the well-aimed cannon of the French defenders. The ship found itself under fire from heavy ordnance to which it was impossible, in a lightly armed vessel, to reply.

Not that a hundred gunner would have fared any better than a sloop; the bay commanded by those guns lacked the kind of deep water that would allow bombardment from the sea by the capital ships, depth of keel being confined to a narrow channel right by the inland cliffs. It was blessed with a very strong citadel sat on a high promontory above the fortified city, with only one flat avenue of approach by land, and thus had to be a hard nut to crack.

From what Furness had told him, the siege was entirely land based, with several batteries of naval cannon being hauled ashore and set up to pound the walls from the surrounding heights, which had humbugged the defenders, who thought such a thing impossible. The premier was of the opinion that if it was progressing slowly, given the amount of shot expended, matters there should be approaching the point of some conclusion.

Finished reading, Hood put the letter on the table, sunk down and sat back in his padded captain's chair, his face rigid and thoughtful. 'Do you know the contents of this communication, Pearce?'

'No, sir, I do not.'

'D'ye hear that, Parker, the fellow gave me the courtesy of a "sir".'

'Not before time, milord.'

'You'd best peruse this, Parker, given it will likely affect you as well.'

'My instructions were quite specific, milord, in terms of who was to read it.'

'Never mind, Pearce, I will tell Billy Pitt that you allowed me to disobey them.' The admiral took a deep breath, which coincided with a frown from Parker as he began to read. 'Was anyone else present when you took possession of that?'

'Henry Dundas was there.'

'Ah yes, the arch manipulator himself. Minister of War be damned, he's minister of wherever he chooses to poke his finger into. I wonder, Parker, how much of what that implies stems from that damned Scotsman, may God strike down them all?'

Pearce stiffened involuntarily; if not a rabid Scot he was enough of one to see offence in any insult to the entire race. About to check the admiral he bit his tongue; to speak would increase the level of insults, not diminish them, and that was when he was sure he saw a twinkle in the old sod's eyes. This was a man who knew his antecedents only too well.

'There is no more than a recommendation in this, milord,' Parker said, vigorously waving the letter.

'I believe you will know the expression "a nod is as good as a wink".'

'If you have no further need for me, milord, I would wish to be on my way.'

'On your way, Pearce! To where?'

'Back to England, of course.'

'I do not think so.'

'I am sailing under an Admiralty pennant, milord, and I hardly need to explain to someone of your rank what that means. No one can give me orders once I am at sea.'

'If you were to read that letter, Pearce, which you will not be privileged to do, you would see a superscription at the bottom, I suspect in Dundas's own hand since it does not match the rest, which tells me quite plainly that once it is delivered your mission is over. As soon as you are back aboard that armed cutter you must strike that blue flag and hoist the one under which you will serve, namely mine – at least, that is, for the moment.'

'If I cannot read the letter I cannot be expected to suspect anything other than malice in such an interpretation.'

Hood responded with a scornful laugh. 'You are as a flea on an elephant's arse, Pearce, and not worthy of an ounce of my malice, even if you have brought me what amounts to a dismissal from my command.'

That got a loud cough from Parker, to which Hood responded with a growl.

'Oh, it is couched in polite language, Parker, and it is only hinted at by the excuse that with my years and time at sea I must be in need of some leave. But there is no doubting what has brought it on and to whose benefit it is directed—'

'Milord!' Parker exclaimed, in order to interrupt his superior. 'It is not a fitting subject for discussion with an officer of the lieutenant's rank.'

'Don't you think the messenger should know the stench of politics that he carried all this way?'

The older man did not wait for a reply and nor did he seek to hide his anger as he sat forward and barked at Pearce.

'In order to appease the Duke of Portland and his damned parcel of Whigs, and to secure their support for the continuation of the war, so feeble is the parliament of which I am a member, that I must surrender the command of my fleet to that dolt Hotham!'

Pearce was not really listening; instead he was ruminating, and not happily, on how Hood's blast was going to affect his ability to get back to Leghorn, where he had left the lady with whom he was deeply enamoured. If that was bad enough, the name Hood blurted out did little to help matters if he was not going home; if there was one admiral he was less keen to serve under than Old Sam it was Sir William Hotham.

'My Lord, I must protest.'

'Protest away, Pearce,' Hood said, suddenly looking deflated. 'Your protest will do you as much good as to do so would accomplish for me.'

That required a touch of quick thinking. 'Then, milord, I request permission to sail for Leghorn to make good my lack of stores.'

'That,' Parker insisted, 'will only take place once I know what are your present levels, Pearce. So if you will fetch your logbooks aboard I will let you know once my clerks have examined them.'

'Sir, I—'

'Don't tell me,' Hood responded acerbically, cutting right across Pearce. 'You protest, which seems to me to be a permanent state.'

'With good cause, sir.'

'There he goes again, Parker, there's a bit of politesse under that haughty Caledonian exterior.'

As Pearce bristled under the slur, Parker moved quickly to lean over Hood and whisper in his ear, which, after a few seconds, had Old Sam slowly nodding, his mouth compressing and his lower lip becoming prominent, it being fairly clear he was not enjoying what he was hearing. As Parker moved away he fixed Pearce with a glare.

'It has been pointed out to me, Pearce, that in my indiscreet outbursts I have obliged you with information to which you should not be privy, namely the contents of the letter you fetched from London, something I would not wish to be bandied about the fleet.'

'And I would point out to you, milord,' Pearce snapped, 'that I take it very amiss that you doubt my ability to be discreet, which I will be, however shabbily I feel I am being treated.'

'Yet,' Parker interjected, somewhat relieved by what Pearce had just said, 'it would be best if you were absent for a short while. I still require that you present your logs to be examined, but once they are I will issue orders to proceed to Leghorn to make up your stores.'

'Thank you, sir.'

Pearce ran into a waiting Furness as he exited the great cabin; the premier was not going to let him go, especially since it was very close to the time for the wardroom dinner. With the door closed and Furness speaking he could not hear what was said inside.

'Do you think we can trust him, milord?'

'Absolutely, Parker.' Seeing a questioning look, Hood added, 'I know my man – indeed, if he wasn't such a touchy sod I could get to quite like him, for whatever else Pearce is, there's not a craven bone in his body. He's his father's son, man, and even if Adam Pearce was pestilential in his rantings about equality and the like, he was no coward. King George might not have all his marbles, but he did not do a disservice to the navy when he promoted old Adam's son.'

'And this?' Parker asked, waving the letter.

That produced a particular look in Hood's eye, one Parker had seen many times and one that implied a great deal of thought was being processed by a very acute mind.

'Portland may propose, but it is Billy Pitt that will dispose. When I have his ear it will be to tell him that he is mistaken in giving way.' The voice rose discernibly and added to that was a rasping growl. 'I am not ready for the knacker's yard yet.'

CHAPTER THREE

The party that marched out of Calvi under a truce flag had taken great care to look elegant: the French general, as if to underline that he had been a soldier in pre-Revolutionary times, wore a freshly powdered wig under his tricorn hat, while his junior officers, several of them naval, looked fit for a sovereign's parade. The party that moved forward and down from the Royal Louis battery could not match them either in dress or carriage, General Stuart particularly looking positively ill, while Captain Nelson had a bandage under his hat that covered one of his eyes. The third member wore no recognisable garb that could be called a uniform.

If the British officers and their lone Corsican could not match the French in dress they were quick to equal them in determination: the garrison must surrender forthwith, while the requests for the sailors to be allowed to take their own ships back to the mainland, with the soldiers as passengers, was quickly squashed. One of the vessels sheltering in the deep-water channel under the fortress guns was a very fine frigate named *Melpomene*; Nelson was determined it should be forfeit.

In the end it was agreed that the garrison of Calvi, having put up a good fight and in a way that left no taste of bitterness, could march out with their arms. A cartel, a British transport vessel, would be put at their disposal to take them back to their homeland. In the meantime no guns were to be spiked and nothing was to be done to the naval vessels that would diminish their immediate usefulness as they came under the Union Flag and a British crew.

'Though I am damned if I know where we are going to find the hands to man them.'

Nelson said this as he, General Stuart and the Corsican representative, made their way back to the Allied lines to prepare for the forthcoming act of formal surrender. If he had expected a cheerful and reassuring response from the red-coated bullock he was left disappointed, not that such came as much of a surprise.

Malady was not the only thing that made Stuart a less than endearing fighting companion in this siege; his manner had been abrupt throughout and he was wont to treat any sailor, however successful, as a burden with which he was unfortunately saddled. It was generally held by those on the receiving end that his pique was caused by his discomfort at being dependent on the tars to both get him ashore and to provide and man the guns necessary to subdue the place.

None of what had occurred could be observed from the cell shared by the prisoners, but their spirits were raised by the lack of gunfire, something that had been a constant for a whole month now. Then the French army bugles blew and Buchanan knew enough to identify the calls as signals for the garrison to stand down, donning his shirt and dust-streaked red coat as the sounds faded away.

Silence promised freedom and that was borne out within the hour by the arrival of their sergeant gaoler, who roughly told them, more by gestures than in his halting and very bad English, to gather their possessions and be prepared to leave. Not that what they owned amounted to much, no more than the garments with which they had arrived. Buchanan immediately enquired about the prisoners in the dungeon, to be told that they would be released at the same time.

Toby Burns had not worn his blue midshipman's coat for weeks and, despite what he had said to Buchanan about longing to be out of this cell, when he put it on now – service dignity demanding that he do so – it was with reluctance, not only for the fact that it was too hot for such an article, but for the way it underlined to him that he was back in the navy, his hat, once donned, highlighting a fact that made him miserable.

Buchanan, full of good cheer, displayed the same level of kindness he had shown since he had crossed swords with Watson over the slops pail, singling him out for an honour. 'Since you were first to occupy this damned cell, Mr Burns, I think it fitting that it should fall to you to lead us to freedom.'

The glowering face of Lieutenant Watson gave the lie to the word 'freedom', making it hard to respond with the appropriate animation; Toby Burns now realised that this cell had represented liberty; outside these stout walls was where he was really a prisoner for here he had been safe from harm – and not only from the risk of death in fighting the French. The malevolence, which he knew animated Admiral Hotham, would once again be in play.

Added to that there was the mad insistence, from the same person, that Burns should sit for promotion to lieutenant, an inquisition he was bound to fail. There was some hope that such an examination, to which a goodly number of senior midshipmen would have been invited, had already taken place; they would not wait upon him, but laying that minor worry to potential rest did not induce any feeling of ease.

Hotham would volunteer him for some new and dangerous duty, just as he had already done at Toulon and twice at Bastia, once with an army column and secondly with that madcap and fearless fool Nelson, who saw nothing stupid in manning posts that were well within enemy range. He had found himself ashore here at Calvi under the command of the same fellow, who was responsible for the very action that had not only put him in mortal danger but had led to his incarceration. What would the old goat, Hotham, come up with next?

Added to that was the situation regarding his uncle's flawed court martial, or to be more accurate a fellow called Lucknor, an attorney employed, he assumed by John Pearce, to probe Burns about his actions in lying under oath. He claimed to have been present at the illegal impressment of Pearce and his friends from the Pelican Tavern when, in fact, he had been aboard *HMS Brilliant*, his uncle's frigate, berthed at Sheerness on the night in question.

That lie was compounded by another more serious act, taking upon himself responsibility for a navigation error that had landed the press gang and his uncle at the wrong location on the River Thames, putting them ashore in the Liberties of the Savoy, a place in which the navy was forbidden by law to operate, when the intention had been to land by Blackfriars Bridge.

If it sounded false to his ears as he had said it, the statement had been enough to ensure the censure of Ralph Barclay was no more than a wrist slap for an act that, had it been laid at the door of the man responsible, which would have proved it to be deliberate, could have seen his uncle in serious trouble.

Such false testimony had only been possible because there was no one present to refute the lies being peddled, and again Hotham was the villain of the piece. He had staffed the trial with compliant officers, men who looked to him for advancement and opportunity, as well as sending away on an extended mission to the Bay of Biscay anyone, John Pearce in particular, able to tell the truth.

All these worries, easily diminished in captivity, were resurfacing to haunt him again. The letter he had sent in reply to Lucknor's enquiries, seeking to exculpate his sin, seemed feeble in recollection, hardly enough to lay the blame where it squarely lay, with his Uncle Ralph. Composed weeks before, it would surely have arrived in Gray's Inn by now. Would the attorney believe his excuses, that if he had perjured himself, it had been done under the duress applied by those who had coached him on how to respond to questions? And even if he did, what would happen next?

'How in the name of the devil can you look so gloomy, young sir?' Buchanan demanded.

Toby Burns, when he felt threatened, had one trait that never failed him and that was the ability to produce quick and easy-to-believe excuses, often ones that expressed worthwhile sentiments utterly at odds with his true feelings. Out on the battlements now he made a point of looking at the town of Calvi, which lay below the fortress, destroyed by endless bombardment so that hardly a single building stood and none intact; given that aspect he could conjure up words to cover his apparent misery.

'How many died or were maimed for this place, sir, and was it worth it?'

'Worthy lad, very worthy,' Buchanan replied, gravely. 'Does you proud to think that way. But that is war and there is no gainsaying that folk, innocent and guilty alike, suffer in any conflict.'

'How right you are, sir,' Toby replied, not thinking of Calvi but himself.

The arrival of an armed cutter sailing under an Admiralty pennant did not go unnoticed aboard *HMS Britannia*, being unusual enough to cause much comment on the quarterdeck, given most despatches came by civilian packet from Gibraltar. The flag officer aboard being a stickler for things being done proper – and he was the sole arbiter of what that might be – obliged the officer of the watch to send a midshipman to the great cabin to appraise the occupant of the approach.

Vice Admiral Sir William Hotham saw no need to stir, given it would head for Hood's flagship, not his own, while whatever messages it bore would only be passed on to him if and when his superior thought it necessary. Yet such an arrival could do naught but stir unhappy thoughts: no job was as thankless as that of being second in command of a fighting fleet, made doubly disagreeable when the man to whom you must defer was one of questionable tactical skill, as well as being a commander unwilling ever to listen to sound advice.

In his darker moods, William Hotham felt that the only way he would get a proper hearing, or have his notions of strategy adopted as policy, Hood being so contrary to him both personally and professionally, was to propose the precise opposite of what he truly believed. These were grievances he had often penned and sent home to his Whig friends and supporters in London, most potently his patron, the Duke of Portland.

Hotham had doubted, and still did, the present siege of Calvi, for the very same reason that he had opposed that popinjay Nelson's assault from the sea on Bastia, for Corsica was not worth the wax off a candle. Such adventures were unnecessary, the soldiers were against them and it stood to reason that they knew more about such matters than sailors. What was the point of asking the general in command of the troops for an opinion on an operation then utterly ignoring it, which is precisely what Hood had done?

Success at Bastia had not dented his belief that the whole endeavour had been in error, not an act of supreme military necessity, more a sop, and a bloody one, to please the Corsicans, as well as the King's proposed viceroy of the island, Sir Gilbert Elliot. Yes, Calvi too would fall, but at what cost and to whose advantage when all the fleet needed was the bay they already occupied?

At least he had gained something from the farce, finally having got rid of an irritation that had caused him concern, namely Midshipman Toby Burns. The youngster had gone out on a night raid on the fortifications of Calvi and had not returned, so he was assumed to have perished, a satisfying result given the trouble Hotham had gone to in getting the lad into harm's way. Time and again, since the siege of Toulon, he had volunteered Burns for service where the shot and shell flew, only for the little sod to emerge, if not unscathed, with wounds nowhere near fatal.

What had the world come to, he wondered and not for the first time, when a man of his rank, age and experience had to worry about a lowly creature like Burns? Yet the little toad had impinged on his consciousness for the very simple reason that he had the power to cause serious trouble.

In the process of cracking a walnut, the thoughts on which he was ruminating made him apply too much pressure, which shattered the kernel as well as the shell. Thus the same midshipman who had knocked earlier, to enter on his command, found his admiral crouched down and picking up pieces of nut from the carpeted floor.

'Signal from *Victory*, sir, requesting that you repair aboard.'

If the position in which Hotham found himself could be described as humiliating, the thought could not be avoided that he was being invited to suffer yet more of the same.

'Acknowledge,' he snapped with clear irritation, which sent the lad, a mere stripling, thirteen years of age, scurrying out.

If John Pearce had serious reservations about the King's Navy and his place in it, there was no gainsaying the fact that they could be a hospitable lot. His boat crew were on the lower deck, having been handsomely looked after, chinwagging with their fellow tars and no doubt boasting away about the action they had taken part in off Portugal, in which they had saved a postal packet from being taken by privateers.

If their commanding officer was sure they would be gilding it, turning what was a skirmish, albeit a satisfying one, into a great and deadly battle, he was equally certain he was not, for when it came to recounting his own exploits, weariness of repetition was added to a determination not to show away.

He had eaten well and drunk of wine better than that aboard most naval vessels, for the town of San Fiorenzo had been under French control and they never stinted on the supply of such luxuries, which had naturally been taken over wholesale. He was likewise much taken by the fact that, since the last time he had dined in this very wardroom, there were so many new faces among the fifteen lieutenants present, one more being on watch.

Polite enquiry informed him of those who had been promoted out and to where – not that he truly recalled their names or their faces – as well as the fellow who had died of the bloody flux after a marathon session to taste as many of the bottles as possible that had been looted from the French stores.

All this was related before he was drawn into describing the successful battle in the English Channel that had seen him promoted at the hand of King George himself from midshipman to his lieutenancy. What he feared was approaching and Pearce knew there was no avoiding it: a raft of questions would follow his deliberately dull recounting as these young men, and they were all that, Furness included, plied him with enquiries as to the details he had left out.

They wanted to know to the final dot the calibre of guns on the *Valmy*, a seventy-four, and how efficiently they had been plied by the revolutionary sailors working them. How by his actions had he saved the fifty-gun *HMS Centurion* from the certainty that she must strike her flag? Details of wind and the run of the sea and how that affected the encounter were deemed essential to make a full picture and these he would have to invent, for, in truth, these were facts he could not recall and was too ignorant at the time to note.

With deliberate intent he moved the conversation on to the recent battle in which Lord Howe had trounced the French in the Western Approaches, news of which had set the bells ringing in England, which had been named, since there was no land nearby to provide one, as the Battle of the Glorious First of June.

Yet, in truth, Pearce was in no position to add any more than could be gleaned from a study of the newspapers. To cover for that he milked the fact that he had been on the periphery of the action, albeit without a shot being fired, having inadvertently sailed through a convoy of American vessels bringing much needed wheat to France only days before Howe's victory.

'Sailed through them, Mr Pearce?' Furness asked, his brow creased. 'How so?'

Damning his own stupidity, Pearce was drawn into telling of his recent mission to the rebels of the Vendée, though he was able to name it as something less than a success, given the people fighting the Revolution on the western coast of France did not, to his mind, have either the means or the will to impose a check on the madmen of Paris.

There was much, too, that had to be left out, not least that in the encampment occupied by the Vendéean rebels he had come across a woman who had, at one time, been his mistress. Questioned on that would reveal their liaison had taken place in Revolutionary Paris, albeit before the outbreak of war, and that was a time and a place to which he had no desire whatsoever to go.

Likewise he could not mention that in sailing with his despatches, he had, without permission, detoured to Leghorn, and there dropped off his present mistress, Emily Barclay. She being the estranged wife of a serving naval officer and a post captain to boot would not sit well in such a gathering.

So he stuck to the bare bones of his mission, yet there was no escape from seeming enterprising as he outlined the parameters of the Vendéean assignment and what had happened ashore, nor of the favour he continued to enjoy by being entrusted with such a mission.

'But the grain convoy?' Furness insisted, when Pearce thought he had said enough.

'I found myself right in the midst of that by accident, given we were sailing away from the approaches to Nantes without lights, while they were likewise in darkness, seeking to avoid detection by Howe's inshore frigates.'

'Could you not have sunk a few?' asked a marine lieutenant.

'Not without alerting the French escorts, added to which, we had an important envoy aboard and could not risk capture. We had a couple of close shaves when it came to collisions, but I was able, by calling out in French, to get us clear without the escorts knowing of our presence.'

'You speak it well enough to fool them?'

'I was talking to Jonathans, but yes, I do, so had they been French the result should have been the same.'

'Must be a fine thing to be able to speak French.'

This was mouthed, and gloomily so, by one of the more junior members of the wardroom, no doubt a midshipman freshly promoted to lieutenant, a fellow who looked so fresh of face as to be barely breeched, while one or two of his companions gave their guest a look, quickly masked, that hinted that the ability to speak the tongue of the enemy so well might amount to treason.

Other reasons for disapproval lay, in some cases, very shallow under the surface of good manners and Furness, well able to read an atmosphere that had ceased to be as perfect as he wished, quickly covered that as he ordered the glass before Pearce to be refilled, following with a question designed to fully concentrate the minds of his inferiors.

'I don't think you have fully entertained us with the story of the *Valmy*, Mr Pearce, and if I admire your desire to be modest regarding your achievements, a fuller account of the action would not go amiss.'

'Hear him, hear him,' cried the assembly.

A young fellow, very flushed, who had clearly run all the way from the quarterdeck to deliver his message, rushed in after a very perfunctory knock and, in addressing Furness, saved him.

'Compliments of the officer of the watch, sir, but Admiral Hotham's barge has set off from *Britannia*.'

Looking around the faces, all seeming disappointed that this gathering would be required to break up and they would miss the nub of a good story, he was sure they were silently damning Hotham. They would not do so openly and vocally, that would be too disrespectful, yet their pinched expressions underlined to Pearce just how unpopular that particular flag officer was, especially aboard this ship. Not that he was too concerned; the sod had got him off the hook and now he could return to *Larcher*.

'Mr Furness, I need my boat crew to be brought to their duty.'

'Of course, but you must come and visit again, Mr Pearce, given we are agog to hear more of the good fortune you have enjoyed.'

'Hear him, hear him,' was, this time, accompanied by the majority of hands slamming hard on the table.

That repeated noisy and hearty chorus, which included marines, the surgeon and the master, had Pearce redden and duck his head with embarrassment. In this gathering of young men there seemed very little hint of the hidden malice he usually encountered in the company of his peers; this accolade appeared genuine and that induced in him an odd feeling, unaccustomed as he was to unfettered acceptance.

CHAPTER FOUR

The distance between the two first rates was not great, and the men from *HMS Larcher* were not keen to depart, taking their time to assemble, meaning Hotham's barge came too close to allow Pearce to take precedence over the arrival of an admiral. This obliged him to wait to one side while the men he had just dined with, plus Captain Knight, the commanding officer of *HMS Victory*, as well as the entire complement of marines, lined up for the ceremony of receiving a flag officer.

Sam Hood was not there personally to greet his immediate inferior, which good manners demanded, if not actual protocol, and neither was Rear-Admiral Parker, which if it was not an insult from the executive officer of the fleet was damned close to one. Though his knowledge of admirals was slight, John Pearce had been at sea long enough to glean from gossip and a certain amount of exposure that they were more like a bunch of warring fishwives than sober and wise men able to easily cooperate; right now and before him was a living example.

The first sight of Hotham was as a stocky silhouette in the entry port, which he remained as the courtesies due to him by the pipes and marines coming to attention were acted out. Then he stepped forward to be formally greeted by Captain Knight, with Lieutenant Furness at his superior's elbow.

If Hotham noticed that his fellow flag officers had declined to attend he gave no indication of being troubled by it and, after a brief exchange and the requisite inspection, he began to make his way aft, escorted by Furness. This obliged John Pearce to raise his hat in salute and the premier to make an introduction.

'Lieutenant Pearce, sir, captain of *HMS Larcher*, newly arrived this very day.'

The effect was immediate: Hotham, stopping abruptly before him, was too pallid a fellow to ever let it be said the blood drained from his round and unblemished face, but he was visibly shocked. 'Pearce! What in the name of the devil are you doing here?'

His hat was held above his head and he was feeling foolish, yet the temptation to reply with mockery never occurred to John Pearce, for which he cursed himself later as several bon mots of a derisory nature came to mind. As it was, delay meant he was not required to respond at all, given Hotham barked at him.

'You, was it, under that Admiralty pennant?'

'It was, sir.'

'Navy's gone to the dogs, Furness,' Hotham snorted, before stomping aft, muttering under his breath, while the greeting party noisily began to break up behind him.

'Hard to disagree with that,' Pearce said, as Furness looked at him questioningly.

'Not popular in that particular quarter, I take it?'

'Mr Furness, I have yet to meet an admiral in whose favour I can be said to reside. Now, if you will allow me to get into my boat.'

'Of course,' Furness replied, calling to one of his juniors to make it so, before scurrying after Hotham.

If John Pearce, making for the entry port, could have seen into the mind of the admiral with whom he had just exchanged words he would have been gratified by the turmoil his presence had created. Toby Burns had been a bane but then the midshipman had been no more than a tool, there to be manipulated by the spite of John Pearce. This Hotham had gleaned from the letter Burns had written in reply to an attorney called Lucknor, which had been intercepted by Toomey, his clerk.

Given the little fool had damn near confessed to perjury and named those who had encouraged his testimony, albeit with grovelling caveats, there was no way that missive could be allowed to proceed on its way. Toomey was sure that Lucknor, never having communicated with Burns, would not have any knowledge of his correspondent's handwriting, so the clerk had composed a suitable and far from damning reply in his own hand, purporting to be from the midshipman.

That should have put matters to rest, but the presence of the principal upset those calculations and caused the comforting feeling he had harboured earlier about the demise of Burns to evaporate; Pearce presaged a potentially much greater threat and it was a providential God that had so arranged matters that the two would not meet again – whatever disclosures Burns was willing to make had gone with him to the grave.

Even in his present state of turmoil Hotham could not fault

Barclay for what had been a questionable impressment. Such a thing was a common enough event at the outbreak of a new war and normally nothing with which to trouble anyone: such complaints as arose, and there were many, could usually be brushed off by the pressing need of the nation to get to sea a fighting fleet.

Sense dictated that those who had connections enough to make trouble were quickly identified and let go with an apology. The rest, once they were at sea, where they would stay for the duration of the conflict, could be ignored. Yet in Pearce, clearly not a seaman and quite obviously an educated fellow – though Hotham would take exception to naming him as a gentleman – Ralph Barclay had broken that golden rule and in doing so had caught a tiger by the tail.

The man was clever, determined and, what was worse, inside the service and a lieutenant in rank, a position from which it would be hard to divert any protest, indeed it had taken all his authority and no shortage of guile to do so at Toulon. To renege on that as matters seemed to spiral out of control, to let Ralph Barclay face the consequences of his error, was tempting, but had to be put aside for several reasons, not least because he was a client officer.

Leaving him to swing on his own would not go down well with those who enjoyed the same standing, for if captains depended on the good opinion of admirals it was not a one-way trade; it would be a wounded superior who might struggle to rely on support should they feel one of their number abandoned. Hotham was not only honour bound to protect Barclay, he was obliged to do so professionally as well.

For once, being kept waiting by Hood – normally something to induce rage – gave him time to recall the way he had arranged matters, though he had done so without even thinking that the consequences would turn out to be so troubling. The transcript of the court martial he had arranged, of which Pearce had somehow procured a copy, would not stand up to too much scrutiny and might be seen for what it was, a put-up job, especially in the light of his actions in sending away anyone who knew the truth.

Toomey had taken depositions from three of the men with whom Pearce had been pressed and they too had been got out of the way, so that the testimony they had provided could be quietly buried. If they, in a court of law, relayed that fact to a jury it might not just be Ralph Barclay who would face censure. That train of thought, as well as the chilling possibilities it had opened up, had to be abandoned as he was shown into Lord Hood's cabin, to find his superior standing awaiting him, a look on his craggy old face that promised added turmoil.

The officer so troubling Sir William Hotham was waiting in the anteroom of the huge town house owned by the Duke of Portland, looking out at the rainswept square that bore his name, as well as the number of elegant, tall buildings that had been erected around the central garden. Despite his impatience he was trying to calculate how much such a slice of property was worth in terms of rents and leases; that it was not the only bit of land the Duke had developed, indeed there were several streets and squares on what had once been inherited farmland, only fed Ralph Barclay's envy.

The amount of time he was being kept waiting served to try his patience, that being a commodity with which he was not supremely gifted. But on this occasion he had good reason to fret as well: as a ship's captain in an active command Ralph Barclay was obliged by the rules of the service to sleep aboard his ship: like most regulations it was one observed much in the breech but it was taken seriously.

Being in contention with both his commanding admiral and Lord Howe's executive officer over his own actions in the recent battle made just absenting himself from his sleeping cabin unwise. He had been obliged to request permission to do so, on the grounds of needing medical advice in London. This he had received from the captain of the Channel Fleet, Sir Roger Curtis. To ask the admiral himself was impossible: the old sod had left Torbay and his responsibilities for Bath, where he was taking the waters and no doubt wallowing equally in praise for his recent victory.

That Portland was in the capital provided a bonus; it would allow him to catch up on certain matters with his prize agent, yet the time to do that was diminishing rapidly, which fed his irritation. To find such an elevated personage in London at this time of year, when men of property ritually decanted from the capital to their country estates, spoke volumes for the state of politics in the nation; even with a war on it was rare to find anyone in town during August. William Pitt, too, more likely to be found gardening at Walmer Castle in Kent during the high summer months, had returned to London to deal with the pressing matters that troubled his administration.

The Duke of York had been soundly beaten in Flanders mid May, which, if it had left the royal Commander-in-Chief of the British Army open to much ridicule about marching up and down hills, had put pressure on the government over the prosecution of the war, not least because of the cost. This fiasco had been compounded by the subsequent crushing of York's Austrian allies at Fleurus, which had left the forces of the French Revolution in control of the Netherlands, including a coast too close for England to feel secure; the memories of the Dutch Wars and their incursions up the Thames were still fresh in the minds of many.

To counter the gloom and soothe parliament there had come news of the welcome defeat of the French fleet by Lord Howe, which removed for a time the most pressing fears of any trouble from the Netherlands, while there was hope for good news from both the West Indies and Corsica. But the most telling event was political: the sudden fall and execution of Maximilien Robespierre and an end to what had come to be called the Reign of Terror naturally led to hopes of peace.

Such desires faltered on one simple fact: the new men in charge in Paris, too many of whom were old revolutionaries, had the stain of King Louis' blood on their hands. They appeared just as keen to prosecute the war, as had been the now defunct Committee of Public Safety; indeed several had been members of that murderous body. So feelers put out to Paris had met with a sharp rebuff and now there was a renewed clamour in the country for either a disengagement from a war that few saw as vital to Britain's interests, or at the very least some positive means of prosecution that would bring it to an end.

Charles James Fox, the great Whig orator, if in his private life a sybaritic character, was a wily politician, well able to exploit any political weakness, and he was snapping at the heels of the government, abetted by a Prince of Wales keen to prove his father the King was too mad to properly rule. Prinny was sure that he should be appointed Regent, and if he was then it would be Fox he would appoint to lead the government, not Pitt.

The barrier to loss of office for the Tories lay with the Duke of

Portland. He had led a section of the Whig party away from Fox and into alliance with William Pitt. This had, of course, come at a price to the administration: Portland's supporters now held several ministries, while keeping them onside was paramount to avoid an election, the outcome of which could not be predicted in a country far from united.

If any of this impinged upon Ralph Barclay, his only hope was that the war would go on, advancement in the navy at a time of peace being slow, whereas conflict naturally sped things along. Well into the top half of the captain's list, he kept a sharp eye on the names of those who died and were ahead of him, mostly admirals expiring from old age. But in war there were those who perished from fighting as well; all he had to do was avoid a similar fate and one day he would top the list and have his flag.

War had also brought him prosperity. The expansion of the fleet had led to his first command in five years, time he had spent languishing 'on the beach' on half pay. Barclay recalled the period with the sour feeling brought on by the struggle to make ends meet and at the same time maintain appearances. If it had not been poverty, his life then had been far from comfortable, with the constant need to postpone the payment of bills, to the point when more than once he had been obliged to deal with a bailiff.

All that was behind him now; anyone who observed him at present would see a highly successful naval officer who could afford to buckle his shoes in silver and hire a carriage in which to travel, of a quality that indicated his position. He had garnered prizes enough to make him comfortable and to live in the manner he felt to be his right; if he was looking at the obvious Portland wealth with envy, he was also calculating if he should take a lease of one of those imposing mansions himself, perhaps when he had forced his errant wife back into the family home?

That was the only gremlin in this confident reflection: the state of his marriage was not sound, for his young wife Emily had disappeared. The complications of that were enough to darken any mood of confidence and not only for the loss of her presence in the marital bed. She had turned against him in a very troubling way, threatening to expose his transgressions, so much so that she posed a threat to his otherwise blossoming career.

Such a situation could only be resolved when he had her once more under his roof and his conjugal control, for she lacked the means to live an independent life. Through his prize agent he had employed a one-time thief-taker to find her, yet for all the fellow's supposed expertise weeks had gone by without any apparent trace.

The door behind him had opened noiselessly, so the voice came as a slight surprise. 'His Grace will see you now, Captain Barclay.'

The temptation to say, 'About time, damn him,' had to be suppressed. The man who had kept him waiting had the power to break a mere naval captain with a click of his fingers, indeed enough power to make admirals quail. Limping along the long hallway – he was still constrained by a wound to the thigh – he passed what he assumed were the portraits of Portland's ancestors.

The most imposing was a fellow in a full-bottomed wig that dated him from a distant past, the previous century, in fact. Perhaps this was the Bentinck who had come from Holland with William of Orange and set the family on its upward path. In the features, most notably the long and sharp nose, there was something of a resemblance to the man waiting to greet him.

Not that the welcome was in any way warm: Portland, sat

in a high-backed armchair, was a cold fish who rarely made any attempt to temper his air of innate superiority, a haughtiness he eschewed for very few people, and certainly not for this particular visitor. Pale of skin, with dull eyes under greying hair, he looked like a man who saw daylight as inimical to good health, which had Ralph Barclay thinking that to such an aristocrat, his ruddy complexion, his features weathered by a life spent at sea, must appear coarse indeed.

'Leave us.'

This dismissal was aimed at the fellow clutching in his hands a sheaf of papers – there were more on the table before him – which he began to add to those he already carried. Such a sight made Barclay seethe even more; he had spent over an hour waiting so that Portland could see to his business affairs, which surely could have been put to one side. It was a repeat of the disdain with which the Duke had received him the first time they met and it did nothing to stifle the feelings of exasperation.

'You will wish me to leave this letter, Your Grace?' asked the factotum, producing the article. 'It is the one from Captain Barclay.'

The reply was a languid nod, before Portland took the missive and, using a lorgnette, looked over it, this while his man disappeared; his visitor was left to stand in silence for a good minute.

'What you say in part of this letter, Barclay, is of some interest to me.'

'I had hoped it might be, Your Grace.'

'Not very flattering about Admiral Lord Howe, though, wouldn't ye say?'

'I have reported what I observed—'

The interruption was sharp. 'And have written to me, since you do not feel that the gentleman in question has given you the credit which you are sure you are due?'

'In that I am not alone, Your Grace. As I have detailed in my letter, I am not the only captain who fought on the First of June to feel his honour and abilities impugned, a matter I raised with Sir Phillip Stephens at the Admiralty.'

'And how did the secretary respond?'

'With the kind of reserve that one would expect from such a functionary. He seems far more interested in the King's joy at the victory than any investigations of impropriety that might temper that. I am assuming you have read Lord Howe's despatch?'

'Dreary stuff to a landsman, Barclay, but yes, I have read it.'

Ralph Barclay waited for a ducal opinion; he waited in vain, which forced him to speak again. 'While the conduct of the battle raises certain questions, Your Grace, you will see, as I have detailed, that there is some doubt as to whether it should have been fought at all. If I may refer to recent events in France, can we see a connection between the fall of the tyrant Robespierre and the lack of bread to feed the denizens who elevated him?'

Portland put the back of a hand to his mouth, as if stifling a yawn. 'I think not, Barclay. More likely those who guillotined him did so to avoid suffering a similar fate themselves. Have we not seen this damned revolution eat its own already? I doubt the mass of "citizens" had much say in the matter, with bellies full or empty.'

'And yet we have no sign from Paris of any moves to make peace, which I humbly suggest would not be the case if the country was starving.'

His letter was waved again. 'I read your opinion on that.'

Barclay was seeking some indication of his host's attitude,

but with his indolent delivery it was impossible to form a view. Was what Portland had read useful to him or not, for whatever arrangements had been made with Pitt, the Whigs were ever keen to curtail the powers of the monarchy and even more so to force an election which would propel them to untrammelled power.

'Do I need to remind Your Grace that Lord Howe got his command through the direct intervention of His Majesty King George.'

'No, Barclay, you do not!'

That reply was sharp, it being a fact well known, added to the unproven one of why that particular admiral was so favoured. Many believed, on what was flimsy evidence, that Howe was a blood relative of King George, albeit born on the wrong side of the blanket to the mistress of the previous monarch. To a Whig politician, schooled in the tenets of the Glorious Revolution of 1688 and a Bentinck to boot, the exercise of such royal interference in government or the affairs of the military was anathema.

The pause that followed was one Barclay felt once more he could not break. Howe had given unstinting praise to many of the men who had officered his fleet, but not to Ralph Barclay, indeed he had questioned his actions in the battle, naming them as tardy. Yet he had suffered least in that regard: several of his fellow officers had been castigated in writing to the point where it sounded like an accusation of cowardice.

Those Howe praised, many of them long-time client officers, were to be the recipients of specially struck medals celebrating the Glorious First; Ralph Barclay had been one of those omitted from the list of those to be so favoured, which was not a slight he was prepared to let pass.

'I seem to recall that you received a wound in the action?'

The question, as well as the manner in which it was conveyed, made Barclay wonder if Portland had even noticed he was a one-armed captain, having suffered a left-arm amputation after taking a bullet at Toulon, one which shattered his elbow. Tempted to refer to that, he saw sense in sticking to the subject under discussion.

'To the thigh, Your Grace, and I lost so much blood I passed out. But this was at a time when *HMS Semele* was fully engaged with the *Vengeur du Peuple*, which as you no doubt are aware, we damaged so severely she sank.'

'Yes,' Portland actually yawned this time, as if such a thing as a vessel going down with in excess of six hundred men was trivial. 'If you would be more comfortable seated, Captain, please feel free to do so.'

With a contrariness compounded by stupidity, even though his thigh was paining him, Barclay's reply was firm. 'I am happy to stand, Your Grace!'

'So be it. Now, about this damned grain convoy?'

'I fear I need to provide a full explanation, Your Grace, so perhaps with your permission I will sit down.'

That got a wave of the lorgnette and once seated Barclay launched into his case, which was, quite simply, that Lord Howe, well aware, as was his government, of impending famine in France – the harvest had failed for the second year running – should have sought out and destroyed the American convoy bringing relief in the form of hundreds of vessels full of grain, rather than fought an action with the French battle fleet. Even if he was privately glad Howe had not done so, it provided a lever by which he and those like him could seek redress.

'You maintain, in this letter of yours, that he was deliberately drawn away from the grain convoy and the fact was, if not obvious, then plain enough to warrant consideration?'

'I recorded that very opinion in my own log at the time, which now resides within the vaults of the Admiralty.'

It could not be said that Portland sat up when Ralph Barclay said that, but there was a definite movement, a physical reaction, followed by a slightly querulous complaint as the letter was waved once more.

'You did not say so in this.'

'I did not want to commit that to writing, Your Grace, without having spoken to you first. If such information is to be of any use, then it is best that it not be disseminated too freely.'

That mollified the man, as it was intended to do, even if it implied his correspondence was not secure, which allowed Barclay to detail what he had seen and how it had been played out.

'Are such logs not first examined by the flag officer?'

Given a chance of a bit of his own condescension, Ralph Barclay could not resist the temptation to employ it; his tone was positively fatherly. 'Not personally, Your Grace, they go to his clerks and their examination is cursory, more concerned with beef and pork in the barrel than battle tactics.'

There was no doubting Portland's tone when he replied; it was positively incensed that he should be so addressed. 'So your observations were missed.'

Barclay took refuge in being matter of fact. 'Our outer screen spotted the topsails of a lone frigate on the horizon, which immediately put up its helm and fled westward. Lord Howe, informed of this, ordered a general chase in pursuit, which I found to be a questionable course of action. Not that I had anyway to communicate that to the flagship and affect the admiral's thinking.'

'You infer by that a ploy to draw the fleet away from the convoy?'

'That is how I saw it at the time and how I recorded it, as I say, in my log. Whatever success we enjoyed it is without doubt true that the real purpose of putting the Channel Fleet to sea was to interdict that convoy and to ensure the grain did not reach France. If that is so, then for all the praise being heaped on Lord Howe, not least from the King himself, it is possible to question if he acted properly, given we are still at war with the Revolution and the populace of France has the food to keep going.'

'And now that you have passed this information on to me, what is it you hope to gain?'

'Redress, equity, perhaps to let it be known that Lord Howe is something less, an idol with feet of clay rather than the flawless hero that is being claimed. If that can be used to political advantage, there is only the question of how that is to be achieved, and for that I seek your advice. Is it something that should be handled with discretion . . .'

'Or?'

'Do we who feel slighted, especially Captains Bertie and Taylor, along with myself, demand a court martial to establish the truth and clear our names and our reputations?'

The Portland chin rested on the aristocratic chest as the peer digested that remark and considered its consequences, none of which were a mystery to his visitor. Would such a course serve the interests of the Whigs or should he put what would be an embarrassment to the government of which he was a member before party advantage? Ralph Barclay did not care which course would be adopted, only that something should be done; he deserved praise not censure and he most certainly wanted that medal.

'Leave this with me for consideration, Captain Barclay.'

'Am I allowed to say to you, Your Grace, that there is a matter of time to be considered?'

Portland knew he was being warned not to just sit on what he had heard and, powerful enough to rarely be threatened, he reacted with palpable irritation, his voice now a hiss.

'Be so good as to ask my man of business to return on your way out.'

CHAPTER FIVE

John Pearce was re-examining his logs prior to their transfer to the flagship, not least those covering his detour to Leghorn, to make sure that they met the requirements of the service. The worry that they would not was a bane that plagued every captain of a King's ship in the navy, for these ledgers were not just a record of his course, speed and location, with details of sails set as well as the prevailing wind, tide and sea states: other books listed everything that had been used since he had sent the previous set in from Buckler's Hard to the commanding admiral at Portsmouth.

The powers that ruled placed little faith in the honesty of their officers, which was just as well given the lengths many went to in an attempt to circumvent the restrictions placed on them for private gain. The master and commander of *HMS Larcher* was well aware of his lack of the kind of nautical knowledge acquired from serving for years at sea; he was even more acutely conscious of his ignorance when it came to the art of capperbar: the ability to compose logs in a way that hid from the admiralty clerks – they being the final examiners – things that could be justifiably lost in the maze of figures.

It was bad enough just having to account for what had been properly consumed: beef, pork and peas in the barrel, small beer and rum, as well as the wear on sails, cables and rope. God help you if you lost an anchor and it was reckoned as carelessness! Even if you had engaged in a successful action, as he had off the coast of Portugal, the amount of powder and shot he had expended, accounted for to him by the gunner, as well as the timber, canvas and cordage needed to repair any damage, would be pored over to ensure he was not gilding it and selling that dishonestly claimed on to the first merchant captain he encountered.

The banging of the distant gun that penetrated into his tiny cabin was only remarkable when it was repeated, that deep boom bringing home to him that it was not a recognition signal being fired – too common to be remarked upon – but a main armament weapon. Standing up he stopped short of hitting his crown on the low deck beams above, this based on much previous experience of the sharp pains induced by too much haste, just as Michael O'Hagan knocked and entered, his smile broad and his green eyes alight.

'There's a frigate – that captured Frenchie *Lutine* I am told – coming up hell for leather, John-boy, and firing away like it were a royal birthday.'

Still crouching, for the doorway was even lower than the cabin roof, Pearce followed O'Hagan out on to the deck, to find the side lined with most of the crew, all gazing to the north and the headland that formed the western arm of San Fiorenzo Bay. For a moment he considered ordering them back to whatever duties they had left uncompleted but to do so, when they were at anchor and nothing could be said to be pressing, would be churlish.

'The flags *HMS Lutine* has aloft, Mr Dorling?'

'Enemy has struck her colours, Capt'n, which I take leave to mean that Calvi has fallen, her being part of Captain Nelson's squadron. Wouldn't make no sense otherwise.'

Overheard by those closest, which on such a vessel meant a goodly number of the crew, the beginnings of a hurrah began to sound out, which Pearce killed off with a sharp command to belay.

'It wouldn't do to tempt providence, lads, best wait till you are sure of the good news before we start cheering.'

'Permission to send a boat alongside, sir, and gather that in?'

'Granted,' Pearce replied, again on the grounds it could do no harm, 'though I must go back to my damned logs.'

Which he did while the boat was launched and it was not alone; nearly every captain in the fleet was agog to hear the news and too impatient to wait for it to be disseminated from *HMS Victory*. John Pearce heard the noise, as the boat was hauled alongside and manned, somewhat jealous of the freedom enjoyed by those who served, as he had once done, before the mast. They obeyed orders instead of issuing them and had no need to record their every action as well as every drop used of cleansing vinegar with quill and ink.

The cannon fire did not go unnoticed aboard the flagship, though Hood did not stir from his chair, continuing what he thought of as his conversation with William Hotham: to the recipient it was more like a lecture. In this Hood had first advised him of his intention to take some leave at a date yet to be established, with the insistence that he would be returning to the Mediterranean and his command in due course, which allowed him, as he took care to point out, to dictate how he wished matters to proceed in his absence.

It had been instructive to see how Hotham reacted, for if he thought himself a master of dissimulation he was far from correct. The truth of that was not in his face, the features of which he managed to control; it was evident in his hands and the fidgeting thereof, no doubt caused by the thoughts of what he would do once Hood had departed, never mind any orders that were issued. That Hotham twitched even more at the sound of gunfire made the pleasure of keeping him seated and still all the greater; not that Lord Hood would have stirred, it being beneath his rank and dignity to display such obvious curiosity.

It had been hard, when giving Hotham instructions, not to hector him, to keep his orders strictly professional, for Hood was not a fool: he suspected they would be disobeyed as soon as his topsails disappeared over the horizon. For that reason he had his clerk present, as well as Admiral Parker, writing a verbatim record of the conversation.

A copy of this, once neatly written up, would be delivered to HMS Britannia along with the papers Hood had accumulated during his tenure in command. Hood had struggled to keep out of his voice the disdain he felt for his second in command, for his tactical appreciations as well as his manner of going about his duties, an area in which, to the thinking of Admiral Parker he had signally failed.

'It would be worthwhile to hold to it, Sir William, that you have the overall command out here, and while you cannot instruct the likes of General Stuart to undertake operations which he declines to support, you have the right to apply a great deal of pressure, as I have, I think, demonstrated. I have set a policy of taking control of Corsica, on behalf on the indigenes, of course, and I expect that to be followed.'

Ignoring the hands and looking into that smooth face and those, to his mind, shifty brown eyes, Hood wondered if the sod was paying true attention. As it was he himself was distracted by the knock at his door.

'Enter.'

'Captain Knight's compliments, milord, but *HMS Lutine* is approaching under full sail and flying the signal, enemy has struck.'

'How long before we have their boat alongside?'

'Half a glass, sir.'

'Very well, signal the captain to repair aboard and let me know when his barge is in the water.' Hood began speaking again as soon as the door closed. 'Now we must discuss the French fleet and what you must do about it.'

'I find it insulting, milord, that you think I do not know.'

'As if I give a damn about that,' Hood snapped. 'You had a chance to stop them while I was occupied at Bastia and missed it. It would pain me, Sir William, as well as the British people, if that were to happen again.'

Hotham reddened at that reminder and his voice went lower in tone as he defended himself. 'I took cognisance, milord, of the facts as I saw them, not least the state of our ships.'

'It has ever been my policy,' Hood replied, with a weary tone that was all the more insulting for being so, 'to take more cognisance of the state of the enemy's ships.'

'Yet I think you will agree, milord, that we are short of

overwhelming strength and our vessels have been at sea for at least a year, some for near eighteen months, with the concomitant wear that implies. Our allies choose to stay too far off to give us immediate support, while we are ill placed to sustain any losses. It is an undeniable fact that every vessel in the fleet is short on hands.'

'That is so, and many of our ships may be in need of a dockyard, but the French are not worked up as we are, having barely been at sea. They will not sail their vessels with a proficiency that can match our own, added to which they cannot handle their guns with anything like the skill our fellows can bring to bear. Cease to worry about the state of your timbers, Sir William, or the whereabouts of the Spanish fleet and put yourself and *my* fleet alongside the enemy should the opportunity present itself, and that, sir, can be taken as a direct order.'

Hood looked at his clerk to make sure that was noted, gratified by the nod.

Parker, hitherto silent and not entirely lacking in sympathy for Hotham, spoke up in order to bring an end to what was beginning to sound like a baiting. 'I think we can assume, milord, that *Lutine* brings us positive news from Calvi.'

'Very likely, Admiral Parker,' Hood replied, with a wicked twinkle in his eye, added to which came a twitch of those straggly, prominent eyebrows. 'Perhaps it calls for a toast to celebrate, one in which Sir William will no doubt join us, given he was so positive in his support for that particular operation.'

If Hotham was furious, and to Parker's mind he had a right to be, he hid it well, the only sign a clenching into fists of those fidgeting hands. It had to be admitted, though, that if he carried questionable ability as a fighting sailor he had never lacked the skills of the natural courtier. He stood and smiled, as if he had not just been reminded of his real position on Calvi, and spoke with an even voice.

'Settle for my congratulations, milord, if indeed such news is in the offing, but do not let me dampen any high spirits that ensue. Also, before I return to my own ship let me offer you my hope that you have a safe passage home and a good and fruitful period of leave.'

He might as well have said, 'I hope you damn well drown!'

'Mr Burns,' Horatio Nelson cried, his normally high-pitched voice made even more so by his obvious delight, 'you have no idea how it pleases me to see you alive and well. We were sure you had made the sacrifice.'

Greedily drinking from a butt, Toby Burns had water dripping from his chin as he looked up and responded, his glance automatically taking in the half-closed right eye, still showing signs of bruising. 'You did not know I was captured, sir?'

'No we did not, young sir, for our French friends did not see fit to tell of anyone they had taken, although we forbore to pronounce you were definitely dead as we were lacking a corpse. But let us say it was assumed to be true and I was mightily cast down by the fact, blaming myself entirely.'

There was a moment then, a flash of a thought – that, had he known, he could have just disappeared – one that had to quickly be buried regardless of how it momentarily lifted his spirits. That was replaced with one of annoyance; he was indeed being hailed by the very man who had put him at risk of being killed. If Nelson observed the look that crossed Toby's face it did not register; he had come closer and as he did so his nose twitched, followed by a look he made no attempt to hide, one that took in the state of the midshipman's clothing.

'I see that the French adhered to their normal standards of cleanliness.' Nelson turned and called to another officer. 'Lieutenant Farmiloe, be so good as to escort your old friend to a place where he can certainly wash and get his breeches cleaned, and on my purse let us advance him a new shirt.'

'Lieutenant, Dick?' Burns asked, as an arm shepherded him in the direction of Farmiloe.

'Newly minted this very month,' Nelson responded, his good cheer once more evident, 'and very deserving of his elevation.'

'Might I point out, sir,' Farmiloe said, 'that Mr Burns missed his examination through his incarceration.'

'Bless me, I had forgotten that, which makes me doubly sorry for the troubles with which I have assailed you. On my word I will speak with Lord Hood and see if we cannot make amends.'

'Do not go to any trouble on my behalf, sir.'

'Mr Burns, once more your reticence does you credit. Now go with Mr Farmiloe, get busy on your return to the human race and do not keep him too long – I need his aid in getting my guns back aboard *Agamemnon*.'

'If ever there was a duty to avoid, it is that one,' Dick Farmiloe whispered, as they moved away, past the tars toiling to move cannon that had been in place for a month and had trunnions well sunk into the soil. 'Do you recall what it was like getting the damn thing up here in the first place?'

'I do,' Toby murmured, though he was not really thinking on that. 'How hard was the examination?'

'I was sure I had flunked it. If I replied to any of the questions without a stammer I cannot recall it, in truth I would struggle to remember anything that happened clearly, except that my knees were shaking so hard it must have been visible, even seated with hands seeking to hold them steady.'

'And yet you managed to study your books, I suppose, during the siege, I mean?'

'As much as my duties here allowed, Toby, and it is to be thankful that night falls early in these parts, for if it had stayed light as it does at home in summer, we would have been plying those cannon until ten of the clock.'

'The town is totally destroyed, I saw it as we came out from the citadel.'

Toby was guided into a building that had once been part of a monastery, the interior cool after the heat of the open, to find and pass the servants of the military officers busy breaking down campaign cots and packing the chests that lay beside them with the possessions of their masters, finally stopping next to a series of hammocks slung from the roof beams, with a battered chest below picked out with Dick Farmiloe's initials.

'This is my berth, so strip off your things, Toby, and I will see to your breeches.' The question being implicit in the look he got as he removed his blue coat, Farmiloe added, 'We have local women who clean them up amazingly well and in this heat they dry in an hour. There is a place to wash in that little room over there, though it's damn cold, being spring-fed. I will see about some stockings and a shirt, for those you have are beyond saving.'

'Are such things to be had here?' Toby asked as a block of soap was placed in his hand.

'Oh, yes. The possessions of those who have perished are for sale. I will try to get you a shirt that belonged to a fellow sailor, but I fear you might have to settle for a bit of cambric that was once in the possession of a bullock, or even worse, Frenchman.'

'Did many of our own perish, Dick?'

'No more than was necessary, Toby, and if I have not yet made it plain I am glad you were not one of them.'

'Despite my worries?'

'Yes!'

The two young men exchanged a look then, regarding the knowledge they both possessed but had no need to openly discuss. Richard Farmiloe too had been a midshipman on *HMS Brilliant*, indeed he had been with Toby's Uncle Ralph on that ill-fated night when they pressed those men, John Pearce included, from the Liberties of the Savoy. Farmiloe had likewise received a letter from Gray's Inn, couched differently from that to Toby Burns, merely asking him to confirm his presence at the incident, plus one or two salient facts that were required to be established, careful to point out that whatever else, given his lowly rank at the time, he bore no responsibility for what had occurred.

'I take it you wrote a reply,' Farmiloe asked, 'as I advised?'

'Yes, I did.'

'Then you have cleared your conscience, Toby, and no man, or even God, can ask more of you.'

'How I pray that you are right, Dick, and I know that should matters take a turn to the bad I can rely on you to support me.'

'Make yourself presentable, Toby.'

In that reply Farmiloe succeeded in keeping out of his voice his true feelings: he had no desire to get involved in the troubles of his one-time fellow midshipman. Toby Burns seemed to have latched on to him as a bosom friend, which was far from being the case; Farmiloe found the younger man an awkward companion at the best of times and a bit of a nuisance at the worst. If there was sympathy for his plight it came from the kind of fellow feeling that could be extended to anyone with whom he had once shared a berth and not come to actively dislike.

Added to that, Farmiloe knew Burns was not the hero he had been acclaimed; knew the truth of what had happened on the coast of Brittany and who it was responsible for the actions that underpinned that false reputation. In being honest about his lying at his uncle's court martial, Toby had not seen fit to be open about the previous misrepresentations that were the bedrock of his reputation as a brave and resourceful young fellow who had been hailed as an example to follow.

'Put all that out of your mind for now, Toby,' Farmiloe said finally, 'and get yourself decent. Then I will take you aboard *Agamemnon* where you can dine as my guest in the wardroom.'

The cheering, which resounded around the whole fleet, finally brought Sam Hood onto the quarterdeck of *HMS Victory*, a raucous cacophony that assailed the ears of Admiral Hotham as he barged back to his own flagship. Not every captain had seen fit to man his yards, but none, even those who saw Hood as a bar to their own personal prosperity, had sought to stop their men from letting their commanding officer know how heartily he was regarded and how the success at Calvi added lustre to his reputation.

Aware that on every vessel, every telescope would be employed for a sight of him, Hood, several times, raised his hat and it was a demonstration of the clear-sightedness of those he commanded – young men in their prime mostly – that such an act raised the hurrahs to a crescendo.

'Damn me, I will miss this, Parker.'

'I too, milord, since I will be returning with you.'

'Aye, Hotham will want his own captain of the fleet, but I am sure he will give you a ship and command of the rear squadron if you ask him.'

'Let us just say, milord, that after so long at sea, I too could use some respite.'

Hat in the air, Hood replied, 'Best get Pearce away quickly, Parker, I don't want Hotham to get any inkling that his position is anything other than temporary.'

'With respect, you are not the only one who receives letters from home.'

'True, no doubt the likes of Portland will be keen to tell Hotham he has nothing to fear from my return. But I have made it plain that I intend to cause trouble, Parker, and that is also something I will make just as plain to Billy Pitt. Politics is the game that has led to my present position and it will be politics that will reverse it.'

'A very different kind of battle, milord.'

'Yes, Parker, but once home I will be a participant, which will make all the difference. Get Pearce away to Leghorn.'

'He cannot stay there for ever, milord.'

'We need not issue any order for his return and, who knows, perhaps Hotham will forget about *HMS Larcher*, for I cannot think either the vessel or the person who commands it are of much import to him.'

Hood replaced his hat and looked at the somewhat pinched face of his executive officer, his face breaking into a wide grin. 'No need to look like that, Parker; if anyone knows me for a devious sod it is you.'

'There, milord, I cannot but agree.'

The grin settled into a frown. 'No need to be so hearty in that, is there?'

CHAPTER SIX

Quite unknown to Hood, his second in command had asked that *HMS Larcher* be kept under observation, an instruction seen as odd by the ship's officers, but not one to ignore with such an irascible superior. When the deck of the armed cutter turned from celebration to the kind of activity that preceded departure, Hotham was informed and was on deck with a telescope to his eye as she was hauled over her anchor.

In the glass and at no great distance the admiral could examine quite easily the face and features of John Pearce standing by the binnacle. He was certain he could see endemic malice and rank self-interest, this against most folk – there were some very notable exceptions – who took him to be a fellow who could be termed handsome and, if they had dealt with him, fair of mind.

Pearce was tall, which to a man of truncated height like Hotham, was enough alone to induce a degree of resentment, but harbouring such feelings would not answer the pressing question of what to do about him. And why, having just arrived, was he being sent away? There seemed no apparent reason for his not remaining in San Fiorenzo, yet, flying a flag that identified *Larcher* as now being part of the fleet Hotham was about to inherit, he was preparing to weigh.

Hood had employed Pearce in some questionable undertakings before and seemed to repose some kind of trust in his abilities. Hotham wondered if he was on some kind of mission and, if so, could the purpose be detrimental to him? Such a possibility had him call into his cabin, once he had returned, his clerk Toomey.

'I have a need to know where Pearce is going and, if possible, why.'

Toomey needed no telling of the kind of trouble Pearce could cause and his presence here was just as unwelcome to the clerk. But he was quick to tell the man he served, and on whose good fortune his own prosperity depended, that he had less to be concerned about than he thought.

'Without Burns, and with the reply I sent on the young fellow's behalf, there is good reason to hope that the matter will be closed.'

'And if not?'

'The case requires a willing witness.'

'You do not see the possibility of others coming forward?'

'Might I remind you, Sir William, of your rank and station, soon to be enhanced by the titular command of the fleet—'

'Once in my hands, Toomey,' Hotham growled, 'it will not be wrested back, take my word upon it!'

'And I heartily hope that to be the case, sir, and much honour to follow. But to continue, now Burns is no longer with us the only credible witnesses Pearce could call forward have to be serving officers and ones with no known bias, for who would believe any of those lower-deck fellows that he calls his Pelicans? A cursory examination would show their attachment to Pearce personally and thus render their testimony suspect. Now, for a serving officer to risk traducing the name of an admiral—'

'Hold on, Toomey, it is Barclay who is at risk here!'

The clerk had to suppress a sigh; his master was a sailor and confident in his nautical abilities, about which the clerk was willing to admit to ignorance. In Toomey's experience sailors were, as a breed, less secure once they let their feet touch land, and the case being outlined fell into that category.

'And he, Sir William, is a client officer of yours and known to be so. To seek to impugn Barclay is to do the same to you.'

'They would fear to risk it?'

'If they care about a career in the service, they most certainly would, especially if the risks they were embarking on were pointed out to them. I would also add that the only two we need be now concerned about, Lieutenants Digby and Farmiloe, are both serving in what is soon to be your command.'

'You're sure they can be silenced?'

'It is my business, Sir William, to be diligent on your behalf, so yes, I am sure.'

Hotham nodded slowly as he digested that and it was pleasing to Toomey that he saw the sense of what was being advanced; he was in little danger now. 'I still wish to know what Pearce is doing.'

'And you shall, sir. I see Lord Hood's clerk frequently, given we have much to discuss, and with what is proposed for his master that will apply tenfold. That gives me an excuse to call upon him and I am sure he will tell me what orders have been issued to *HMS Larcher* if I ask.'

'And?'

'Let us say if he does, they will be routine and then we have nothing to concern ourselves with. If, on the other hand, he does not; if he ducks what is a seemingly harmless enquiry, then it will be enough to put us on our guard, which is all we need to be.'

Even if he had suffered nothing from being anchored within sight of *HMS Victory*, John Pearce was happy to see her upper poles diminish the further north he sailed; his lack of trust in Hood and his machinations was total and all the time he had been within hailing distance he had conjured up, based on past experience, any number of schemes into which the old sod could embroil him. It had happened too many times in the past to induce comfort, though Pearce had never thought to wonder why he was so often called upon to undertake some delicate or dangerous mission.

A lack of vanity would never allow him to think it was based on trust or his ability; more likely he had certain skills, not least a fluency in French that could be said to be in his favour when that nation was the enemy. In addition, Pearce supposed Old Sam saw him as expendable, not really a naval officer and also a fellow without parents or important connections, thus someone who would not command an explanation should he be lost on what could be seen as some hare-brained adventure.

Yet there was another side to the matter; if he had ever been reluctant to comply with Hood's orders, John Pearce could not deny that he took some pleasure in the risks involved, as well as the overcoming of them. Running over such missions in his mind, going ashore at Toulon to help facilitate the surrender of the port, the various adventures since, he wavered between a remembrance of how nip and tuck many of the situations had been, mixed with satisfaction at having seen off the various difficulties.

Such self-regard fell apart as he recalled Gravelines and what had come from that escapade, which had nothing to do with Hood or the King's Navy! He had put his life in danger as well as those of his friends to such an extent that it had come to haunt him after it should have died a death. Stood on the tiny area of planking that made the term quarterdeck risible, his knees giving and straightening with the rise and fall of the ship, he found another reason to rebuke himself.

The one overarching mission he had set himself, namely to get his friends their freedom from the navy had failed, for they were serving under him and doing so as volunteers. That would have been possible to live with if he had not been the cause. They took the King's bounty that locked them into the service for the duration of the present war to save his skin!

Not being a fellow to excessively berate himself and long before they had raised Cape Corse, his mind had turned to the future not the past, only to settle on a matter that was utterly lacking in certainty, thus no more comfortable in contemplation. First there was the question of Emily Barclay, with whom he envisaged spending that future, for he could not for a moment believe her husband would just accept their affair.

The Ralph Barclay he knew was not that kind of man, this witnessed by the lengths he had already gone to in seeking to secure the copy of the papers from his court martial. If he had not personally broken into the offices of the solicitor where his wife had lodged them, then he had certainly engineered the attempt at recovery.

Added to that there was money, which if he was not on his uppers was not so plentiful that he could provide himself and his paramour with security – her notion that her now well-heeled husband should support her was not something the Pearce pride would countenance.

He was owed some prize money but it was not sufficient to support them both for long and, in truth, the only income he could boast of was his naval pay. The irony that he might need to maintain that was not lost on a man who had stated many times his desire to be shot of the uniform he wore and everything associated with it.

It seemed all his life he had lived on the wing, first endlessly traversing England in the company of his father, aiding him in disseminating his radical message – an end to monarchy and aristocratic privilege, universal suffrage for both men and women and a fair distribution of the wealth of the nation. He could see now, in his mind's eye, his father on the stump, hectoring his listeners, often berating them for their own apathy, which sometimes was taken as truth but more often went down like a flagon of cold vomit.

He could smile now at the way they had often been obliged to flee, though it had been far from funny at the time, and even if they were still in one place long enough for Adam Pearce to drive home his message, his son, collecting in a hat the contributions necessary for them to eat and pay for shelter, had to keep a lookout for lads close to his own age who had an eye on the takings.

There had been other occasions where some local worthy had been keen to engage Adam Pearce in meaningful debate or even one who saw the radical orator as a soulmate: the latter had often led to a comfortable bed and regular food. Several winters had been spent in such ease, times when, instead of being paternally instructed in his letters and numbers, son John had been sent to a local school to continue his education.

Even being arrested and locked up in the Fleet Prison could be recalled without a true memory of the utter misery such a place represented. Incarcerated by a government who feared his words and ideals – many might have hailed the Revolution in France, but it was not seen as encouraging by those in power – good friends had got Adam and his teenage son free.

If the administration had hoped to silence the man they called the Edinburgh Ranter, they had spectacularly failed: if anything, confinement raised Adam Pearce's profile more than his numerous and profitably selling pamphlets until eventually the government acted in a way that left no alternative for both father and son.

The King's Bench Warrant for seditious libel had forced them to flee to Paris, for that was an offence which, with malice, could end up at Tyburn. Initially hailed by the men who had toppled their king, those who assumed power in France found Adam Pearce just as much trouble as King George and his ministers, for he was as keen to remind them of their failings, not least their recourse to the guillotine.

For all his ranting against privilege Adam had never advocated that anyone, monarch included, should die to see a more just world, for it could never be that if stained with blood. His growing son, taking the pleasures of Paris in his stride as he turned from youth to manhood, held even more jaundiced views on the fallibility of the human race, so that the admiration of childhood had morphed into that period when the child rarely agrees with the parent about anything.

A distance had grown up between them that John Pearce now deeply regretted, for he had loved his father deeply and respected him, even if he had disputed with many of his Panglossian notions of the innate goodness of their fellow man. Time and circumstance had put paid to the kind of relationship they might have enjoyed as adults and that was regrettable. Yet if old Adam had now gone, nothing seemed to have changed for his son: he was still living from day to day without any kind of settled future.

'Sure that's a brown study you're in, John-boy.'

Pearce lifted his chin from his chest at the sound of that soft remark, to where it had sunk in contemplation, aware that his worries must have been evident in his expression. Habit, the need to hide those feelings even from his closest friend, made him force a smile.

'How good it would be, Michael, to be able to see a clear path ahead.'

'Me, sure I put my faith in God, and let him see to it.'

There being no reply to that, which would not cause an upset, religion being a thing they fundamentally disagreed about, Pearce cast his eyes over the prow, to see that they were about to come abreast of Cape Corse so it was nearly time to change course: how easy it was to do that on a ship and how difficult in life.

'Leghorn at sunrise Michael, if this wind stays true.'

John Pearce was not the only one thinking on the future; Emily Barclay was wondering where life would take her now that she had made such a dramatic and irreversible choice, this driven home forcibly by being alone in a foreign city. In the world in which she had been raised a woman did not leave her husband and certainly never for a lover, which could only lead to her being ostracised by decent society; that there was another assemblage, a demi-monde who would turn a blind eye to such a state, was poor compensation for a girl brought up by respectable parents and inherited standards.

Set against that was the fact that she had decided to elope with John Pearce, and the happiness to which such an association had introduced her – the truth that it was possible to love and be loved and take pleasure just as much in the physical manifestation of same as the emotional. There was a time, not very far past, when such lubricious thoughts would have brought Emily to the blush but she was a fully grown woman now.

Long gone was the naivety that had led her into matrimony with a man twice her own age, along with the notion that he might be a person of some honour to go with his status as a post captain. The more she thought on Ralph Barclay the more she saw a beast instead of the being she was thinking of on the day of their nuptials, a man of parts who would give her a life of respectability and comfort.

He was a person of mean spirit, a captain who flogged his men with what she saw as scant justification, as well as a conspirator prepared to stoop to any level to gain his ends. But more than in any other sphere she rated him as a beast when it came to claiming his matrimonial rights. Disenchanted prior to the demonstration of that characteristic, Barclay had provided the final straw needed to break with him, though not for another – there had been no John Pearce; indeed, that she had been attracted to him was a mystery.

Walking the quayside under a floppy bonnet, very necessary to keep at bay the glare from an early morning sun, she was examining the endless tables full of the fruits of the sea, wondering if she should buy something to take back to her lodgings; would the woman who owned them be offended and if she was would it be obvious or disguised?

If her hometown of Frome was inland, it was yet provided with fresh fish, so Emily knew to look at the eyes, which would tell her how long the creature had been out of the sea. These examinations were, at each display, accompanied by a pitch from the vendor that the bella signorina must buy and the price would be special because of her beauty – or so she assumed, given they spoke a local Tuscan dialect incomprehensible even to their fellow Italians. If they comprehended her refusals in *Inglese* they were very adept at pretending they did not.

When it came to the heaped crustaceans, still alive and crawling over each other, their bodies shiny from the water with which they were periodically doused, she saw in the lobsters and crabs – and she admitted to herself it was fanciful – something of her own dilemmas: they were unsure of which way to go in an environment utterly alien to them; even those remaining still waved their claws in seeming despair.

'Can I help you, Miss?'

The voice slightly startled her, first speaking English, being mixed, as it was, with yet more exhortations from the man selling the seafood. Then there was the appellation itself for she was in truth a Mrs, not a Miss. In the act of turning to face the enquirer certain impressions emerged: the fellow must have been observing her to know she was entitled to be addressed as a young Englishwoman, and since she had removed her wedding band long ago it was possible to assume that the lack of that had added to the way he had addressed her.

'These fellows will dun you as soon as look at you, I'm afraid.'

The bonnet Emily was wearing flopped to the sides, which did much to hide her face, so that it only became truly identifiable full on. The moment when that happened shocked both her and the speaker, he the first to react.

'Mrs Barclay?'

'Lieutenant Digby,' she replied, certain the nervous tremor would be obvious in her voice.

His hat was in the air now and he could not help but look out to sea at the various British men-o'-war that lay in the offing, as well as numerous transport vessels. 'Forgive me, madam, I did not know Captain Barclay was even in the Mediterranean.'

In an act of physical defensiveness Emily had crossed her hands over her stomach, left fingers hidden by right, so that when Digby's eyes dropped the lack of a wedding band was hidden. Had he observed that before he spoke to her? She did not know, but Emily was aware that however it was phrased the mention of her husband was a question and one demanding an answer.

'You are, I assume, here with a ship, Mr Digby?'

The deliberate prevarication worked, for he was obliged to reply. 'I am, *HMS Leander*, here from San Fiorenzo to revictual.'

'And how do you find service in her?'

That creased Digby's features somewhat and Emily guessed why. Was she asking in comparison to his time of service with her husband? She must be aware that had been a less than wholly edifying experience for a newly employed lieutenant, not too long in that rank, nervous and unsure of his abilities, these not being traits that brought much sympathy from Ralph Barclay. When he did reply it was with something of a stammer.

'Let us say that service aboard *HMS Brilliant* was easier.'

'Pray, Lieutenant Digby, replace your hat. The sun.'

He had been unaware of his still raised hat and it was to his credit that, found looking foolish, he laughed. Thinking back to the times she had previously met Digby, Emily reckoned that this signalled improvement for he had struck her as too serious a fellow, especially when he had dined at her husband's table; shy, nervous and seemingly terrified of making some gaffe. Then, of course, there was the man at whose table he was eating: Ralph Barclay tended to make many people anxious.

'If your husband is here, Mrs Barclay, it would be only fitting that I pay him my compliments.'

There was no getting out of that enquiry, though she had looked into Digby's eyes to seek to discern if it was as innocent a comment as he had made it sound.

'He is not.'

'Ah!'

The sound was singular, especially after the slight pause that preceded it, suggesting that if he were not here, then it would have been natural for her to have continued and said where he was. For Emily Barclay, and Digby could not know this, meeting him had created for her a moment of truth.

Up till now she had never had to confront anyone who knew both John Pearce and Ralph Barclay, never had to admit to the true situation in which she found herself. If Leghorn was full of English sailors, and it was, they were strangers to her, and if that had led to admiring glances over the last few days, as well as deliberately flirtatious passing comments, it had not been taken to a point of proper conversation.

Finding that she was biting her lower lip, Emily immediately desisted and then, with a voice as strong as she could make it, issued what sounded like a declaration. 'I must inform you, Mr Digby, that Captain Barclay and I no longer live under the same roof.'

That got another slowly delivered, 'Ah!' and she searched his frozen face to see if such a statement made sense. Had Digby thought them a mismatch aboard her husband's frigate? Had any of the officers and mids thought that she, being half the age of their captain, closer to their years than his and given his character, reckoned it was a relationship doomed to be unhappy?

'Would I be allowed to refer to that as unfortunate?'

That surprised her. 'Why, pray?'

'It is never a happy state of affairs when a man and his wife are . . .'

He could not find the word he wanted so she supplied it for him. 'Incompatible?'

'Unable to stay within the bounds of their vows, was what I was seeking to say. Do I take it you are alone here in Leghorn?'

How should she reply? Tell the truth, or would the God in which she utterly believed forgive a lie to save her face and blushes? The sound of signal guns was no less rare in the roads of Leghorn than they were in the Bay of San Fiorenzo and the boom of that now had them both looking out to sea, over the tables of shiny fish, at the outline of the tiny ship coming in under topsails.

If it was an unknown quantity to Digby, it was not to Emily, who had sailed in *HMS Larcher* from England. It was one of the only two ships in the world she could have positively identified and the sight meant that there was no point to even thinking of lying.

'No, Lieutenant Digby, I am not alone. A comrade of yours from a previous commission brought me here.' That confused him until she added, 'I believe you are very well acquainted with Lieutenant John Pearce.'

Digby went bright red then, for the implications were obvious. 'Forgive me, Mrs . . . Madame, I must be about my duties.'

'Lieutenant Digby,' she said as he turned away, 'I would be obliged if you would treat what I have just told you with some discretion.'

His reply was too indistinct to be easily heard.

CHAPTER SEVEN

There were two people at the wardroom table who were drinking too much: Toby Burns was one of them and it was moot, when they were called upon to speak, who made the greater exhibition of themselves, he or Horatio Nelson! In the case of the captain of *HMS Agamemnon*, the senior of the guests, it was partly due to the need he had to dull the continuing pain he felt from his wounded eye.

This, weeping slightly, was under regular attention from a large handkerchief. Yet there was another element to contend with: pure mischief on the part of his officers, Nelson being a well-known lightweight in the article of drink, a trait they acted upon for the enjoyment to be had from his behaviour. There was no lack of respect in this – to a man they esteemed him highly – but such tomfoolery was the very stuff of life to young men of high spirits engaged in a dangerous occupation.

Never one to overly mask his feelings, wine made him a trifle boastful, not for himself but for the British tar and especially his ship. Nelson was eager to remind his inferiors that he knew what it was like to serve before the mast, having done so aboard a merchant vessel in his early youth, to let them know that he understood how an able seaman or topman thought, knew how to get the best out of them, which was why his sixty-four gun ship of the line was the best fighting vessel in the fleet.

'Hear him, hear him,' came the collective cry when his praise was extended to those present: they too were proud of their ship and their abilities.

Only when he began to praise his wife did the eyes of his fellow diners glaze over and not just because of the effusion with which he spoke of Fanny Nelson. To hear her described as a paragon, the very essence of marital rectitude and the bosom companion of his heart flew in the face of both his deeds and other statements he was wont to use after too frequent attention to the decanter. He had been heard to say more than once, 'East of Gibraltar every man is a bachelor.'

Ashore, there was no plying of Nelson, quite the reverse, for in drink he was a worry; in the hothouse atmosphere of the kind of entertainments to which his rank got him invited, adulterous temptation was something he found hard to resist, his most recent fancy an amply bosomed Italian opera singer. There was no regard for his wife then and it was doubly dangerous in that he was often attended upon by his stepson Josiah Nesbit, serving aboard as a midshipman; who knew what the lad was telling his mother!

Toby Burns, the sole guest of that rank at the table, was being plied by Dick Farmiloe in order to get him to loosen up; he had seemed like a wound spring since he had been released and even if his one-time fellow mid thought he knew the reasons, there seemed no need to avoid a celebration of his freedom. Farmiloe's attention, which kept Toby's glass well topped up, backfired when the youngster was called upon to recount the past heroics for which he was famed.

Normally, when it came to recounting the events in Brittany for which he had been much lauded, Toby could trot out a well-worn tale liberally sprinkled with the kind of becoming modesty that deflected repugnance. Excess wine altered that and induced a degree of boastfulness that many found embarrassing, Farmiloe most of all; only Nelson seemed to drink in his every word, rapt in his attention.

'To find yourself ashore,' Toby slurred, in conclusion, 'with half a dozen seamen in a panic is terrifying, sir, given I was on my first ever voyage. But I soon took charge and began to formulate that which I must, a way to get us back to *HMS Brilliant*.'

'Which you achieved with a brilliant stroke,' Nelson hooted, looking around the table for approval of his telling pun.

'Indeed it was,' Toby responded with seeming glee, even if he had heard the same words ten dozen times, in being a jest too obvious for many to avoid.

'Did you not have help?' Dick Farmiloe asked, seeking to temper the swank, which he knew to be pure invention. 'Some of the men you led aided quite substantially in the affair, did they not?'

'Useless!' That reply was spat out along with droplets of wine. 'And a damn radical in one case, Dick, a true Jacobin.' Toby's voice dropped and his face took on a look of what he supposed was cunning; it made him look like a particularly dishonest horse vendor. 'But I saw to him and no error. You know the fellow I speak of—'

The voice from the door interrupted to tell all assembled that *HMS Victory* was in sight, which made Nelson sit back in his chair; it also prevented a stony-faced Farmiloe from dishing the whole fiction of what Toby Burns had just imparted.

'Gentlemen, I must resist any more of your hospitality, for Lord Hood will want me aboard to hear from my own lips about the fall of Calvi. And you, gentlemen, need to be about your duties.'

There was no mystery in his listeners as to what that meant: their commanding officer needed to sober up and they had to pretty the decks so that their ship would pass muster under Hood's basilisk and very critical gaze. Every eye was upon Nelson as he said those words and they stayed there as he got unsteadily to his feet, his servant Frank Lepeé stepping forward to get close enough in case he stumbled.

This was even more amusing than anything that had happened at dinner. Lepeé drank like a fish and was often in need of a hand on his elbow himself and here was such an occasion, for the servant, with glazed eye and unsteady gait, had clearly been tippling hard in the wardroom pantry.

The pantomime that followed, as the pair staggered towards the doorway trying to measure the pitch and roll of the ship, meant no one was looking at Toby Burns, which was just as well given he had taken the news badly, so much so that, head in his hands, he had begun to cry. Those who passed his shaking shoulders reacted in different ways, some embarrassed, others patting his shoulder and issuing reassuring words. Farmiloe, having been first out the door, even before Nelson and Lepeé, had not noticed and would probably not have expressed sympathy if he had.

The last to pass him was the premier, who ended up utterly

nonplussed by the reaction to his kindly delivered words, an even greater shuddering of the shoulders. 'Never mind, lad, we'll get a boat to fetch you back to *Britannia* before the next watch. Nothing like your own berth, eh?'

With all secure aboard *HMS Larcher*, John Pearce could prepare to go ashore, a list of his present stores in his hand, as well as what he needed to bring them up to requirement for what lay in the future. Where he would be going next he had no idea, for in his orders bringing him to Leghorn there had been no mention of what he should then do. They might be here for a while, which was a not unpleasant prospect given what was awaiting him.

'Mr Dorling, I need you to work out a list for some shore leave – no more than eight hands at a time and none to spend a night out of the ship. I trust we have no one foolish enough to run.'

'Not likely on a foreign shore, Capt'n.'

Pearce nodded, even if he knew that there were sailors in the fleet, though he doubted on *Larcher*, who would desert regardless of where they were. That was more the case on the larger ships; the intimacy of a smaller vessel meant the binding connections were more personal.

'I will grant that once I have seen to the revictualling.' Looking over the side at the dozens of boats that had surrounded the armed cutter almost before she had hove to and anchored, Pearce added, 'The men may trade, but no women to come aboard. If the men want their pleasures they will be granted time to take them ashore.'

Pearce suspected that would somehow be circumvented for he had no marines in his complement to prevent it, not that the lobsters were beyond the odd backhand bribe to allow what was every commanding officer's right to ban, though many did not bother to do so. Often they took quite the opposite course, which flew in the face of Admiralty instructions.

A glance around the inner roads, just before he entered his cabin, showed just what a predicament it was; every warship had its quota of bumboats close by and there was a seventy-four not far off, with open ports, from which it was possible to hear the sound of fiddles and flutes, while he had no doubt the local whores had clambered through those openings to service the crew, even if there were guards set to stop them.

'*Leander*,' Michael said when Pearce alluded to the seventy-four and the sounds of merriment. 'Sure it's the devil ship. Me, Charlie and Rufus was put aboard her to come out here the first time.'

'Not a happy time?' Pearce replied, not without a strong stab of guilt, for that had been his fault.

'Sure, the captain was never to be seen outside a foray on deck of a morning and the ship was run by that bastard Taberly, who I have told you of enough.'

It was rare for Michael O'Hagan to overly complain; he was a man who tended to take life as it came, but he had done so and very vocally about serving aboard *HMS Leander*. The aforementioned Taberly, premier of the ship, was a flogger and a gamer, who had put Michael to bare-knuckle fighting, bouts on which he had creamed off goodly sums, a small reward going to the man who had earned him his winnings. He felt no need to give away more: if Michael did not do Taberly's bidding there was always the grating to help persuade him.

'Then let us hope you do not run into him.'

'We will be going ashore, John-boy?'

'You will. I'll arrange it, Michael, that you, Charlie and Rufus are ashore at the same time as myself. Then we can find somewhere quiet to share a drink without the need for any of you to go forelock touching.'

Even in his private space both Pearce and O'Hagan had spoken very softly; it was a truism that the average sailor could hear a whisper through ten inches of planking and generally knew what their officers were about to propose well before they gave out any orders. If the crew knew that there was a special bond between these Pelicans it was not something to be too blatant about; any hint of favouritism could lead to resentment in the confines of a ship and that was a problem, once it took hold, very hard to counter.

The response came in the same hushed way and with a hint of humour. 'Sure I hope not too quiet, John-boy. We Pelicans are as minded to pleasure as any man aboard.'

'Just as long as you get back by the last dogwatch, Michael.'

'No problem there, as Jesus is my judge.'

That got O'Hagan a jaundiced look, for he was a man too fond of the bottle for the liking of his friend. Then there was his other habit of seeking to knock some poor soul's block off his shoulders; when Michael was in drink, violence was never far off, which might have been acceptable without his massive size and considerable ability.

Pearce worried that one day O'Hagan would be so far gone he might maim or even kill someone, which past experience had shown was not beyond him, albeit in the act of near murder when he had been stone-cold sober and needing to defend himself.

'Boat's ready, Your Honour,' Dorling called, 'and Bellam requests that he go ashore with you, given the parlous state of your personal pantry.'

Tempted to point out, that with Emily Barclay in the town, he was more likely to eat ashore than aboard, Pearce held off. If there was a golden rule in the navy, regardless of your rank, it was never to upset the cook. Fishing in his purse, he pulled out several coins, more than enough to allow Bellam to purchase what he thought he needed. There was another truism Pearce was aware of: he would see no change and it would be a far from sober one-legged cook who came back on board.

There was a momentary distraction as a frigate that had been in their wake made to anchor, the calls to do so floating over the harbour from an officer using a speaking trumpet. *HMS Dolphin* had first been spotted well out to sea and Pearce knew it to be British after they had exchanged the private signal and their respective numbers.

He had assumed it to be on course for Leghorn and for the same reasons as he, and the only thing unusual now was the number of redcoat officers crowding its quarterdeck and poop as the crew went about their duties, which brought an aside from Dorling.

'Bullocks gettin' in the way, Your Honour, an' it was ever thus.'

'Not for long, Dorling; they will be as eager for the fleshpots as any of our lads.'

'Best, then, they don't frequent the same, for it will be knives out an' no error.'

'Let's hope, as officers, they seek out a higher grade of establishment.'

For a second, before he stepped down into the boat waiting to take him ashore, Pearce wondered about issuing an instruction to his crew to avoid any army officers if they encountered them; that he also put aside, for it would be a waste of breath and might have the reverse effect of what was intended. They might start to seek out those bullocks as a fitting target for a good brawl.

Emily he spied well before he made the quayside and his heart lifted at the sight of her, for she had changed out of her everyday clothing and bonnet; now she was dressed in fine clothing and under a parasol, with her long auburn hair pinned up showing a slender neck. Every one of her features was plain to see and heart-stoppingly beautiful they were. Facing forward Pearce declined to respond when she waved, for before him were several sets of rowers. He was damned if he was prepared to see them grinning at him, indeed he waited till the cutter swung round to tie up before merely lifting his hat.

As it was, Emily did not call to him, but to those very same oarsmen. 'Gentlemen, it is good to see you again.'

That had them grinning all right, to the mind of John Pearce akin to baboons. Yet there was no disguising the pleasure they took in being acknowledged. In the voyage from England Emily had endeared herself to the whole crew, after one unfortunate incident, by her obvious lack of airs and graces as well as her consideration for the extra burden she placed on them by her mere presence. Added to that, she made their commander happy and a man in that state was a sight easier to deal with than a misery guts like the fellow John Pearce had replaced.

He had only a brief moment to touch Emily's hand before he was obliged to help the rotund, one-legged Bellam out of the boat, watching him as he stomped off along the quay, then he was required to address the oarsmen.

'I must ask you to return to *Larcher* and wait for our cook to signal his need to return. There will be leave, but not until I have seen those in command here and found out what places you should avoid.'

Pearce did not hear the grumbles as the cutter pulled away, too taken as he was with his paramour; the places the Leghorn consul and the senior naval officer would wish them to avoid would be the very places they were most keen to visit.

'How it would please me to kiss more than your hand, Emily.'

'Which must wait, John,' came the hurried reply, for she knew him to be impetuous, 'until we are somewhere more private.'

There was something of a growl in his throat then, a signal to her that when they were somewhere more private there would be more than kissing to do. That she understood exactly what that sound meant produced a flush to her cheeks that made her even more attractive to her lover. Yet the way her fingers tightened round his sent another signal, to say she was not inclined to resist such a notion, which made it doubly hard to point out the need to attend to his duties first. It also made what followed, as they set off along the quay, sound very banal.

'You have been well since I left you?'

'It has not been long enough for anything untoward to occur, John.'

For all the weeks they had now spent together, Pearce was still in that state of early infatuation that made it necessary to examine every word Emily said and the way in which it was delivered; he also knew that she still harboured doubts about her actions in agreeing to depart England with him, and such acute sensibility allowed him to detect a hint of a false note in her voice.

'If something has, it would be as well to tell me.'

That got a slight pout. 'It must have occurred to you that my situation here is far from ideal.'

To agree with what was a palpable truth was to open a box of problems best avoided; in truth, her circumstances would be far from perfect wherever she was, but it took no great leap of imagination that here in Leghorn they could be acute. For the estranged wife of a post captain to be resident in a port much frequented by the Royal Navy, even on her own, was far from being ideal; to be there openly in his company would be damning. Quick-witted as ever, he produced a reply to that point with what he reckoned to be a convincing tone.

'Such a fact occurred to me, Emily, while we were apart, and it may be that we need to find somewhere less frequented by anyone who might know . . .'

He had to pause; what was appropriate to describe her circumstances? Did he say 'know your husband'?; 'know you are married and not to me'? What?

'Why do I get the impression, John, that what you have just said has come from the kind of sudden inspiration to which you are somewhat prone?'

Tempted to lie, or at least bluster, he could do no more than smile. 'You have come to know me too well.'

That got him a squeeze on his arm. 'Not true, I need to know you much better than I do.'

There was a pause before he spoke again, as he sought to distract himself from the feelings running through his body, that being far from easy. 'Yet you have an immediate worry, I sense, and on that score.'

'While I was walking the quay this morning, just as you were entering the roads, I met someone we both know, Henry Digby.'

'Ah!'

'You sound so very like him when you respond like that. He asked about my husband, expecting if I was present so was he . . .'

'And you told him the truth?'

'I was about to proffer some excuse when I spotted *Larcher*. With you about to land it seemed pointless to lie.'

'And if he makes that public . . .'

'I asked him to be discreet. I have no idea if he will abide by that request.'

'He is a good man, Digby, and I believe he will. In any case I will seek him out and explain our position to him.'

'And if it happens again, with another officer acquaintance?'

'I will not let anyone insult you, Emily.'

'And what difference will that make to their opinion of me?'

There was no doubt that the conversation had killed off the happy feeling apparent at the moment he stepped onto the quay; it was equally plain that it was not just going to suddenly disappear. Emily could not stay here if such knowledge became common; she would be exposed to, at best ridicule, and at worst, if he was not there to protect her, being importuned by men who saw any woman who had acted as had she as more than fair game.

Their forward progress, which had slowed in any case, was brought to a near halt by the redcoats piling out of several boats that had brought them ashore from *HMS Dolphin*. Boisterous in the extreme, they were milling about in a way that made passing through their ranks far from easy, which irritated John Pearce, even as it obliged him to put a cap on that as he uttered a series of the necessary polite asides to get them to clear a path.

'You sir, there sir, by the devil stop!'

Unaware of who was being addressed, John Pearce paid no heed until a hand grabbed his shoulder and roughly spun him round. He found himself staring into, under a wide-brimmed tricorn hat, the bright face of a redcoat major, a man oddly familiar, who wore an expression of deep fury.

'I told you to stand, sir, and you will oblige me by doing as I command.'

That was the wrong word to use to John Pearce. 'Sir, you have no right to command me, and if you dare to ever dare lay a hand on me again—'

The major cut right across him. 'You did not fear to do so to me in Gibraltar, sir, an act for which, had you not run off like a damn coward, I would have had satisfaction for the very next day. But then you are scrub enough to get others to see to your honour!'

It is hard to react properly when faced with the sudden realisation of an uncomfortable and truthful memory. The familiarity of the face – the confusion came from it being under that hat – lay in the fact that he had, in first acquaintance, landed on it a hefty punch. He had then received a challenge from the same fellow on their second meeting many months later. On their third encounter, the very next morning high above Gibraltar, he had seen him take a ball in the shoulder from the originator of the original quarrel.

Right now he was struggling to recall the major's name, while an added complication was the presence of Emily, not to mention a clutch of the man's companions now crowded round them, this while Pearce concluded that there was only one possible way out of what was bound to be an embarrassment.

'I have, however caught up with you . . .'

'And you will find me eager now as I was on our second encounter to apologise for what was an untoward act. And I would add that to my mind you fully satisfied your honour in facing Captain McGann.'

'Apologies be damned, I say, and as for that bastard dwarf—'

'Sir,' Pearce shouted, struggling to keep his emotions, mostly anger, in check. 'Can you not see I am in the presence of a lady?'

The face, now no more than two inches from his own, went puce.

'I do not recall you showing such consideration to my wife when you took leave to land a blow on me, sir! Added to which I will not be set from my course, and that is to demand satisfaction from you, merely because you have some whore in tow.'

Pearce, who in any case had been fighting to control his emotions, was not about to have Emily so traduced. Unhooking her arm, his fist took the major on the side of his jaw and sent him flying backwards, while his hat spun off his head. Misfortune followed: he struck a bollard and lost complete control. As his companions grabbed Pearce they would have been better employed seeing to their major, who, with helpless cries, fell backwards into the harbour with an almighty splash.

'Satisfaction, sir,' Pearce shouted, as he struggled to get his arms free. 'You may as well have need for it twice rather than once.'

'Damn you, sir, he will slice you to ribbons come the morrow.'

'Not,' came the reply from a heaving naval chest, 'if he drowns.'

That concentrated the military minds; they detached themselves and set about rescuing their major – a man who obviously could not swim and now struggling in the filthy quayside water – this done with more useless cries and suggestions than actual physical practicality.

'An address, sir, where you can be found?' asked a fresh-faced lieutenant, who had forborne to go to the aid of his superior.

'*HMS Larcher.*'

'And your name, sir, for when Major Lipton's second calls upon you?'

Lipton! Now he recalled the name. 'Pearce, Lieutenant John Pearce.'

It was with a quicker gait that Pearce led Emily away while behind them the major was hauled out to drip water all over the cobblestones.

'What, John, was that about?'

'Later,' came the glum reply.

CHAPTER EIGHT

Very little attention was paid to the boat bringing Toby Burns back to his ship; every eye was on *HMS Agamemnon* as if, by careful examination, the story of the successful conclusion at Calvi could be extracted from her timbers. Added to that, Nelson's barge had set off just before the midshipman and that had to be tracked to the entry port of the flagship.

Sitting under his hat, leaning over his sea chest and still feeling the effects of too much wine, the youngster was far from easily identifiable, and since the boat was not seen to be fetching anyone of importance there was no party on the main deck of *Britannia* to welcome him aboard.

The main deck, with anchor watches set, was quiet and he had to wait for what seemed an age till a seaman appeared to shift his sea chest, and hard on that fellow's heels he nearly got to the mids berth before he was spotted. The greeting, if loud, from the senior midshipman raising the question led to some doubts as to the sentiment behind it.

'Good God, is it you, Burns? Damn me, we were told you were a goner.'

The speaker was lit only by the fitful light that made its way down the companionway, and peering into the eyes of a fellow dressed in working garb whom he knew to be a bully, as well as a superior who would scarce be upset by his demise, Toby observed no evidence of joy.

'Taken prisoner, Mr Fletcher, or,' Toby added with a hesitant stammer, for the fellow had been up for the same examination board as he, 'are you now a lieutenant?'

'No, I am not, Burns, and it would have better fitted your manners to have found that out before you had the temerity to ask.'

It was foolish to state the obvious, but drink was still affecting his tongue. 'So you failed again?'

If he had set out to rile Fletcher he could not have picked a better or more sensitive spot. The eldest mid had, if the one Toby had missed was included, sat for lieutenant four times and had been rejected for promotion by the same number. Already in his late twenties it seemed he was destined to spend his life in his present rank, unpaid, with only a hope that a fleet action or some stroke of heroic genius would get him his step or a bit of prize money.

'Report to the premier the second your dunnage is stored,' Fletcher barked, before stomping away.

Is that how I will end up, Toby asked himself, in silent contemplation of a fate he saw as akin to death? Fletcher was trapped and if he was an oppressor by temperament that was made more telling by his situation. He held his position through some sort of favour owed by the ship's captain, a reciprocal arrangement whereby the sons of fellow officers, distant relatives or the offspring of local worthies, were taken aboard to learn a trade in which they might prosper at little or no parental expense.

Fletcher was fed and provided with a bed; he could, through his age and seniority, extract, especially from nervous and newly appointed mids, enough in the way of sweeteners to fund an occasional trip ashore, a night of ale and a whore. But should he find the lack of promotion too hard to bear what was he then to do? Life ashore and the prospect of having to live and eat from his own endeavours probably held even less of an attraction than what he faced afloat, ever the butt of his superior's temper and now, surely, aware that he would never rise in the service.

Toby had tried to point out his own unsuitability to the navy on his first visit home, but that fell very flat. The exploit in Brittany had made him a hero and the whole town wished to fete their young Lysander as such, a situation that gave prominence to his family and made them proud. Any hints that he might leave the service were brushed aside and he had lacked the willpower to overcome parental dismissals.

Knocking on the wardroom door, he was brought to think on what would have happened if he had taken the lieutenant's exam; probably he would, like Fletcher, have failed but as of this moment, entering the berth to which he would have aspired, he had no ambition to be any part of it.

'Enter.'

With the ship at anchor there were few of the normal duties being carried out so the room was close to full, most of the lieutenants with the marine officers present as well as the doctor and ship's master. Their collective cry of sheer amazement brought the first lieutenant out from his tiny cabin and he stared at Toby, eyes popping, as if he was seeing a ghost. The only thing that prevented an outburst was the need to preserve his self-esteem in a domain of which he was the leading light.

'Mr Burns, I see the news we received of you was mistaken. Let me say on behalf of the wardroom how very happy we are that it is so.' That was not greeted with loud huzzahs, but a low murmur. 'You will oblige me, and I daresay us all, with an account of how you come to be alive.'

Toby's mouth felt like the inside of a yet to be cleaned horse stall; he had a sour taste on his tongue and a dry windpipe, so that his response made him sound, and the tone did nothing to diminish it, as if he had just come back through death's door.

'Which I will happily do, sir, if I may have something to ease my throat.'

That got a raised eyebrow; in the premier's navy midshipmen did not ask for a drink in the wardroom.

'Forgive me for asking, but I was most splendidly entertained aboard *Agamemnon*, given they were my fighting companions and eager to celebrate my survival. I fear they plied me with too much wine and I am suffering for it.'

'Well, we cannot do less than a mere sixty-four,' the premier replied. 'Give the lad a glass of wine. Nothing like the hair of the dog, eh?'

Sat at the table, recounting the raid on which he had been captured, not forgetting to add that he had done his best in what was probably a hare-brained effort, Toby could not be aware that the news of his return had reached Hotham. He too was drinking a glass of wine, albeit of better quality than the midshipman and from good crystal.

The crash as that hit the casements above their heads made everyone in the wardroom look towards their own stern windows, but it was a momentary interruption and in a blink they were back, engrossed in the youngster's tale. The gap between the breaking glass and the message was short.

'Mr Burns to repair to the admiral's cabin at once.'

The only person not to smile at that was the object of the message; it was well known, and something of a mystery as to why, that Hotham had given this particular youth every opportunity he could to distinguish himself, forever putting him in situations where he had a chance to shine. There was some resentment in the lower levels of the lieutenancy – it was well known there was ten times that in the mids berth – for to see prospects going to one of a lower rank than their own was inclined to cause irritation. Not that it was ever openly voiced; no one in search of favour wanted criticism of an admiral's favourite to reach his ears.

'Better cut along sharpish, Mr Burns,' the premier said, 'Sir William must be agog to hear of your adventures.'

'It was a reaction, that was all, Emily, such as any man might make when they see a friend being struck. What happened after that was as a consequence of my original interference.'

The tale of what had happened at Gibraltar had not come out well and had suffered from having to wait until he had settled matters at the office of the Naval Commissariat. This entailed dealing with an officer, a representative of the Navy Board, who gave the impression of a man who bled if he parted with so much as a nail. Not that he was an exception: every man appointed on a foreign station to see to the needs of the fleet acted as if he was at war with his own side.

The Navy Board saw to the building of warships and supplied the fleet both in peacetime and during conflict. They saw careful husbandry as essential – things cost money, while the serving sailors, answerable to the Board of Admiralty, argued that without the means to fight, freely supplied and the price to the exchequer be damned, they were being emasculated.

No one ever emerged from such an encounter between the twin branches of the service in a good mood and John Pearce was no exception so he was glad to address another subject. Yet telling his tale brought no sense of comfort from Emily, who thought the whole affair absurd or worse.

'And is it true what that man said, John, that you ran away the day after you struck him?'

'I did not run away,' he snapped, only to realise that irritation at the suggestion had made him speak too harshly. This required an apology and a moment to return to the meal they were consuming so he could compose another response.

'The ship of which I was due to sail upped anchor at dawn the following day, and I being on official business could not let it depart without me. Naturally, I thought that the end of the matter. Not so. When we were on our way to the Bay of Biscay, we stopped at Gibraltar to find not only Lipton still there, but also the man who set the whole sorry mess in train was there and drinking in the very same tavern.'

'Captain McGann,' Emily confirmed.

She received in response a shake of the head denoting wonder as Pearce pondered on the personality of the Irish seafarer, a man of whom he was exceedingly fond, as well as the number of times their paths has crossed. The last had been off Portugal, when *HMS Larcher* had come to the rescue of McGann's postal packet, under fire from privateers. Emily, when they met at the conclusion of the action, had been exposed to all of his abundant Celtic charm, flattery and endemic good humour.

'I find it hard to believe that such a cheerful soul could have behaved as you say he did, and as for his prowess as a marksman, well, all I can say is he does not appear to be so gifted.'

'The man you met is a different creature ashore, Emily, and the expression chalk and cheese is fitting in his case. He is a superb sailor and a sober father to his crew on water. Yet he is a danger to himself and those same fellows as soon as his feet hit terra firma. He drinks like a fish, dresses like a Commedia dell'arte prince and thinks every woman on whom his eyes fall is so enamoured of him as to fall willingly into his arms.'

She was not convinced; Pearce could see that and he had the impression he could go on in that vein for ever and not change her mind. It was a trait he had noticed before in women he had known: once they had formed a good opinion of someone it tended to be unshakable until some act of pure outrage allowed the scales to fall from their eyes. Given this was not going to be that telling moment, it was best to change tack.

'As to his ability with a pistol, you would be best to ask our good friend Lutyens about that. He was the doctor who attended to Lipton after McGann put a ball in him and at precisely the place where he had earlier said he would make the wound. A winged Lipton was in no state to fight me and I had sailed on before he could recover.'

'You could do the same here, John, sail away and avoid a confrontation.'

The voice was low as he replied, 'I do hope you do not mean what you say?'

If he had expected her to be repentant, John Pearce was quickly and sadly disillusioned.

'Why not? Do you expect me to welcome the notion that you might die in a duel, and for what? Some stupid expression of male pride and one, I seem to recall, that is expressly forbidden by the law?'

'A stricture that does not even apply at home, Emily, and would certainly not serve out here.'

'So you will put your life at risk?'

'And what would you think of me if I did run away?'

'I would think the man I love and the man for whom I have risked everything is alive.'

Her eyes were wet and soon, Pearce knew, the tears would begin to flow. He came out of his own bench seat to join Emily on hers, putting his arms round shoulders which had begun to heave.

'It will not come to that, my dear. Any effusion of blood settles these things, as it was for McGann, who did not seek to kill Lipton. For me, with, I suspect, swords, it would be a cut at worst, I would reckon. It will mean no more than that you will be required to nurse me. Would it help if I say that I am almost tempted to bleed for just that attention?'

'I know it is selfish,' she snivelled, 'and unbecoming, but what is to become of me if you are wrong?'

'I intend to offer Lipton a more formal apology in the hope that he will settle for that.'

Emily looked up at him, her wet eyes showing a flash of anger. 'You are thinking on the hoof again, John Pearce.'

He kissed her forehead. 'Is that such a bad thing if it calms your fears?'

'Only if it is a lie.'

He had to hold her gaze then, so that she would not see how much such a course would affect him. John Pearce was not the type to seek out a duel with anyone; he saw the whole notion of two men employing weapons to settle an argument as farcical. But neither was he a man to easily walk away from a challenge, for there was the matter of his own pride. Added to that, if he did do so, any stain would not just disappear, it would follow his already troubled name and, he suspected, lead to more difficulties in the future than he would face now.

'Let us put that out of our minds, for now, Emily, let us finish our dinner and then . . .'

He paused, for even John Pearce could be brought to the blush when making too obvious a point.

'As you know, I am obliged to sleep aboard my ship, without I have permission to do so and I have the needs of the crew to attend to.'

'Would it help if I were to say I was no longer hungry?'

For all the peremptory nature of the summons, Toby was kept waiting outside Hotham's cabin, while inside the admiral sought from his clerk some way to deal with a situation that could too easily deteriorate.

'He must be kept away from Pearce, Toomey, for ten seconds in that sod's company and the little turd will be babbling away.'

'Might I ask, Sir William, when Lord Hood intends to depart?'

'Damned if I know and damned if he would tell me. I'll probably only have a clue when he ups anchor.' Seeing the look in his clerk's eye, Hotham was quick to add, 'Don't ask that I enquire, man, I will not demean myself to do so.'

'I was only going to point out that once he has gone you have the power to do anything you wish, and Lord Hood was much given to trusting this Pearce fellow with missions which, if I may say so, bordered on the extremely risky.'

'If I had my way I'd drop the little sod Burns over the side on a dark night with a cannonball in his breeches and hang Pearce from the yardarm.'

The tone of the response was designed to soothe, something at which the clever Irishman was adept.

'Sir William, the lad does not know Pearce is back in the Mediterranean. Can I suggest he be kept in ignorance until the time comes where such knowledge suits our purpose? In which case, you must maintain with Burns the same attitude that you have demonstrated to him so far.' That got a grunt. 'And you will recall, sir, that we set an examination as much for our intentions as any other purpose.'

The plan had been to have Burns promoted, even if he behaved like a dunce, then to send him off to serve with some tartar of a captain, a man loyal to Hotham, who would both keep an eye on any correspondence to and from Burns and, as well as making his life a misery, ensure that if there was danger in the offing, he was sent towards it.

'I can't set another examination so soon.'

'Sir William, I repeat, when you are in command, you can do whatever you wish, and should such an act be questioned by the Admiralty – why, who would be so churlish as to not see it as a favour to a lad, already a hero, denied his right by cruel circumstance?'

'Hero, my foot; Barclay told me the truth of that little escapade. The boy is a damned coward and perhaps it would be best if the truth of that were known.'

Toomey was often given to wondering if endless patience was the lot of anyone who held his position, or was he excessively burdened in that regard. Sometimes it was damned hard to serve a man so blind to his own interests. Allowing his emotions to surface was one thing; not suborning them to the greater purpose was another.

'I should call Burns in, Sir William, added to which I beg you treat him kindly.'

It hurt, Toomey could plainly see that, and it took time to be filtered through Hotham's anger and frustration at having to deal with a situation he thought resolved. But eventually, after a degree of huffing, the admiral saw the sense of the advice and waved that Toomey should let Burns in, which he did with a degree of what looked like quiet flattery mixed with concern.

'Well, Mr Burns,' Hotham said, sure his voice sounded strained, 'no cat has the luck on you, do they?'

'No, sir.'

'I am agog to hear of your latest adventure, as is Toomey, I'm sure.' The man knew what that meant; stay with us and make sure I do not lose my temper. 'Well?'

'It was an action proposed by Captain Nelson.'

That got a deep frown; Hotham made little secret of his dislike of that particular officer, and in waiting, Toby had reasoned that if there was to be any anger directed in his heading the best way to deflect it was by giving Hotham a better target.

'The aim was to spike the guns playing on the battery where I was employed.'

'I do not see it as a job for midshipmen when there are regiments of soldiers available.'

'Captain Nelson is not one to stand aside for a bullock, sir.'

'Captain Nelson is scarcely a fellow to stand aside for his own creator!'

Toomey quickly intervened; Nelson was a bête noire and once Hotham's temper was let loose it could go in any direction. 'I take it you volunteered, Mr Burns?'

The nod made that a good guess on Toomey's part: the youngster was not going to say that he had been presented with little choice in the matter; it was stand to be counted or display open fear and Toby Burns, if he would do all he could to avoid danger, would do even more to avoid being thought shy.

'Was it wise, Burns,' Hotham barked, 'this raid?'

The reply did not come immediately. 'It is not for me to say, sir.'

'Nonsense! From what I hear it was a damp squib.'

'There was a large element of risk, yes.'

Hotham had sat forward and was, to Toomey's mind, being too aggressive in his questioning; he could not seem to accept that Burns was just a youngster who would know little and probably observe less.

'I think, Sir William, it would be best if we just let Mr Burns relate his story.'

That got him a glare, but then a nod and at least the admiral sat back and ceased to appear so threatening.

'Bear what you have said in mind, Mr Burns. It may be that Captain Nelson will be called upon, at a future date, to explain such a foolhardy action. So, tell me what happened and how you came to be a prisoner?'

* * *

Horatio Nelson was closeted with Lord Hood and Admiral Parker, his expressions of regret at the C-in-C's impending departure long aired, as was his refusal of another ship, a seventy-four, to which he was more than entitled. He was content with *HMS Agamemnon* and she was thus to set sail for Leghorn under his command, there to effect some very necessary repairs and make up her stores. Once complete he was to make his way to Genoa with a message for the Doge and his council.

'Which,' Parker pointed out, 'will be couched in polite language, Captain Nelson, but you must make it plain to them that if we are to stop the French, Genoa must do more, and if they cannot provide ships they must furnish us with money and supplies. If they wish us to fight their battles they must dip into their coffers of gold.'

'I take it I am forbidden to threaten bombardment if they show themselves unwilling?'

Hood chuckled, this while Parker frowned: he was not one to trust such jokes and he reckoned Nelson could be a dangerous loose cannon, just as he thought that his superior was too indulgent of this officer.

'We have some despatches for Sir William Hamilton as well. I will give you orders that they are to be taken to Naples by *HMS Larcher*, presently in Leghorn.'

'I would much rather go to Naples than Genoa, milord.'

It was Parker who replied, his tone impatient. 'One needs stature, Nelson, a man who can make the Genoese sweat a trifle, see that we might not support them if they do not oblige us – and, by damn, they are threatened with the French just along the coast. Naples is with us heart and soul, thanks to Ambassador Hamilton. Such a job as sending despatches to him is not a task for a ship of the line.'

Nelson was an enthusiast as well as a man who wore his feelings on his sleeve, so it was of some interest to Admiral Parker that he looked exceedingly crestfallen.

'Then, Nelson,' Hood added, taking up the conversation, 'once you are done in Genoa, we must find what the Jacobins are up to in Savoy. You will hoist your flag as commodore and take a squadron of frigates to see if we can impede the French as they seek to get into Italy, as they are bound to do. Once there you can bombard away to your heart's content and send parties ashore to cause mayhem.'

As usual, the prospect of action immediately lifted Nelson's somewhat downcast spirits; his eyes took on a gleam and he began to move restlessly in his chair, as if he wanted to up and at 'em that very second.

'And once *HMS Larcher* is done in Naples she can join you, for there is bound to be inshore work for which an armed cutter will be useful.'

'As you wish, sir.'

'Now, we must celebrate the fall of Calvi, Nelson, so I will have a message sent round the fleet to assemble tonight for a capital dinner. I'm sure you will be praised to the maintop.'

Parker, listening, was wondering if there was another motive for a celebratory dinner. Hotham would have to be invited as a matter of course and Hood would be able to openly gloat in his presence.

CHAPTER NINE

Lieutenant Walcott of the 63rd Foot was pacing the deck of *HMS Larcher* looking with increasing anxiety to the west, to the point where the sun was slowly sinking towards the horizon, wondering at the absence of the damned fellow he had come to call upon? Surely a ship's captain should be aboard his vessel, not gallivanting about ashore.

Dorling had offered him the use of a chair, which he had declined, yet as he paced he thought on what he had learnt about this John Pearce, who it transpired was no stranger to Leghorn, nor, given what he had earlier had on his arm, to the local ladies.

The navy man had been in these parts before and had got into a scrape with some countess or other, quite a beauty by all accounts, the pair being nearly caught in flagrante by her husband and Pearce forced to flee through the streets in his smalls, carrying his clothing. The information had come about as soon as his name was mentioned at the commissariat, where the bullocks had gone to draw on the stores that were theirs by right; clearly the fellow was a rake as well as a coward and the butt of what was seen as a humorous tale.

The visitor was not to know it was a story also known to Emily Barclay, for, as well as John Pearce she had been in Leghorn with her husband when it happened and she had marked it as shameful. It was now, however, an incident over which they had, with mutual silence, drawn a discreet veil.

Walcott could suppose that whatever was keeping Pearce from his nautical duties was of the same order of business as that escapade. Remembering what he saw of the filly Pearce had been escorting when he encountered them on the quay induced a definite feeling of jealousy: she too was a rare beauty.

'Captain has signalled for his boat, sir, and will be with you in a trice.'

'Thank you.'

Dorling waited a second in the hope he might hear the purpose of the visit, but nothing was forthcoming. The whole crew was just as curious, not sure if Michael O'Hagan was right or wrong when he said, that to his mind, it boded ill and would do their captain no good at all, he being minded to chuck the redcoat in the harbour if given the word.

'Bound to be trouble if Pearce is to do with it,' opined Charlie Taverner.

'No error there, mate,' Rufus Dommet agreed, and since their opinion was held to be more knowledgeable about their commander it was a crew on edge by the time his boat came alongside and he was piped aboard.

'I take it, sir, you know who I am?'

'Not by name, sir.'

'Lieutenant Walcott, at your service.'

'And to what do I owe the honour?'

Both men knew the answer to that question, but it fell to the bullock to speak. 'I am here on behalf of Major Lipton who has asked me, as his second, to tell you that he demands satisfaction for the cowardly way you have struck him on two occasions.'

The whole ship was listening, both on deck and those below, exchanging knowing nods; it came as no surprise to hear that their commander had belted some cove. Twice was seen as a plus, not a black mark.

'He does not feel that experience mitigates against exposing himself to danger?'

'He is a soldier, sir, danger is part of our profession, as it is of yours.'

'His shoulder,' Pearce said softly. 'The nature of our encounter did not allow me to ask if it is fully healed?'

'There is no reason for him to avoid what must be done.'

'And if I offered Major Lipton a full apology?'

That got suppressed gasps from the crew; their man was in no way shy, quite the opposite.

'It would not be accepted. Also, since you struck the blow, Major Lipton insists that should you agree to give him satisfaction he reserves the right to choose the weapons.'

'Very well.'

'All that remains for you to do is to send me your second and we can finalise the arrangements for the time and place of the encounter. We are billeted at the Pensione d'Ambrosio.'

That the man he was addressing then laughed confused Walcott, but he could not know, and John Pearce was not about to tell him, that he would be hard-pressed to find anyone to second him; it had to be a fellow officer and as of this moment he knew no one in Leghorn apart from the Navy Board captain with whom he had spent an hour in dispute.

'My boat crew will take you ashore.'

'Obliged.'

It was getting dark now, pinpricks of light appearing in the buildings that lined the shore. Pearce stood rock still as the army man got down into his boat, which immediately set off. It was almost at the quayside before he moved, calling for Dorling to come to his cabin and to bring with him the lists of men he had targeted for leave.

Michael O'Hagan saw to the lanterns being lit before departing. Sitting opposite each other, Pearce knew that the ship's master was dying to ask him about the recent conversation on deck, which had his captain concentrating on the paper before him, about which he had only one reservation.

'I see you have put O'Hagan, Taverner and Dommet down for the very first batch. Better leave them for a day, since I would not want them to appear specially favoured.' Even if he did not look up he knew that had been received with an understanding nod. 'I must also tell you that I will be spending most of my time ashore, so I will be able to keep an eye out for our lads.'

He did look up then, into a face that had gone utterly blank; Dorling would never say it or even give a hint of what he knew: if John Pearce was ashore, the only thing he would have eyes for was not going to be male or naval.

'I have indented for the following,' Pearce said, passing over the list of stores they could expect. 'I will leave it to you to stow the holds with what hands are left aboard.'

'Aye, aye, sir. Might I enquire as to where we are headed next, the lads are agog to know?'

The temptation to say bollocks had to be suppressed; only Dorling would care about that. To a man, the crew of *Larcher* would be thinking of wine and women, as well as counting out what coin they could muster and setting that against what pleasure it would pay for. Thinking on that reminded him that Charlie and Rufus had been taken from a receiving ship straight onto a warship. They might be utterly bereft on that commodity and he owed it to them to provide the remedy.

'I have set an anchor watch, sir, if that is acceptable.'

'Of course, but we will need sentinels as well, and rig lantern aloft, for we are sure to be given a visit from the local villains.'

Michael O'Hagan entered as soon as Dorling departed and there was no need, given the look in his eye, for him to speak: he expected to be told what was afoot and he was indulged, wearily but fully, leaving Pearce a little nonplussed that his predicament seemed to amuse his friend.

'I don't know what's so funny!'

'Sure, John-boy, we're not much alike, 'cepting when it comes to trouble. If it don't follow us about we seem fitted to go out and find it.'

If the connection was tenuous, that brought to him an image of his actions in La Rochelle and with that the face of the man who had commanded *HMS Faron*, the ship on which they sailed to the Bay of Biscay. Henry Digby had been gifted no knowledge of what had happened in Gibraltar when they were there together, but he was in Leghorn, and surely, given the adventures they had subsequently shared, he would not decline to act for him.

'I had a thought while talking to Dorling,' Pearce said, still thinking on that while he fetched out his purse. 'Charlie and Rufus are probably a bit light on coin, so I'd best give you some to see them right.'

'What about pay?'

Pearce shook his head, that having been another discussion he had been obliged to undertake while ashore and if he had complained it was to no avail: the man who held the British Government funds in the Grand Duchy of Tuscany had seen him off; when it came to sailors' pay, bigger and better fish than he.

'There's not enough specie in Leghorn, or the whole of Tuscany if what I am told is true, to pay ships' crews, and if it is a lie there's damn all I can do about it. So the best you can ask for is a pay warrant to discount with the locals. I would say it's better to spend what you have than be dunned for a good half of what you are owed.'

'It so happens, John-boy, that I am a trifle light myself.'

On previous occasions, John Pearce might have just chucked his purse to Michael and told him to help himself, but in discussing pay he had become acutely aware that he was bearing a degree of expense now that was greater than hitherto. He had to shell out for Emily's board and lodging, with no certain knowledge of how long that would last, the only conviction being whatever it was it must be met. So he doled out a couple of guineas, which brought from his friend a weird look.

'Leghorn is cheap, Michael, and also, if I leave you on a rein it is for your own good.'

'Jesus, this servant lark is no good at all, lest you can't stand the man you're seeing to.'

'Meaning?'

Michael stood up, or rather crouched over, a look on his face that mystified his friend, for it was not kindly. 'Then you can steal what you require instead of asking for it.'

Once he was gone, Pearce got out paper, ink and set to sharpening his quill. He had logs to complete, but also he needed to write to London, first to Alexander Davidson, his prize agent, to see if he could remit some money to the Mediterranean, then to his attorney, Lucknor, to inform him he would not, as he had supposed, be returning immediately to England and to send out to him any progress he had made in the case against Ralph Barclay.

That reminded him: one of Lucknor's letters had been to Henry Digby. Was it a subject to raise with him, or one better left dormant, given his needs? What did Digby think of Barclay?

Still in London and continuing to claim the need to seek medical advice, Ralph Barclay was in receipt of better treatment than he had received from the Duke of Portland, but then the man in whose office he sat had seen him for some time as a source of profit, for the fees to be gained from handling the prize money of naval officers could be lavish, while the income that came from then investing and managing those monies was even more lucrative if properly handled.

That Ralph Barclay had been part of the recent successful action only added to his lustre; the total payout for the Glorious First was reckoned at over two hundred thousand pounds, and even if he were at odds with Lord Howe regarding his conduct, he would get his full share.

To this partner in the firm of Ommany and Druce, matters had been set up to guarantee satisfaction, for Barclay had as a clerk and secretary a fellow called Cornelius Gherson, a man who had a less than honest past and could be bought; he was as keen to see his own pockets bulge as that of his master.

It was not, however, a wholly happy interview. Edward Druce had managed to deflect Barclay for some time as he listened to his litany of complaints regarding the recent battle, during which the captain kept glancing over the prize agent's head to a painting of another fleet action in which he had been present, if, as a frigate commander, less closely involved. This was the Battle of the Saintes, an encounter in which his one-time patron, the late Lord Rodney, had trounced the Comte de Grasse.

'And that was a proper fleet, not like that parcel we encountered off Ushant,' Barclay declared, when he finally made a comparison and pointed at the huge canvas. 'The flower of the Royal French Navy was what Rodney beat, not some suddenly elevated numbskull tainted by revolution!'

He's had too much claret, Druce thought, but if his glass was empty, and it was, there was little choice but to top it up, this in the hope that his client would burble on about naval battles and stay off the subject of his missing wife. When Emily Barclay had disappeared, a thief taker called Hodgeson had been employed, through Druce, in order that she should be found and returned to the matrimonial home, forcibly if necessary.

There had been a worry, voiced by the thief taker, a very experienced and canny fellow, that Barclay could not be trusted; that he might, when his wife was located and he was told of her whereabouts, act outside the law and that was voiced before there was any mention of the involvement of another man, which was bound to heighten whatever feeling Barclay had. Though it had never been openly stated, there was the possibility of harm coming to the lady, of which Hodgeson wanted to be no part and neither did the man who had engaged him.

The other worry for Druce was the fellow Gherson, sat in the basement as of this very moment, going though the list of investments, as well as profits and expenses, even the odd small loss, so that he could reassure his master that the Ommany and Druce activities were sound.

God forbid Hodgeson should ever find him, for Edward Druce's brother-in-law definitely wanted Gherson dead, indeed he had tried to dispose of him previously, with his relative by marriage unwittingly supplying the thugs, moonlighting members of the Impress Service, this to satisfy the way Gherson had dallied with the man's wife.

Druce had also agreed to find Barclay's clerk, then sent Hodgeson off on entirely the wrong scent with a description at total odds with Gherson's very obvious appearance; the fellow was too profitable to the business to be put at any risk. He had described him as dark, swarthy and unprepossessing, instead of being what he was: near white of hair and with an absurdly handsome countenance. Such unwelcome ruminations were brought to a halt as Barclay's voice rose to a pitch of irritation.

'Medals to be struck, pensions granted, promotions to flag rank all around and what do I get? Nothing but spiteful lies.'

'It is to be much regretted, Captain Barclay, for if I was not myself present, I cannot but believe you acted with noble endeavour. Were it in my power to alter matters I would put all my efforts to doing so.'

'Just as I hope you have put in such efforts to find my wife! I had hoped, on my return to shore, there would be some information, indeed the place where she is skulking.'

His glass being drained again, Druce topped it up, thinking two unrelated thoughts: that it was a good thing Barclay did not have two hands and, though contentedly married himself, that matrimony could be a cesspit. In both the cases he was reluctantly dealing with, a great difference in age seemed to lie at the root of the trouble.

His brother-in-law had married a much younger bride and one whose attention had wandered with handsome Cornelius Gherson sharing the household. Barclay likewise had wed a woman half his age and it seemed as if it had resulted in the same sort of consequence.

'I am happy to say, Captain Barclay,' Druce replied, reaching into a desk drawer, 'that information has come in this very day.'

That was a smooth lie; Druce had been in possession of Hodgeson's report for weeks, now in two parts: one complete, the other a filleted one that would, it was hoped, avoid future difficulties landing on the prize agent's desk, for Emily Barclay had not been at all hard to find. Leafing through it now he read the thief taker's words: she had been staying in London at Nerot's Hotel and, thanks to a servant easy to suborn with drink, so had a young naval officer who went by the name of John Pearce.

According to the man who had observed their behaviour, she had been sweet on this Pearce, indeed they departed on the same day, if in separate conveyances. Too long in the tooth to fall for that ploy – Pearce was a fine-looking cove by all accounts – Hodgeson had merely enquired of a source at the Admiralty, one of the doormen, fellows who would sell their mother for a silver coin. Did a John Pearce, lieutenant by rank, have a ship?

Indeed he had and it was berthed at Buckler's Hard, down at the bottom of the New Forest, whither Hodgeson had gone, only to find *HMS Larcher* had set sail some days previously and, lo and behold, as the good folks of the shipyards watched it weigh, they could not fail to notice the presence of a very comely young lady on the deck who very much fitted the description Hodgeson had. No genius was required to put two and two together, so it was back to his Admiralty doorman for information as to where *Larcher* was headed.

'Well, Mr Druce?'

'Just refreshing my memory, Captain Barclay.'

Druce was lying again; in reality he was still wondering how much it would be wise to say, which report to read out? Was it prudent to tell this man that he was being cuckolded and that his wife was on the way to the Mediterranean with the guilty party, or should he just say where Emily Barclay had been sighted? As a naval officer Barclay would surely have no trouble in finding out about the ship on which she had sailed, but that would not tell him about the fellow Hodgeson assumed had snatched her away.

'Have you had any communication with Mrs Barclay?' he asked, prevaricating.

'I had a letter on my return and one that changes nothing, despite her protestations that our union is ended. Once I have found her—'

'Your wife may no longer, we think, be in the country.'

'Damn it, man, where could she have gone?'

'It occurred to my man that you would be better placed to find that out than he, given after she left Nerot's Hotel she travelled a goodly distance, then set sail on a naval vessel.'

That nearly had Barclay's eyes popping out of his head, the

conclusion being obvious: if she was on a King's ship a fellow officer must have facilitated that flight.

'She sailed from a place called Buckler's Hard, which is—'

'I know where it is!'

'Quite,' Druce replied, taking refuge by dropping his eyes to the reports. 'Aboard an armed cutter called *HMS Larcher.*'

Barclay shook his head, a clear indication that whoever commanded her was not someone he could recall, indeed he had probably never even heard of the vessel. Caution being one of the Druce watchwords, that was when he decided to suppress the name of Pearce.

'My man questioned the locals as to where she was bound.' Druce surreptitiously slipped out the full report and let it drop to the floor where it was hidden by the bulk of his desk; the one he had prepared and did not mention a naval lieutenant was handed over. 'It was felt that you would be in a better position to find that out than anyone I employed.'

Barclay's good hand came out and he took the single sheet of paper, which he stared at for some time before speaking.

'Armed cutters tend to be inshore vessels, Mr Druce, tasked to catch contrabandiers and protect small merchant vessels on the coastal trade from privateers, and they rarely go in deep water. This leads me to suspect that if she has been transported in one, and God would only know the whys and wherefores, then she has been taken to some port or fishing village along the south coast and dropped off, not out of the country as you suggest. That may mean, when I find which waters the *Larcher* is set to cover, sending out your man again.'

'He is, of course, entirely at your disposal, Captain Barclay, should you need him.'

'As for the fellow who has aided her to escape me, I will see him drummed out of the service, for I cannot believe he did it without knowing who he was dealing with.' That brought forth a deep sigh. 'As you will no doubt have gleaned from our previous discussion, no naval officer, however hard he tries, can go through his years of service without some people taking against him.'

A discreet knock allowed Druce to look away from a man he expected made enemies easily, that followed by the door being opened, to reveal one of the agency's liveried servants. He announced that Captain Barclay's man had completed his examination and was waiting outside.

Druce picked up the nearly empty claret bottle. 'Do you wish to cast an eye over them here, Captain?'

'No, I will examine them later. Right now I must get to the Admiralty and find out the name of the scoundrel who commands this *HMS Larcher*.'

'And then?'

'I must get back to my ship, since my leave of absence is not unlimited. I will write to you with what I find out and you can set your hound on her trail again.'

Druce was thinking that having settled one problem, Barclay's departure would now deal with another: he was anxious to get Gherson out of his offices and away; as long as he was in the building, who knew what could happen and his brother-in-law did sometimes just drop in. One thing Edward Druce did know, he was damned if he would knowingly be a party to murder.

CHAPTER TEN

Pearce was obliged to go aboard *HMS Leander* in search of Henry Digby and was thus presented, close up, with the kind of activities that took place on a man-o'-war when the captain was lax about allowing women aboard. It was not just noisy whores and paid-for fornication: there were lute players, magic tricksters and jugglers skilful enough to ply their skill under low deck beams, as well as barking traders who were so established that several mess tables were set up as stalls selling everything from trinkets to monkeys, the whole ensemble setting up a cacophony of noise exaggerated by the confines of the available space.

The marines on duty, he found, seemed tasked only to make secure the parts of the ship where no stranger was allowed to go – the various cabins, naturally, the powder, bread and private storerooms. But that still left plenty of places where they could extract some coin from a man that sought privacy for his carnal activities; the marines off duty were, Pearce assumed, as likely to be found indulging themselves in pleasure as the ship's crew. Judging by the raucous singing, there was drink available, too, and in quantity, which no doubt led to endless problems with discipline.

Having found his man he was immediately aware of the reserve with which he was greeted and that was off-putting. Here was a fellow with whom he had sailed into dangerous waters, indeed with whom he had faced a risk to his very life; Digby had also taken the time and trouble, and with patience, to fill many a gap in his subordinate's nautical knowledge, a kindness over and above his responsibilities.

Pearce thought Henry Digby a thoroughly decent fellow, if blinkered in an Anglo-Saxon sort of way; strong in his Anglican faith, an upholder of the Thirty-Nine Articles of the Act of Settlement and proudly conscientious in his morals; no doubt the latter, the case of he and Emily Barclay, was the cause of his cold manner. So instead of engaging him in the subject on which he had come, Pearce entered into an opinion of the entertainments through which he had just progressed.

'Seems like the Feast of Saturnalia on the main deck.'

'The premier is a man fond of the cat,' Digby lamented, his detachment lessened by a subject that probably affected the very same tenets by which he was no doubt judging his visitor. 'He is of the opinion that the crew must be allowed their pleasure, then if they step over the mark, which as you know any tar is bound to do in drink, he has them up at the grating and I cannot but believe it is for his pleasure.'

Digby dropped his head slightly so that Pearce could not see his eyes, which gave the impression that he was ashamed of what he was saying.

'We are also burdened with a commander who does not interfere, a fellow of stunning indolence, more interested in butterflies than his duties. He's ashore right now with his nets and his servant, running around the Tuscan hills seeking to augment his collection. This ship, in his absence, is run entirely by Lieutenant Taberly.'

'I know what he is like,' Pearce replied, which got him a look of enquiry. 'Don't you recall, my Pelicans served aboard *Leander* before we sailed for Biscay? They told me about Taberly.'

'Well, today he too is ashore, so I can invite you into the wardroom without the risk of upsetting him. It's one of our premier's strictures, no one to be a guest in his domain lacking his personal permission.'

'Actually, I wish to speak to you on a private matter, so if the wardroom is occupied . . .'

Digby frowned, giving his visitor the clear impression that he knew what was about to be discussed, but he did not demur. 'If you want, we can talk in my cabin, though one of us will have to sit on the twenty-four pounder that has a greater claim to the space than I.'

To get to Digby's cabin meant traversing the wardroom and that required introductions, every face examined by Pearce as his name was mentioned to see if it registered. One or two of the occupants did pull on their mouths – having been at home when Pearce got his elevation they would have been part of the general buzz of disapproval at his promotion – but no one said anything and courtesies complete they went into the cramped space of Digby's home, a somewhat noxious one behind a canvas screen, given it was too close to the quarter gallery that acted as the wardroom latrine.

'I think I best say at the outset, John, that if you have come to seek my approval I cannot grant it.'

'Approval for what?'

That caused Digby to hesitate for a split second, his discomfort obvious. 'I met Mrs Barclay on the quayside yesterday.'

'I am aware of that.'

'And much as I have regard for her as a person—'

Pearce interrupted. 'Does that regard include me?'

'I have no idea of how you came to be conjoined, John, so I cannot speculate on who is to blame.'

'Blame?'

'You can hardly see the situation as regular.'

'How I see the situation, Henry, is my affair and that of the lady with whom I am, as you put it, conjoined. While your disapproval of it does not surprise me, it would be best that you know such an attitude will have no bearings on what I will do in the future. So it is thus best a subject that we do not discuss.'

'If we are not to discuss that I am at a loss to know why you have come a'visiting?'

Pearce produced a wry smile. 'I am not allowed to call upon an old friend?'

Was it the word 'friend' that made Digby's expression change? Pearce had no idea and was sorry to think it might be, for they had become, if not as close as he and his Pelicans, familiar enough for such an appellation to seem appropriate. As if to underline that such intimacy was in doubt, Digby's hesitant reply lacked any reassurance.

'Of course.'

'As it so happens I have come to see you on another matter

entirely. I have been challenged to a duel and I lack anyone to second for me.' Digby's head moved and his lips too, but no words emerged. 'I have come to ask you to be that person.'

'It is against the law.'

'That will not stop it taking place,' Pearce insisted, which received a gloomy nod; there was a spot outside every town in England, Hampstead Heath being the London favourite, where duels took place on a daily basis. 'Perhaps it would be best if I told you the circumstances.'

Which he did, aware as he spoke that what he was saying did not put him in a very good light. Digby, he was sure, was filtering the words through the prism of his own standards and that meant an intuition that no such thing could ever occur with him; for a man, especially a naval officer, to so lose control as to strike another officer, regardless of the nature of his service, was close to an abomination. There was also the point that he had been in Gibraltar when Lipton was shot and had been kept in ignorance of what was taking place.

'I plead that I was defending another.'

'Who does not, to my way of thinking, sound worthy of your interference.'

'I will not defend Captain McGann, Henry, but I will say that if you knew him you might understand.'

In saying that Pearce was wondering if that was true: the short and drunken captain had practically had his nose buried in the ample bosom of Major Lipton's wife and had ignored all attempts that he should desist. Perhaps, in similar circumstances, Pearce would have belted him too.

'Anyway, there you have it, so can I ask you to act for me?'

'If I do, John, I must tell you I do so unwillingly.'

'If I had a choice I would accept that, but I do not, so I am obliged to press you.'

'There is another caveat. I cannot do so without I have permission from Mr Taberly.'

'And will that be forthcoming?'

'I cannot say, he's such a contrary fellow that he could go either way.'

'Can I give you the details, in case his reaction is positive? The name of Lipton's second and where he is to be found.'

Digby's head was on his chest, Pearce thinking he was seeking another reason to refuse, but he lifted it eventually and looked his visitor right in the eye, without much in the way of affection.

'There are writing materials in the wardroom.'

'No need,' Pearce replied, pulling a piece of paper from his pocket. 'I took the liberty of noting them down before I set off.'

Taking it from him, Digby spoke softly. 'On the subject of Mrs Barclay, John—'

'It is one we best not discuss. I am in enough hot water as it is.'

He so much wanted to say to Digby that Emily's name was no longer Barclay as far as he was concerned; she had reverted in their relationship to her maiden name of Raynesford. It was, he decided, unwise to point this out; it would only fan the flames of Digby's disapproval.

The offer that he be shown off the ship was declined and Pearce made his farewells, with a hesitant comment from Digby, given he had never done anything of this sort before, that if Taberly agreed he would need to establish certain facts in the forthcoming encounter: weapons, timing and how the fee for the attendant medical man was to be shared out. He would send a boat to tell of what was happening.

Making his way across the main deck Pearce ran into another lieutenant coming aboard, who literally stopped him with a stare, so full was it of enquiry. There was also the fact that he practically blocked the way to the entry port.

'Pearce,' came the response. 'Commander of *HMS Larcher*.'

'Taberly, Premier, and what is *Larcher*, pray?'

'Armed cutter and part of the fleet, here to revictual.'

'How singular,' Taberly replied, with something close to a sneer. 'Must be the only vessel of its kind on station – a tiddler, indeed. And what are you doing aboard my ship?'

'Visiting Lieutenant Digby, who I previously served under.'

'That Biscay affair.' Pearce nodded; it had been Digby's only command so the connection was not difficult. 'Given our Digby ideas above his station. Having been in authority once he finds it hard to act the subordinate.'

'As would anyone.'

'So your business was purely personal?'

The nodded lie was easy, but it produced a frown. The premier of the seventy-four seemed an unnaturally inquisitive cove, unwilling by that expression to merely accept that Pearce was renewing an old acquaintance. Best he find out from Digby what it was about!

The lack of any response caused Taberly to rub his chin, in his case a very prominent one. He was of average height and without that feature he possessed a face that could be described as unremarkable: brown eyes, rather dull, and a button nose. But that jaw he was fingering hinted at a natural belligerence and that was supported by the tone of his voice, which seemed to imply that the man before him had overstepped some invisible mark.

'I like to know what my officers are about, Mr Pearce.'

'Very commendable.'

The face came a fraction closer. 'Not looking to shift, then?'

'He did not tell me so, sir, and I would hardly pass that on if he did.'

Taberly was being nosy and, in effect, John Pearce was telling him to mind his own business. But he made sure to sound polite, for he needed this man to approve what he was about to be asked.

'Pearce? Name rings a bell – now, why would that be?'

'I daresay Lieutenant Digby will be only too happy to tell you. Now, sir, if I may, I have duties to perform aboard my own vessel.'

'Very well,' Taberly replied, standing marginally to one side. 'But I will add, that if you are in the habit of visiting *Leander*, I would take it as a courtesy that you enquire of me first if it is suitable.'

There was no need for that, which made it easy for John Pearce, who had a low opinion of the name in any case, to decide he did not like this Taberly at all, especially since he was obliged to manoeuvre his way round a man who was not going to entirely get out of his path. Yet still he raised his hat a fraction, given there was no point in letting the premier know how he felt.

Henry Digby came aboard at sunset with the required information instead of doing as he said he would, sending a note. Given he knew the Pelicans almost as well as Pearce, that led to the kind of greeting always exchanged when old shipmates met, albeit with all the courtesies due to the difference in rank. Then Digby was taken into the cabin and invited, on a hot night, to divest himself of his coat.

'Lord, John, this is tighter than *Faron*, and the accommodation there was snug enough.'

'Can I offer you some wine, Henry? My cook fetched aboard some very decent stuff.'

'Then he is a better man than any of our wardroom stewards. What they have bought in Leghorn is undrinkable. Mind, Taberly controls the purse strings, so I suspect it is he who is too mean to pay out for anything good. The man is indifferent to food and drink and thinks what the navy provides is enough.'

A certain amount of lip-smacking appreciation followed that, as Digby tasted the local Tuscan wine, a very heady and full-of-flavour red that went by the charming name, he was told, of Chianti.

'Speaking of Taberly?'

Pearce asked this in a near whisper, thus frustrating any of his crew close enough to hear the primary exchanges. Knowing as much about eavesdropping tars as his confrère, Digby likewise spoke softly.

'John, not only does he give permission, he asked if he could be present as a witness. I said yes.'

'I can see no reason to object.'

Digby suddenly appeared embarrassed and hissed, 'He also asked if you were likely to win, which tells me that he will be trying to wager with Lipton's supporters as to the outcome. Taberly does so love a bet.'

'That seems to me somewhat ghoulish.'

'Nevertheless, I would take it as practically a condition.'

'Allow me to impose one of my own, I would not want him running a book on my demise.'

'I will pass that back to him.'

'And the rest?'

'There are some old ducal hunting grounds out to the north-east of Leghorn, in the Tuscan hills. Lipton's man Walcott has named a glade off the road to Pisa, hard by a post house, where we will not be disturbed, and I have arranged for a hack to take us there before sunrise tomorrow. The bullocks have found a medical cove and will take him along with them.'

'Weapons?'

'Swords, army issue.'

'I would prefer a finer blade.'

'Sadly, John, the choice is not yours.'

'With your agreement I will take Michael O'Hagan along with me.'

Having been very serious, Henry Digby, who knew what Michael was capable of, sought to lighten the conversation and he spoke more loudly than previously. 'To start another set of fisticuffs?'

'No, Henry,' Pearce replied in a quiet, mordant tone. 'To carry me back to the ship if I cannot walk.'

'I have to tell you, John, I made enquiries as to Lipton's competence with a sword and not only is he that, he is also something of a habitual duellist. I got the impression that he has, at least once, killed an opponent.'

Pearce nodded, and to cover his ruminations on that he poured some more wine, which for a few minutes both men consumed in silence until Pearce said finally, 'Henry, if you will forgive me, I do not intend to spend tonight aboard ship.' The face Digby pulled then meant there was no need for further explanation. 'I take it the hack you have hired will be on the quayside, so I will find you there.'

'I am bound to ask, John, if you want a priest to be present. We are in a papist country and as you know there is an Anglican church in Leghorn. The vicar there would be happy to confess you either at the church or the duelling ground, should you desire it.'

'And what sins, Henry, would you have me open up to him about?'

'We all carry the burden of sin.'

'Not all of us allow it to weigh us down.'

It was a discussion they had engaged in before, many times aboard *HMS Faron*, for John Pearce was in this respect his father's son. Old Adam was a man who, for all his own scepticism, would not deny to others their need for some kind of faith. But he would ask why those who administered to them, in a religion founded on the lack of material greed of their saviour, had priests and bishops who needed to live in such luxury.

If the divines of Britain were not as greedy as their French counterparts, who in pre-Revolutionary time had counted their mistresses in multiples and their incomes in millions of *livres*, it was yet a justifiable question as to why whoever held the See of Canterbury needed £25,000 per annum to live on, when all around his cathedral there were people he was set to administer to who rarely ate meat for the lack of the means to buy it.

'Your soul is your affair, John, but I will pray for you, nevertheless.'

'Drink your wine, Henry, and be assured I have bought some spirit also, which if it is not brandy is fiery enough to warm our cockles in the morning.'

Both men knew that the purpose of such a spirit was not for drinking, for it was a handy thing to have along to cleanse a wound or, at the very worst case, to ease into the next life a dying man so he would feel no pain.

When it came to prayers, Michael O'Hagan was the master, crossing himself immediately Pearce alerted him to his duties in the morning, with his friend supposing that he spent the hours in between praying for divine intervention. Not that he knew; he went ashore to spend the night with Emily, who when she enquired about his dispute with Lipton was told that it was, for the moment, in abeyance.

When he rose very early the next morning, while it was still so dark he had to dress by moonlight, he left her abed and happy in her somnolence, she assuming it was because of what he had told her; he must be aboard at sunrise and be seen on the deck. The soft kiss he placed on her brow, just before departure, was responded to by a low and murmured expression of affection.

CHAPTER ELEVEN

It was a slow and piecemeal gathering on the busy quayside: the fresh catches from the overnight fishing were being laid out on the trestles. First there was John Pearce wondering at what the day might bring, the letter to be delivered to Emily should matters go awry feeling like a weight in his pocket; it was certainly one on his conscience for she would be bitter at the lies he had told so that she should not worry. Then there was the guilt, the knowledge that in leaving all his worldly possessions to her, as he had done in a final testament, everything he owned did not amount to much, certainly not enough to maintain any kind of independence.

In addition, having been seen with him in Leghorn, there was no chance that their liaison could be glossed over or that it would remain a secret; the navy was a hotbed of gossip and over time it would become public knowledge, which would make life difficult for someone seen as a scarlet woman who had deserted the marital home.

Not that he thought she would ever go back to Ralph Barclay, even for the purpose of restoring her reputation, for there was a situation in which Emily's feelings had turned from dismay at his behaviour, through dislike of his character, to an utter detestation of his person.

In his peripatetic wanderings with his father John Pearce had seen, as a growing boy, more of life than most and part of that had been an acute observation of the perils and ubiquitous nature of poverty, a state into which too many were born and never had a chance to escape, which was at the base of Adam Pearce's so-called ranting about inequalities.

Yet just as obvious was the fact that it was a way of life into which people could too easily fall, folk he had observed who had obviously enjoyed a degree of comfort in their lives forced to become beggars on the street by altered circumstance. The debtors' prisons were full to bursting with men and women of that ilk, many there not because they were feckless but as victims of chicanery by others or just a lack of luck.

Fate could play anyone a cruel hand and in his mind's eye it was all too easy to imagine the woman he loved suffering that kind of misfortune. Against that Emily had her own character, strong and resilient, and she also had her obvious beauty, a priceless asset that would remain with her for at least a decade and probably many more years after that. But would she use it to her advantage? There had to be doubt, given her views on morality, so much at odds with his own.

The sight of Michael O'Hagan climbing onto the quay was not one to lift his spirits, though there was an amused irony to be had when his friend, having handed over fresh linen for the coming encounter, presented him with his sword, showed him the case of pistols he had fetched along as well, before he produced from inside his short jacket a marlinspike to deal with, as he put it, 'Anything that might go amiss.'

What would become of the Pelicans without him to offer them some protection? At present he had a ship and could ensure their lives were not made a misery but that would not persist should he perish or suffer a debilitating wound. They were stuck in the navy for the duration and that meant they could be shipped anywhere the whim of the service took them, with all the dangers such a life entailed.

'If anything happens to me—'

The interruption was quick and, given they were alone, loud as well as delivered in a way that told John Pearce that he was not the only one who had considered the consequences of what he was about to engage in.

'Now don't you go concerning yourself about that John-boy. Sure, the Good Lord had mapped out my course afore we met and has done the same for Charlie and Rufus. What that is we are not to know, but live it we must, for it is the Lord's will.'

Looking beyond him, Pearce saw Digby approaching, but just ahead of him was Taberly and that had him touching Michael so he turned to look, his response a whisper. 'Sure, there's a face only a mother could love, and short of sight to boot.'

'Good morning to you, Lieutenant Pearce,' Taberly boomed, looking at a sky in which the deep blue was turning to pale, with only the strongest stars still twinkling. 'We are to have another fine day of weather it seems, perfect for the purpose.'

Taberly then looked up at Michael O'Hagan, whom he knew

well. There was a moment when his expression gave the notion he was about to address the Irishman before he seemed to decide against it, no doubt because his pride did not allow him to do so.

'However,' he said instead, 'before we set off you will forgive me. I have a need to relieve myself.'

Taberly went to the very edge of the quay, walking between two tables laden with fish, and despite the glares of the locals, began to unbutton the flap on his breeches. While he was pissing into the harbour Pearce could engage an embarrassed Digby in a whispered exchange.

'I tried, John, and made no bones of how reluctant you were to have him along. But he was equally adamant that if he were denied the chance to be a spectator I would not be permitted to leave the ship. I did, however, get an agreement that he would keep his purse in his pocket.'

The sound of iron hoops on cobbles signalled the arrival of their transport and the three officers clambered aboard into what was an extremely cramped space, Michael obliged to stand on the platform at the rear of the hack and to hang on to the frame of the lowered canvas roof.

'Damn me,' Taberly cried in a jolly tone, 'I ain't been so jammed up since I slept in a mids berth.' Aware that the men on either side of him, for he had bagged the central seat and the most space, were exchanging gloomy looks, he added in an even heartier manner, 'Come along, there's no need to be so down, surely? It is a fine thing to be doing what we are about – manly, don't you know.'

'Tell me, Lieutenant Taberly,' Pearce asked, 'what is your attitude to a public hanging?'

'A fine thing, Mr Pearce; I never miss one if it is available and it is at its best when the miscreant is racked with fear of his fate. Why, I have seen many a victim soil himself before he even had the rope placed round his neck. Not that I am repelled by a pretty speech, you understand, and a degree of indifference in the accused. It is good to watch the ladies when the fellow is a handsome cove and romantic with it, for if they shed tears, I daresay it is not the only part of their being that is dampened.'

Was Taberly being deliberately crude, aware that his inferior, Digby, was squirming at his side, though that could perhaps be put down to the lack of space? In the increasing light his face was red; would that merely be put down to the heat caused by enforced proximity? Pearce was also curious to know if such enthusiastic rejoinders to his mordantly posed question were aimed at him, for he had to assume that if he disliked Taberly, the feeling was probably mutual.

Hanging on to the back of the hack, Michael O'Hagan was sorely tempted to fetch out his marlinspike and, having knocked off the lieutenant's hat, use it on Taberly's exposed head.

The sun was up by the time they made their destination, achieved over a surprisingly good road, given it was not something for which the Italians were noted. But it was a main route to Pisa and judging by the traffic well used to bringing goods from the interior to the port for both sale and onward shipping, a fact Taberly commented on in amongst what was a constant stream of inconsequential chatter; if Michael wanted to clobber the man he was not alone, John Pearce was close to creating another duelling partner, so sick was he of the sod's grating voice.

Walcott had left another officer at the point where they had to leave the road and he led them to the rendezvous, a flat bit of land covered in sunburnt grass, shaded by high pines at this hour of the day. Lipton, it seemed, had brought along the entire commissioned mess of his regiment as well as several servants, for the glade was occupied by a good number of redcoats – all the officers, as Pearce examined them, keen to be seen to be indifferent to the occasion, more than one even going to the trouble of a false yawn as he alighted from the hack.

There were several coaches too: at the door of one a fellow was laying out cloths, bandages and the instruments needed to treat any wounds on the floor. Dressed entirely in black, even to his wide-brimmed hat, with a long cloak that reached all the way to the ground, the medico, only if in half view, showed a hooked nose and a complexion pockmarked and swarthy. The man had a suitably funereal air for the task he had been engaged to carry out.

Digby immediately went to consult with Walcott, Taberly making straight for the clutch of army men and engaging them in an animated conversation. Michael, having got down, placed the pistol case on the luggage ledge, then came to help Pearce off with his coat. Lipton himself was close to the trees, his sword in his hand, swinging away and parrying the blows of an imaginary opponent, with one swipe at a trunk leaving in it a deep cut. That done he turned and looked right at Pearce as if to imply he would suffer likewise.

'Sure, he's not short of faith, is he?'

Looking at Lipton, and noticing that in his shirt he carried a bit of a paunch, Pearce pulled his shirt over his head. 'Then let's hope he's short on puff, Michael.'

His Irish friend handed him the replacement. 'I have seen you swing a blade, John-boy, and if it helps I have no fear for you.'

The reply was given in a low voice and it was dismal, made more so by the muffling of fresh linen, this as Digby came back from his talk with Walcott. 'Then it will not reassure you to know that you are on your own, Michael.'

As Pearce's head emerged from the garment he noticed his second was slowly shaking his head.

'He will still not accept an apology. John, he wants your blood.'

Looking past him, Pearce could see that Taberly was breaking his promise; if no actual money was exchanged the slapping of hands indicated wagers were being laid, he assumed by the enthusiasm of the bullocks, against him. Drawing the attention of Digby to this the response was a useless, 'what could he do' sort of shrug.

Bets agreed, an unashamed Taberly came to join them, his voice full of faux good spirits, this as he pulled a watch from his coat pocket. 'I have you down to last at least five minutes, Pearce, the bullocks have you down for a maximum of two, so don't you go succumbing too quick, d'ye hear?'

'I will tell you now, Taberly,' Pearce hissed, 'that my first act at the conclusion of this fight might be to slice off the hand you would use to collect your winnings.'

It was now Taberly who produced a studied yawn, speaking in a derisory tone as he turned away. 'Then it is as well my largest wager, Pearce, is that you will not survive the encounter at all.'

'Sure I'll see to him afore we depart this place.'

'Don't, Michael, he's not worth hanging for. There's a letter in my coat pocket, if the worst occurs make sure my lady gets it.'

Walcott had gone to the centre of the glade; in his outstretched arms lay two swords and it was time, obviously, for the contestants to choose their weapons. O'Hagan crossed himself as Pearce walked towards the spot, Lipton doing likewise. Once there Pearce looked into the man's eyes and saw there not a trace of emotion; he could only hope he sent the same impression out as that to which he was being exposed.

'I leave it for you to choose, Lieutenant Pearce,' Lipton said, pulling a cloth from his waistband and wiping off what small traces of sweat had accumulated from his practice. 'It is a matter of indifference to me which blade I employ.'

There was no discernible difference between them and as he took the guarded hilt of one, with the royal coat of arms prominently embossed, Pearce felt the weight of the weapon. That told him it was lighter than the naval hanger he was accustomed to employ in the rare training exercises he engaged in aboard ship, but heavier than the rapier on which he had been schooled.

The blade was thicker than the latter and longer than the hanger, coming to a sharp point, and he could see that it had been honed all along the leading edge, as it would be for a fighting engagement. Designed for cutting as well as stabbing, it was very far from the lightweight weapon on which he had learnt swordplay, the sort which he would have expected to employ in a duel, not that he had ever fought one or intended to do so.

But he had received proper instruction in fencing: when his father, lodged safely in Paris, had said he wanted his only son to be coached in the arts of polite society, it was based on the conviction that such abilities should be gifted to all. This was in addition, of course, to lessons in mathematics, Greek, Latin and French most of all, as well as horse riding, dancing and the skill of conversation.

The city might be in the throes of Revolution but it had yet to descend into the chaos of the Terror and such schooling was still readily available. The whole process of learning had refined a rather rustic John Pearce and, added to his increasingly fine appearance, had made him an attraction in the salon with both men and women. In the latter case it had led to many a bedroom; what it would do on a duelling field had never been part of the exercise.

Lipton had taken a step back and was swishing again, his sword blade hissing as it cut the air, but his eyes never left those of Pearce, who, when he sought to do likewise, was treated to a sort of executioner's grin. Walcott, with Digby just behind his shoulder, was droning the rules of the encounter: these being simply that the first drawing of blood would be the sign of satisfaction and that the weapons employed were the only ones allowed. Then he produced a pistol and gave it a slight wave.

'Should either party produce a knife, or any other instrument capable of causing a wound, should they resort to picking up and using a rock, then it will be my painful duty to intervene by use of this, and though I will aim to wound, I will not give a thought to the fact that my intervention might be fatal. Do I have your word, gentlemen, that you will abide by what I say?'

In tight breeches, close-fitting stockings and a loosely flapping linen shirt, Pearce was wondering where anyone could conceal anything, never mind a weapon, but he nodded and growled his assent, in the corner of his eye observing the medical fellow was now close to the area of the contest, a towel over one arm and a length of leather trailing from his hand, no doubt the latter to be used as a blood-stopping tourniquet.

'Mr Digby, do you wish to add anything?'

It was with a strained voice that his second responded. 'No, nothing.'

'Then once I give the call,' Walcott announced, 'you may commence. God be with you and may the best man win.'

Walking backwards, both Walcott and Digby got well away from any initial swing of the metal before the major's second called out in a loud voice to engage. Lipton had adopted the classic fencer's pose, legs spread fore and aft, front knee bent, his sword held out at an angle in front of him; it was clear he was inviting Pearce to make the primary assault and he showed deep annoyance when his opponent did not even raise his blade.

'Are you going to fight, sir, or is your intention to hold out so your fellow tar can collect his wagers?'

'The first time I met you, Major Lipton, I thought that you might be short on brains – a typical bullock, in fact.'

'Fight, damn you,' the major spat.

'On the second occasion,' Pearce responded, keeping his voice even, regardless of the difficulty in doing so, 'in your refusal to accept a sincere apology you confirmed it. You took a ball in Gibraltar and, given you lost, if that does not mark you out as a dunce I do not know what else would.'

He had set out to rile Lipton, to throw him off his carefully adopted demeanour, assuming that for all his appearance of calm his blood must be in just as much turmoil. Yet it was not the insults from his opponent that launched the furious Lipton assault, but the call of Taberly echoing through the glade.

'Come along, my hearties, or are we to expire from boredom?'

Lipton came forward, two fast paces on his front foot, his blade held steady till he could get close enough to swipe. But Pearce was not there; he had taken an equal number of steps back and still kept his weapon away from a fighting posture.

'It takes a man of spectacular stupidity to do the same thing twice and, having failed at the first attempt, to expect a different outcome in the repeat.'

Lipton lost it then and came on at a rush, it was in his eyes, the holding of which Pearce had never surrendered, for in those, his instructors had told him, lay the intentions of an opponent. Hold his gaze: watch the sword hand and be alert for the drop of a shoulder, the twitching of which will send you a message of intent; trust to instinct for there is not time to think of how to respond.

The blades clashed for the first time as Pearce parried Lipton's heavy swipe, sending out a ringing sound and sparks, as well as a tingling sensation up the defending arm. Pearce had to work hard not to have his blade swept so far to one side that he opened himself up, and he also was obliged to retreat in the face of Lipton's furious onslaught. The blades clashed repeatedly, with Pearce hoping for that moment when the rush of Lipton blood would leave some part of his body exposed, an upper arm being best.

That such an assault suddenly ceased came as an unwelcome surprise, for Lipton stood back and if he was breathing heavily there was no sign that it was the cause of him breaking off. What was signalled was more worrying, for it seemed as if the army man's brow had cleared, indicating that he had realised how his opponent had set out to put him off, drawing him, by insults, into using brute force instead of skill.

'So I am stupid, Mr Pearce?' he asked, his face breaking into a wry smile. 'Perhaps we shall see which trait is of more use for a fighting man, the brains you clearly claim for yourself or my ability to employ my weapon as a soldier should.'

'Competence in one does not indicate possession in the other, Major Lipton. Indeed it could be said that only a complete fool could be engaged as we are in this place. I, at least, have the excuse of having been pressed into it.'

'Indeed you have, sir, and you have tried to play the coward card by proffering an apology.'

The smile widened but it held no warmth.

'And clever you seeks to put me off my game, but it will not serve, so know this: for the blows that you have landed upon me, delivered in a manner that fits with the shy slug that you are, added to the insults you have advanced this day, satisfaction for me will no longer be served by a mere effusion of blood – in short, a cut.'

There followed a deliberate pause, to give more credence to what came next.

'I now intend, sir, that this should be an encounter, fought as the French say, *à outrance*! That means, Mr Pearce, that one of us will likely perish in this place and I do not intend that it should be me.' With that Lipton resumed his fighting pose. 'Now, shall we continue or are you minded to do as you have done in the past and flee?'

CHAPTER TWELVE

Lipton was good with a blade, something Pearce realised as soon as the major began to fight with a measure of control. Instead of the mad flurry of blows there now ensued a calculated attempt to manoeuvre his opponent into a situation where he would, with patience, eventually leave a gap in his defence. Gone were the flaring eyes and the angry glare, to be replaced with cold reckoning that time was on his side, as was ability. In any contest there is always room for luck, but a good fighter, whatever the weapon employed, will back skill against an unknown quantity like chance every time.

Now the glade rang to the repeated meeting of metal, not the clanging sound of the outset, but the steady tip-tap of blade upon blade, with the occasional scrape as one ran along the other, and given that John Pearce was no amateur himself, those watching became absorbed in what was a fascinating tussle. The words that Lipton had delivered, warning of his intention to kill if he could, had not been heard by anyone other than the participants, so they had no idea of the changed nature of what they were seeing.

Had he been able to look in their direction, and he dare not take his eyes off Lipton, Pearce would have seen a slight concern in the faces of the major's colleagues; they knew his proficiency, indeed he had instructed many of his junior officers, so it came as something of a surprise that the whole thing had not ended within the couple of minutes on which they had wagered. They had expected Lipton to play with the navy man a bit before easing his way past his guard to either deliver a cut to the arm or a point through the shoulder or upper thigh.

'My, my,' Taberly crowed, 'had I known our man was so competent I would have wagered more. Do I have any takers for upping their bets?'

'Surely, sir,' Digby called over his shoulder, his voice tense, 'it ill becomes any man to place money on another's possible wounding.'

Taberly did not raise his voice in reply, but it lacked nothing in terms of reproof because of that. 'You dare, Mr Digby, to check me? Well, be assured, sir, that I will be checking on you and you may find that your career suffers for it.'

It was Walcott who came to Digby's rescue by addressing his own companions. 'I doubt Major Lipton would take kindly to the placing of wagers now. I would therefore urge you, gentlemen, as his second, to keep your powder dry.'

Digby reckoned Walcott too junior to make that a command, but as Lipton's second he had an authority on this day and in this place that transcended rank and so he could go back to concentrating on the fight.

Pearce was sweating, but so, he noticed, was his opponent, the white linen now stained at the armpits, and he assumed Lipton would, like him, have perspiration running down his spine. Yet so cool was his opponent's temperament, so sure was he that he was in control, that he found time to use the cloth he carried, running it across his face and forehead while parrying with apparent ease the opposing blade.

Stinging sweat would eventually get into Pearce's eyes and that would certainly cause trouble, which had him cursing himself for not thinking to carry a cloth in his non-fighting hand. He had only his sleeve to clear his brow and that ran the risk of momentarily clouding his view; he knew he could not afford to lose the lock on Lipton's eyes, for it would be hard to reconnect in time to avoid giving him an opportunity to strike.

The other worry was that his opponent was clearly in a high state of practice, while he was not. He assumed that Lipton was a person to carry out his daily sword drills – he did not know that he trained his juniors – while he had too many other duties to perform, from the mere running of the ship to training in gunnery and boarding, using a variety of weapons. That left little time to work on a skill that any naval officer would reckon to only rarely use and would, when employed, be in a situation close to mayhem where proficiency was less vital than weight.

Most of what had happened so far had taken place in the shade, but now the rising sun was beginning to top the trees. One side of their glade was bathed in strong light and Pearce realised that Lipton was slowly manoeuvring towards that, which told him that he was not, as he had claimed, stupid. The major was content for the moment to keep him moving, to threaten but not to expose himself by seeking to prematurely drive his blade home.

There was some comfort in that: the man was showing respect

to an opponent he had realised was no novice, but that did not alter the fact that the balance lay against John Pearce and that was a situation that could only deteriorate over time.

With a mouth now feeling like rough leather, the last thing Pearce needed was the blazing sun on his back, so from being relatively passive he became overtly aggressive, which forced Lipton to retreat a few paces and allowed Pearce to slip past him, leaving the major with his back to the sunlit strip of grass, an act that brought a smile and a nod of near commendation.

Then Lipton spoke, which was annoying: with a mouth so dry Pearce felt he would struggle to respond.

'It pleases me that you are no neophyte, Mr Pearce, for there is ever a feeling of shame at striking down an opponent who has no chance.' With that Lipton hurried forward and forced Pearce to the side, reversing the gain his opponent had made with ridiculous ease. 'And there is an added bonus in that I am allowed to show them the superiority of my own technique.'

With the man almost laughing at him Pearce felt his blood rise; Lipton was setting out to do to him what he had initially done to the major and rile him enough to put him off his stroke. Yet the thought that occurred was not one of anger, but the notion that if matters went on the way they were progressing now, he must lose.

Lipton was prepared to play with him for however long it took to tire Pearce out. Also, it seemed the man was enjoying the feeling that soon creeping despair would become part of the mental battle. That was as important in this fight as the sword in his hand.

As Pearce knew from his past, when engaged in combat, something happens to the brain – the same sensations that occur in flight – an acute sense of where lie the risks as well as what presents an opportunity for salvation. The angle at which both men now swung showed Michael O'Hagan over the major's shoulder, his height meaning most of him was in plain view and that triggered a mental image.

For reasons he would never be able to explain, and entirely separate from that with which he was engaged, Pearce was taken back to the windswept and cold alleyway outside the Pelican Tavern at a time when the Irishman was unknown to him, as were the rest of the people with whom he had been pressed.

Why had he chosen that doorway when there were other alternatives? Not just because men were pursuing him seeking to serve upon him a warrant. To avoid that he had made a snap decision that had completely altered his life. If it had seemed like a descent to hell at first, he could now see it as a door that had led to a new and better life: a naval career, real friends and not least Emily Barclay.

Instinct had benefited him then, so surely it must be wise to rely on the same now. There was no future in defence but the end sought by Lipton and that might not be so different if he chose another course. Yet it was doubt against near certainty and that caused John Pearce to suddenly take half a dozen backward steps and use his sleeve to clear his brow, the act catching Lipton by surprise so he was too slow to follow.

As he came forward to close the gap once more Pearce attacked and with fury, which threw the major off his stroke and forced a retreat. Now the blades were ringing again as Pearce kept up the assault and if he was happy to be moving forward he was also aware that Lipton was defending himself with real capability. The only advantage Pearce had was that he knew what he was about and the major did not.

The opportunity Pearce gave him as part of his onslaught was too good to turn down; he left his left side open enough for Lipton to lunge forward and run the forepart of his blade along the upper naval arm, having rasped along and glanced off his opponent's metal. Certainly the linen was ripped open and for all John Pearce knew so was he – there was no pain – but the need to take a wound was part of his plan, if a series of interconnected thoughts, impressions and speculative conclusions could ever be so described.

Fully extended Lipton might have seemed vulnerable to those watching; Pearce knew better, knew that the major had not sought the opening without first ensuring that there was no way Pearce could respond in kind – the naval blade had been pushed well out of the way of inflicting any harm. Then Pearce ducked and the thrust he delivered was so unusual and so far from the manual of swordplay that Lipton was thrown for the split second needed to delay his response.

The point that took him in the right foot and drove right through to the ground was different in the sense he was astounded enough to let Pearce haul it out and back away, as he later described it – not with much in the way of self-regard or boasting – more like a scurrying cockroach than a man of honour. In the miniscule pause that allowed him, Pearce had time to look at his arm and see the blood staining his sleeve, this while Lipton, no fool, withdrew himself, not easily, for it was plain he was so wounded in his foot that he was forced to limp: Pearce's blade had clearly damaged bone as well as muscle and skin.

'That, sir, was a coward's stroke,' Lipton shouted.

'I have drawn blood, sir, and so have you, therefore I rest content.'

'Damn you, I do not.'

The fury was back, the eyes alight and the blood rush to the face apparent. Walcott was calling in vain from the sidelines that honour had been satisfied, the blood Pearce was emitting obvious. But his superior either could not hear him or was not listening for he came on, seeking the conclusion he had promised, and Pearce was hard put to keep him at bay. Yet by constant movement, mostly backwards, he was putting pressure on Lipton's wounded foot, and it took no great insight to see in the soldier's eyes that he was suffering pain with every move and doubly so when he was obliged to put his whole weight upon it.

John Pearce had never had any intention of killing Lipton, though he knew and had accepted he would have to if there were no other way to survive. Now he had a better method, which was just to keep moving so that the major would be the author of his own downfall. Another opening came when Lipton, jabbing forward, caused himself so much discomfort that he had to quickly alter his balance and that left him precariously balanced on his one good foot.

With an utter disregard for the tenets of what might be called chivalry or gentlemanly behaviour, Pearce stepped forward and took the good leg from under Lipton with a sweep of his own. The major tried to hop onto his wounded foot, but that would not support him and he went over onto his back, skilled enough to keep his blade sufficiently active to stop his opponent from an easy follow-through.

Somehow he drove Pearce back enough to seek to get to his feet and he was on his knees, having to thrust and parry above his head height which opened him to the next blow. The Pearce boot that came up and took him on the chest sent him flying in a way from which there was no recovery. An incensed Walcott had levelled his pistol, though he was too confused to use it. Did use of any other part of the body constitute a barred weapon? Was it iniquitous enough to allow him to shoot John Pearce?

Digby, seeing a finger begin to depress the trigger, knocked the barrel up in the air, which was just as well for the soldier. Michael O'Hagan, standing only a few feet away from Walcott, had seen what he was about and there was a marlinspike in his hand. Had the gun been used, it was not a shot that Major Lipton's second would have survived.

'Both men have drawn blood, Mr Walcott,' Digby called. 'Honour can demand no more.'

Looking at Digby, then back out to the fighting arena and unable, because of the navy man's upward pressure, to bring his pistol to bear, Walcott was stymied. With his principal now on his back and at the mercy of the sword hovering very close to his throat, while the foot of his opponent pinned the blade of Lipton's weapon to the burnt grass, there was really no choice but to agree, even if he could not hear what was being said between the combatants.

'I will let you rise, Major Lipton, but this contest is at an end.'

'You'd best kill me, Pearce, for as God is my judge, I will do that to you given the chance.'

'What a pity you oblige me to look to my own security.'

With that Pearce, in an act so cold-blooded he was later ashamed, drove his blade into Lipton's upper arm and sliced hard, which brought forth a scream, as muscles were ripped apart.

'I hope, sir, that I have now rendered you incapable of ever engaging in a duel again, though I take no pleasure from having done so. It is, however, preferable to slicing open your heart.'

Behind Pearce, Walcott had sought to bring his pistol back to bear: it was not done to assault an opponent who was *hors de combat*. He looked shocked when the hand grabbed his arm, even more so when he realised the act had been carried out by a common seaman, trebly so when his pistol was taken from that hand as easily as it would be removed from a baby.

'Sure, Your Honour, enough has been done this day to satisfy any man.'

Walcott's fellow officers had gone for their own swords, but the hilts were barely lifted half an inch before Michael O'Hagan had that very same primed and ready-to-fire pistol aimed at them, while Digby had used his hand to stop Walcott drawing his sword. There was a moment when everyone froze, unsure of how to proceed in a situation that was confusing.

That was broken by Taberly, who burst into loud laughter, almost choking when he spoke. 'Damn me, what a to-do, eh? I ain't ever seen the like. It would make for a raree show, and if I am out of pocket for it, then I will say it was worth the price of admission.'

'Gentlemen,' Digby said, addressing the army men, 'I suggest you see to your superior and get him to the local lazaretto.'

The doctor was already beside Lipton, John Pearce standing back to let him administer the necessary treatment. It was then that the first drip of blood fell from Pearce's fingertips and onto the grass.

'Mr Walcott,' Digby said in a whisper, as the soldier edged round him to go and look at Lipton. 'Can I suggest we all depart this place now and in peace, for if anyone seeks to take recourse to arms we will end up with a bloody brawl and someone dead.'

The reply was stiff. 'I suggest, sir, that you get your principal away from here forthwith, for I will not answer for the behaviour of my comrades after such a display.'

'O'Hagan, get Mr Pearce to our hack.'

Michael, walking backwards so that the pistol was still aimed, closed with Pearce and took his good arm. 'Come, John-boy, let us see to your wound.'

'He wanted to kill me, Michael, he said so and I had no choice.'

'Then only God in heaven knows why he's still breathing, for it is sure he would not be so if he had been fighting me.'

Digby went to the coach in which the doctor had previously laid out his instruments and from there he took several bandages. Making for their conveyance, and the stupefied driver who had watched these mad foreigners at their games, he found Taberly already there and preparing to clamber aboard.

'Sir, can I suggest that with Mr Pearce wounded there will not be the same space as there was on the way here.'

'You're not suggesting I walk!'

'No, sir, but unless you intend to take over from me the duty of seeing to Mr Pearce's wound, I will suggest that standing on the rear rack with his servant might be best.'

Pearce and Michael arrived just as Taberly was about to respond and that had him looking from Digby to the wounded man with distaste for both. John Pearce handed Digby the sword he still had, this as his second handed O'Hagan a bandage.

'I leave it to you, Henry, to return this to its rightful owner.'

'If you don't want it,' Taberly growled, 'I will take it as a trophy. It might make up for some of my losses. Mind, there is another way.

Lend me your man O'Hagan for a bout or two and I will make us all a pile.'

Digby had taken the sword; Michael was holding and seeking to bandage Pearce's upper left arm. It was an indication to just how Taberly had got under the skin of a man both wounded and tired that the punch to the point of the jaw was both produced and effective enough to send the premier of *HMS Leander* flying, his hat travelling somewhat further than his body.

'That's your reward,' Pearce spat, 'and by God I hope you challenge me for it.'

Taberly did not respond; he could not, being out cold.

Michael whispered in his ear, 'Sure, 'tis a fine thing you've done, John-boy.'

He was not talking about the sword fight.

If he had hoped for sympathy from Emily he got none; instead she made no attempt to hide her fury at being duped, which left Pearce stuttering justifications that fell on deaf ears, this as she stitched his cut, making no attempt at gentility, and these were assertions, as well as the hissed reactions to the needle, that had Michael O'Hagan chortling from the other side of the door.

His friend's final excuse to escape this physical and verbal drubbing was to say he needed to see to matters aboard ship, and that he would stay aboard overnight, which subsequently allowed the Irishman to relay to his shipmates all that had occurred, a blow-by-blow account that all agreed should have seen a corpse, though it ended in much laughter when they heard how their captain's lady had reduced to jelly a man who was not the kind to shy away from trouble.

When he went ashore again the next day, it was with an agreement that he would meet up with his leave-taking Pelicans later in the day. They were making ready and prettying themselves up to follow, their rendezvous to take place in a tavern well away from what could be called the fleshpots of Leghorn. These bagnios, much frequented by privateers as well as navy hands allowed ashore on leave, were too raucous and too full of prostitution for the kind of quiet talk Pearce had in mind.

Crossing the harbour he saw that *HMS Leander* was in the process of weighing, no doubt to return to San Fiorenzo and the fleet, which produced mixed feelings; he had clouted the premier and the repercussions of that were an unknown for the swine was well above him in rank, merely by service time, and it was strictly forbidden, for obvious reasons, to strike a senior officer.

Then there was Henry Digby, to whom he owed a great deal and if he had been effusive in his thanks he knew that the affair had left his second in a parlous position *vis-à-vis* Taberly. There was nothing he could do, given comings and goings were the very stuff of naval life. He could only hope that Digby would not suffer too much from the man's malice.

He found Emily, if not in tears, with clear evidence that she had been crying. Naturally assuming it to be because of his duel he did not enquire too much, only doing so when, having suggested that they go for a promenade and perhaps to seek out the tavern where he could meet his friends, she flatly refused to leave the lodging house. When he pressed for an explanation that was when tears flowed again and the tale of what had occurred was dragged out of her.

'Who insulted you and what did they say?'

'Best you do not know, John.'

'It is vital that I do, Emily.'

'Why, so you can risk your life again?'

'Tell me.'

'No.'

It took time and much persistence, plus pleading and many a reassuring hug, but eventually the story came out, in fits and starts and only on the condition he would not react to it. Pearce said little as she relayed the tale, seething as he was; to allow Emily to see that would not serve so he had to be content with an agreement to return from meeting his Pelicans to dine with her. He departed carrying with him her good wishes; however, instead of searching for Michael et al, he headed for another destination entirely.

CHAPTER THIRTEEN

The Pensione d'Ambrosio was in the old quarter of the town, in a narrow alleyway of high buildings that cut out the sun, the sign above the entrance naming it, Pearce assumed, as that of the owner. Once through the low doorway he found himself in a room stained dark with years of smoke from pipes added to that from the huge fireplace which, at this time of year, was redundant, given the one used for cooking seemed to be located elsewhere.

That such an activity was in progress seemed obvious from the smells that hit his nostrils: fresh bread mixed with the odour of a dish flavoured with much garlic, something of a surprise given the English aversion to the ingredient.

The army officers, a dozen in number and of varying ages and ranks, were in the lantern-lit room he assumed to be used for dining, for it was a narrow space. They were sat, in shirtsleeves, at a long oak table covered with their breakfast – flagons of wine, filled glasses and an abundance of food: beefsteaks, game birds, a nearly empty tureen of soup and a platter of that fresh bread, the smell of which he had picked up on entry.

The sight of him filling the doorway had a good half of them rising to their feet until a sharp command made them sit down. At the far end of the table sat Major Lipton, his arm in a sling and his face drawn from the pain he must be feeling. He was the man who had issued the order and Pearce assumed him to hold the senior rank present. Having exchanged the appropriate glare with his late opponent Pearce looked around and into the faces of everyone else present.

'A trio of you bastards insulted my lady yesterday, loudly and in public, calling her by a name I will not use, which was overheard by half the local population.'

It was Lipton who replied, his tone jocular as he made a point of addressing the whole table. 'Do the Tuscans know the meaning of the word "trollop"?'

The reply came from one of his inferiors, a young fellow with a crop of blond hair and a plump fresh face, probably no more than an ensign, his words accompanied by a hoot, 'I daresay, sir, they are akin to us in that. They know one when they see one.'

Another officer spoke up, this time with mock seriousness, so grave was his tone. 'The expression they use locally, Major Lipton, is "*puttana*".'

'Which I believe,' another interjected, 'refers to the part of their body by which they ply their trade.'

'I want their names, Lipton, and I want them to know the next person they'll talk to will be acting on my behalf.'

'Good Lord, gentlemen, this fellow means to issue us all a challenge.'

'Can he do that, sir,' asked the probable ensign, 'him being such a low-bred scully?'

The remark was greeted with general laughter and agreement, which left Pearce wondering if this had been rehearsed; it was almost as if the whole thing, including insulting Emily, had been set up to draw him into ridicule. He had to fight to stop himself from yelling insults at them; it took a real effort to keep his voice calm.

'I think your Major Lipton will attest that before you is a man who can fight.'

'I have seen cats in alleyways get into the kind of fighting you practise, Pearce.'

'Lieutenant Pearce!'

Lipton raised his good hand and yawned to imply the barked response had no effect.

'A rank open to any low-born peasant in the navy and for free, which we do not allow in the better service, where it is incumbent that you be a gentleman and have some means in order to gain entry. Be assured Pearce, we would not welcome you into our mess even if you had money, for you lack the attributes as well as the birth to qualify.'

'Give me the names of the culprits and I will show them what a blue coat can do with any weapon they care to choose.'

'I do not think you have yet caught our drift, Pearce; we do not see you as a man entitled to anything other than our contempt. It may be that you are fit to be horsewhipped but there is not a man present in this room who thinks his own reputation would not be sullied by contesting with you in an arena reserved for gentlemen.'

'If you do not grant me the names I will challenge you all.'

'Which, at best, will get you some spittle in your face. I think I speak for the service to which I belong when I say that no officer, certainly none in my regiment, will accept a challenge from a swine like you for fear of having to resign their commission in disgrace.'

'I see I am amongst cowards.'

The ensign piped up again. 'Don't just stand there, man, do what you were bred to and pour us out some wine.'

'Damn you,' Pearce responded, moving towards the speaker through a gale of amusement. 'If you care to step outside the door, you insolent pup, I'll teach you a lesson with nothing but the toe of my boot.'

His way was barred by the men between him and the speaker, so Pearce had no option but to stop.

'Get out of here,' Lipton yelled, half standing too and wincing as he moved. 'For if you do not I will instruct these fellows to beat you like the product of the gutter that you are. Be assured, that horsewhip I mentioned is to hand and will be employed. Then, following a good drubbing, perhaps you will be tossed in the harbour like a bit of offal as a fitting response to the liberty you took against me.'

They were all standing now bar one, and that was Walcott, who had the decency to look downcast. It was obvious to Pearce that if he persisted the threat would be carried out; just as clear was the fact that he could not fight them all with any chance of success, which left him at a stand. He was not prepared to let go what had happened to Emily, who had been accosted in public. She had endured catcalls not only regarding her relationship with him, but with the added insult that her accusers were happy to spare a coin for a bout, though not much, given she was such damaged goods.

'Gentlemen,' Lipton said quietly, 'I believe it would be best if we resumed the consumption of our breakfast.'

'Gentlemen,' Pearce spat in reply. 'I have seen things floating in my chamber pot more fitting for the title than you lot.'

The way they ignored him was harder to take than if they had reacted with violence. With no alternative to feeling foolish, Pearce turned and left. But he heard Lipton call to his fellow diners in a voice so loud that he obviously wanted their visitor to hear.

'Should any of you come across that piece of ordure in the street, you may feel free to belabour him with anything that comes to hand, though I forbid weapons that can mortally wound. Good God, how our regimental honour would be stained by the demise of such a fellow.'

It took an effort to proceed straight to his rendezvous, the temptation to return to comfort Emily being great, and as he made his way his head was full of images in which he bloodily chastised those he had just left, both individually and collectively. Yet underlying that was the obvious truth that there was little he could do if they would not accept his challenge. Could he turn the tables on them and expose them to like ridicule?

There was another point: the information he finally extracted from Emily had been that the insults to which she had been exposed were quite specific and not just a general reference to her being a woman of the brothel, for her husband and the abandonment of him had been mentioned. On consideration of that the only person he could think of from whom such information could have come was Digby, yet he struggled to believe that he, upright by habit, could be guilty.

He was back on the quay now and a minor distraction was caused, with all the usual nonsense of signal gunnery, by the arrival of the very distinctive *HMS Agamemnon*, no doubt to take the place of the now departed *Leander*, and in her wake a couple of frigates and that produced another bit of reflection.

He had to assume Nelson, in a vessel he knew was mainly manned by volunteers, to be a man who would grant his crew leave, so it promised to be a night full of incident ashore, and in cogitating on that he wondered if this was the right time to let the likes of Michael O'Hagan loose on Leghorn.

It was too late to change that; his friends were awaiting him and no doubt wondering where in hell's name he had got to. Turning his back on the sea he made his way out of the old part of town along one of the numerous canals that led to and surrounded the star-shaped fortress built earlier in the century in the style first established by Louis the Sun King's favourite builder of defences, the Marquis de Vauban.

Gravelines came to his mind again here, for the heat of the sun apart and the sense of much colour this gave to his surrounding, the two places were very similar, with the main point of defence located away from the shore along a series of narrow waterways leading to a deep moat. In the case of Leghorn the old fortress still stood on the seashore, but would not hold out against a determined assault by modern ship-based gunnery.

The canals were there to narrow any assault and make it easier to repel but they had an added advantage in that, unlike the alleyways of the old town, full of drinking establishments and brothels which only differed in the degree to which they were disreputable, the air was better, for the open space of the waterways created a wide avenue through which it could easily blow. On top of that, few men of the sea, whether of the service or privately employed – Leghorn was home to a whole fleet of privateers as well as a revictualling base for the fleet – ventured this far into what was a more settled part of town.

Thus the place he had chosen to meet his Pelicans was one used by locals and not by British sailors, who might have been called upon to remark on an officer sharing a wet with common seamen. But just in case, and for the heat as well as discretion, Pearce removed his hat and coat and carried them over his arm.

Sat at a shaded table outside, he could see before he got close that the trio were subject to many a glance from the passers-by, no doubt wondering what fellows who normally came ashore to roger a woman and get drunk not far from the seashore were doing in such a quiet location; they were not alone.

'You certainly picked a right spot here,' Charlie Taverner moaned as his captain sat down, an apron-wearing servitor appearing immediately to take, as much by sign language as words, a new order. 'There ain't a sign of diversion in sight.'

'You'll get your chance for that, Charlie, when we have finished our wet. You must realise that I cannot do this in plain view and I very much want to.'

Rufus, at one time too young to ever cast an opinion, spoke up; he had matured since that night he had been pressed, even if in his freckled face and ginger hair he still looked too young.

'I might not have an hourglass, or for that matter a ship's bell, but I reckon on the last score you are a good two strikes late.'

'Which I will make up to you with as much drink as you wish to consume.'

'It's not where we want to be, John-boy.'

'Michael, can it truly be said that it's a place any of us want to be?'

The wine arrived and was poured, in the case of the others into vessels that had been already emptied more than once. Pearce wondered as silence fell if they were thinking, as he was, of the place where they had first met? It had not been like this, where the shade was necessary for comfort. It had been a cold, windswept night and the Pelican had been a crowded, noise-filled tavern instead of a quiet backstreet affair, part of that clamour coming from folk placing bets on Michael's ability to lift a table using only his teeth.

He had been wildly and blindly drunk that night and he had tried to remove Pearce's head with one of his massive fists, which was a strange way to begin a friendship. The others Pearce had met he recalled, the now departed Abel Scrivens and Ben Walker, lost to Barbary and slavery.

They had been, like Charlie and Rufus, short on the means for a tankard of ale that night and Pearce gathered many another. It was smooth Charlie, who had the skills of a man who could live within or without the law, who had dunned – he would have said persuaded – John Pearce into buying them pots of ale, and as they talked it became clear that they did not reside here entirely out of choice.

The Pelican Tavern lay within the Liberties of the Savoy, a stretch of land beside the River Thames, a one-time part of the Savoy Palace of John of Gaunt and still part of the Royal Duchy of Lancaster, into which those on the run from writs various could take refuge, for no bailiff or tipstaff was allowed to exercise warrants of apprehension within its narrow confines, though that would not have served if the men pursuing John Pearce had followed him into the Pelican, for a King's Bench Writ was a being of a different order altogether.

He had sat with those he had met and mostly evaded their

enquires about where he had come from and where he was going, learning a little of the life they lived, which was one of casual and itinerant employment as well as hot-bedding in a crowded rookery for the lack of the means to pay rent for a space of their own.

Even if they did not list their various offences, it was clear each of his accidental drinking companions were in the Liberties for a good reason, unlike the very noisy Michael O'Hagan. He was a well-paid day labourer who could dig ditches at speed in a city where building was in boom, a man who could spend his wages freely and replace them the next day. He could also afford, and this piqued Charlie Taverner no end, to attract the affections of buxom Rosie, the lady serving their ale.

Then Ralph Barclay had sent in his press gang and all their lives had been altered in that instant; the people with whom he had been drinking went, like him, from free men under a cloud to virtual prisoners of the King's Navy and with no seeming redress. This was the case even if Barclay had broken the law.

'I am bound to ask you what you want for the future?' Pearce said to kill a silence that had lasted too long.

'Christ, John!' Charlie exclaimed, happy to be as familiar as he had once been when they had shared the lower deck. 'Is that not decided?'

'We volunteered, remember,' Rufus added.

'To save me,' Pearce replied. 'What I mean is that things have altered, as no doubt Michael has told you.'

'He has told us we will not be heading straight back home as we thought.'

'And what, Rufus, do you reckon to that and how do the crew of *Larcher* feel, for it shames me to say I do not know?'

'You would if there was discontent, John,' Charlie opined, before he smiled.

Handsome in a fair way it changed his face, for he was a fellow who too often saw the dark side of anything and was wont to voice it. Originally Pearce had taken this amiss, struggling to get on terms with Charlie and the feeling had been mutual. But time and opportunity had led to tales of the Londoner's early life and there was nothing there to bring cheer: no real parents, a street urchin who needed to steal to live, which made sense of his attitude – he had seen too many bad things to anticipate good.

Rufus was different; an apprentice who had run away from the bond paid to his parents and an employer he saw as exploiting him, he was innocence personified, at one time no more than an echo of Charlie, who knew so much more than he about life and its vicissitudes. It had been a pleasure to watch him grow into his own man.

'What I am saying, I suppose, is this. I have no notion of what is going to happen next and there is a very good chance I might be stripped of *Larcher* and ordered to serve in another ship.'

'Will you, John-boy?'

'I don't know, Michael, I have other considerations now than just my own person.'

'Hotham,' declared Rufus as the others nodded.

'You know about that?'

'Christ, John,' Charlie hooted, 'we knew he was to get the command afore he did.'

It was not true, but it was enough to lighten things and provide a shared laugh, that followed by a toast to the eavesdropping ability of tars before Pearce got solemn again.

'But seriously, there's no love lost between us and you and I know why. Added to what he thinks of me, he knows that you carry the truth about Barclay's crimes and are victims of it, for it was he who suppressed your sworn affidavits. He will have the power, with Hood gone, to make your lives as well as mine a misery.'

'And how, John-boy, do we avoid that?'

'I can resign my position at any time, but as for you three – well, you can guess.'

'Run.' Pearce nodded when Charlie said that, but he was looking into faces seriously unconvinced and the same voice underlined the reason. 'In a strange country where we don't know the lingo.'

'The harbour is full of privateers and you are all now prime hands.'

'All of them likely to be boarded by the navy and searched for deserters,' Rufus protested. 'We would be strung up from the yardarm if caught and even service under Barclay weren't as bad as that.'

'Well, think on it,' Pearce said, standing up, donning his coat and waving his hat. 'I have kept you from your pleasures long enough.'

'And you are eager to get to your own,' said Charlie with a knowing grin.

'There's little to be had there at the moment, Charlie, for Emily is severely down and is even refusing to leave her lodgings.'

The looks demanded an explanation, and if it was dragged out of him, they heard every part of his problem.

'And all I can do is hope to find each one on his own and give them a sound beating, all except that fellow Walcott, who had the good sense to look troubled by the way his confrères behaved.'

'You should have skewered Lipton through the belly not the arm, John-boy, as I said at the time.'

'To which Charlie and I agree,' Rufus added.

That got a wry smile. 'Then maybe it would be me that faced the rope, Rufus, for it might have been seen as foul murder.'

'Strikes me,' Charlie said, 'that you have the means to put these swabs in their place without you raise your own hand, John. There's not a man jack aboard *Larcher* that don't think kindly on Mrs Barclay and would take it amiss to see her distressed.'

'Set my crew upon them?'

'That precise,' Charlie replied, having picked up the tone of voice, which was one of distaste. 'If they won't grant you the means to teach a lesson, well . . .'

'No!' Pearce replied, emphatically. 'I may wish them ill with every fibre of my being, but I will not sink to their level.' He tapped his head. 'The answer lies up here, lads, and in time it will come to me.'

'We might happen across them this night.'

Looking into Rufus's eager face he saw what looked like the light of battle and on him it was risible. Charlie was no brawler either, but Michael was another matter and he was about to go out and very likely get seriously drunk, they all were, so it was to the Irishman that he addressed his injunction.

'I ask you, if you encounter any of the men you saw in that glade, to stay well clear of them. This is my affair and I will deal with it.'

Charlie Taverner's reply was crisp. 'Aye, aye, sir.'

CHAPTER FOURTEEN

When he returned to rejoin Emily, John Pearce was surprised to find Matthew Dorling waiting for him and looking anxious. 'We had a messenger from *Agamemnon*, Your Honour, and the commodore wishes you to attend upon him at your convenience.'

The serious look on the young master's face left his captain in no doubt that 'at your convenience' meant immediately.

'Commodore? Is it still Nelson in command?'

'He is, sir, and he has been given his pennant by Lord Hood, which means he has overall command of the frigates with which Old Aggie came in.'

The King's Navy was well known for its peremptory way of demanding that folk shift themselves; orders were usually accompanied by the addendum that anything one was commanded to do was to be carried out with all despatch and Pearce, when he had later examined that footnote, had soon come to the conclusion that it was rarely required, as useless as the other addition, which was that to delay was ever accompanied by the words 'at your peril'.

He could not obey the injunction without first determining if Emily was in a better frame of mind. Not that he would be able to say much to reassure her that it was safe to walk the streets of Leghorn without her being subjected to another bout of public humiliation, certainly not without him on her arm to offer a modicum of protection. Even that was in doubt after his encounter at the Pensione: if there were enough of those redcoats in a group he might find himself involved in fisticuffs with the odds against him.

'You have a boat?'

'Ready and waiting by the quayside, Your Honour.'

'Oblige me, Mr Dorling, by going back to that and waiting. I promise I will not be too long.'

That brought on a frown. 'Am I allowed to advise, sir, that such a course would be unwise?'

'You are,' Pearce replied in a tone that was, while not unfriendly, decidedly firm, 'but not more than that. I will be along presently, and think on this: Captain Nelson, commodore notwithstanding, is no martinet, so a delay of a few bells is unlikely to cause him upset.'

The Emily he encountered once Dorling had been dismissed was no longer the tearful creature he had left earlier, that made obvious by the face she pulled when he admonished her to not go abroad alone. Yet Pearce missed it completely, so absorbed was he in what he thought was a good solution.

'If I cannot be present myself, I will detail Michael to accompany you. I challenge anyone to insult you with him at your side.'

'So I am to be trapped within these walls without I have an escort?'

The pitch of that was unmistakable and it was picked up; it was one of admonishment and Pearce made matters worse by his slightly irate comment that he was only trying to protect her.

'I refuse to be a prisoner, John, and I will not let those worms dictate the way I go about my day.'

'What I suggest is only for a few days. They are soldiers on furlough and surely must soon return to their duties.'

If Pearce had always admired Emily's pluck – she had stood up to her bullying husband and risked everything by eloping with him – what followed was an indication of the way their relationship had matured. Whereas before he had seen courage, he now observed stubbornness. Her face was closed up and determined and the look of which he was on the receiving end boded ill.

'Sure they will depart, to no doubt be replaced by another set of ill-bred scoundrels!'

'Emily, I am trying to look after you.'

'And I am telling you, John Pearce, that I do not want your protection. If I have chosen a way of life that is less than perfect I will not make it more so by hiding my face from the outside world. Or would you have me enter a nunnery?'

Her manner had turned bitter and he sought to mollify her. 'You have a right to regret the life you have chosen—'

'Right?' she shouted, cutting right across him. 'Am I to be told what I can and cannot do, that I am but a chattel, as I was as a wife?'

It was now his turn to sound cross, given he felt he was being deliberately misunderstood. 'That is not what I meant and you know it.'

'Do I?' Emily scoffed. 'Sometimes I have no idea of what it is you mean. You think it is as nothing to lie to me and go and put your life at risk. Did it ever occur to you how I would feel if I was brought news of your death, stuck here in this Italian hellhole at the mercy of every wagging tongue that spoke English—'

'Emily—'

Pearce got no further; she was in a passion and was not prepared to listen to what she obviously saw as his excuses.

'And who told the world of my estate, who made it common knowledge that I am a woman fallen from the required standard, laid so low in the public imagination that any Tom, Dick or Harry feels free to abuse me?'

'I left you a letter . . .'

'A letter!'

'And everything I possessed, with a statement of my love for you.'

The voice dropped now and he knew she was once more close to tears, which made him feel utterly useless.

'That would have kept me warm, John, would it? Your dying protestations of love. How reassuring to be cast into outer darkness and have that as comfort.'

He was at a stand, sure that nothing he could say would resolve matters; his solution was not brave, but it was better than to continue in an argument he could not win. And how alike it was to that which had happened to him earlier in the day.

'I am commanded to go aboard *HMS Agamemnon*. You may have seen her enter the roads and anchor this morning. Nelson has been made a commodore, and even if he were not I must obey, his being so much my senior.'

'Nelson,' Emily replied with some distaste.

Pearce had no idea he was not her favourite officer. She had attended a ball at Sheerness without her husband – he had been away pressing at the Pelican – and greatly enjoyed her evening, being by nature vivacious: dancing, drinking punch and laughing at the sallies of the naval officers present.

This was a fact that Nelson passed on to Ralph Barclay in a way that made her sound more like a scapegrace than an innocent, for which she had been severely chastised by a spouse who was both jealous and careful of his dignity. To Emily, Horatio Nelson was no more than a sneak.

'Anyway, I must be off, I have kept him waiting as it is.'

'Of course, John, do hurry away and do not concern yourself with me.'

He was still seething with the unfairness of that parting shot when he got to the waiting boat. The generally benign looks that greeted him got a glare in return and a sharp command to 'Look lively and bear away'.

Michael and Charlie had taken their carnal pleasure almost as soon as they arrived in the drinking den and were now in the process of imbibing away all the coin they had about them. Rufus had so far avoided the ladies – a loose term certainly – and was far from in a jolly mood, feeling out of place in a low-ceilinged, barred-windowed establishment that was designed to ensure that the difference between night and day was impossible to discern.

His upbringing, if not deeply religious, had been churchgoing enough to imbue in him the need for chastity; in addition Rufus was shy and lacking experience, whereas Charlie and Michael were not, and he felt out of place amongst the noise and excesses. So while he drank, his consumption was much more sparing than that of his companions and no amount of joshing by them would bring him out of his shell.

The place was busy, the taproom and the whores of all ages and shapes doing sound business. It was full of sailors from *Agamemnon*, the frigates *Dolphin*, *Lutine* and the newly crewed Frenchman *Melpomene*. Not too many ordinary hands from the frigates had been let ashore, only the trusted ranks who could be relied upon to return, but Nelson had let a goodly number out of his sixty-four and they made up the majority.

The whole place and the raucous atmosphere, as well as the serious crowding, went up several notches when the midshipmen of the flotilla came to join their lower-rank colleagues. In age they were little different to their fellow tars but the mids of the King's Navy had a reputation for causing mayhem of which they were inordinately proud. The owner, no stranger to the depredations of such creatures, sent out into the public area a number of burly looking coves with barely concealed clubs.

Charlie was in his element; he loved the chance to engage with and josh his fellow humans and he could tell a tale better than most and now he had an audience known to be credulous, and if not that, deeply superstitious. If they were not completely stupid, they were happy enough to be spun a yarn without ever interrupting to point up the improbabilities of Charlie's story: that he was the foundling son of a man of great means, a titled fellow, fallen on hard times, so that instead of enjoying his coach and four as well as the attentions of his servants, Charlie had been obliged to make his own way in the world.

When pressed as to how, he had quick and well-rehearsed answers, for it was a variation on a tale he had told many times as he sought, in places like Covent Garden and Seven Dials, to dun innocents – he called it guiding them – bumpkins who had come wide-eyed to the Great Wen of London, only for them and their bulging purse to fall into the maw of a man who could show them how to spend their coin. Soon, with his fiction taking ever more improbable paths, Charlie had his audience in stitches.

Michael had started singing – wild dancing was sure to follow, then it was possible he would become upset and fists would fly, this caused by some remark he would deem as innocent were he sober – and since some of his fellow imbibers were Irish too, there was much in the way of sentimental ballads in his native tongue. All the while Rufus sipped away and wondered if it was yet dark outside, for he doubted his companions would be keen to meet the strictures set by John Pearce and return aboard *Larcher* before penury forced them to.

Barely listening to Charlie, there not being a tale he had not heard before, he did not realise his friend had moved on from his fictions to the nature of Rufus himself. So he did not hear Charlie tell the Agamemnons that his young freckled friend had yet to lie with a woman and was too shy to do so, even if he had the means in his poke to fund the purpose. To men who had taken their pleasures in every port they visited, and many of whom were the same age or even younger than Rufus, to say such a state of affairs was a red rag to a bull could be taken as an understatement.

If he was aware of the growing level of noise Rufus had no idea of the cause and when he caught, out of the corner of his eye, the coins being tossed into the centre of the table, he assumed it to be some form of wager of which he was not part. The men who grabbed him were unknown to Rufus and had moved without threat so he was unprepared to fend off the half-dozen eager hands. The youngster found himself lifted bodily and just had a sight of a grinning Charlie Taverner as he was borne aloft to the staircase that led up to the cubicles where the whores plied their trade.

His protests were loud but ignored, as ahead of him one of the less ugly ladies, in addition a person close to his own age, was engaged to initiate Rufus into the ways of the world, to take the boy they brought with them and return him a man. To ensure he would not emerge unreformed they took the trouble to remove his ducks, which showed that if he was mentally reluctant, his body held a contrary opinion.

Thrown into the room and on to the cot, with the rickety door left open so they could see that their coin was well spent, his aggressors watched while a girl who knew her trade overcame what were feeble protests. She straddled Rufus, whose facial expressions went from objection, through wonder, to anticipation, then exhilaration, finally settling on what looked like disbelief, the whole short act, for it would not have troubled a clock, accompanied by loud cheering from his supporters, who, having thrown in his breeches, trooped noisily back down the stairs.

When he came down the stairs it was with such a smile, that it was remarked no angel ever looked more beatific.

It was flattering that Nelson came to welcome John Pearce personally and his greeting was full of good cheer.

'Mr Pearce, I have orders for you from Lord Hood.' That such news was not responded to with equal enthusiasm threw Nelson slightly and he looked up at his visitor, his startlingly blue eyes confused. 'I do assure you they are of a pleasant nature.'

'Would I be permitted, sir, to say if that is the case, it is a novel one to my mind?'

Nelson shrugged and gave a sly grin. 'Needless to say, I have heard of some of your exploits and have been rendered envious.'

'I would have given way to you at any time, Captain Nelson, I do assure you, for my "exploits", as you call them, came about more by coercion than any desire on my part.'

'Your modesty does you credit.'

Pearce was about to protest that he was telling the truth, there was no modesty involved, but he thought better of it: to do so would be a waste of time with such an enthusiast as Nelson, so instead he apologised for being tardy.

'I was ashore when I received your message.'

'As are most of my officers as well as a goodly number of my crew, and no doubt they are setting the whole town by its ears. It is one of the constraints of command that such pleasures are barred to us, though I recall fondly some of my own youth. But I am glad you have come aboard at this hour, for you can dine with me, that is if you do not have a previous engagement.'

'Of course.'

'Good, for we have matters to discuss.'

Pearce had a vision of Emily then, not the irate one he had so recently left, but a more benign apparition. Was Nelson about to refer to their liaison? Time to deflect even the chance of that.

'My orders are, sir?'

'To proceed once more to Naples with despatches for Sir William Hamilton.'

The conversation had taken them from the entry port to Nelson's cabin, a large space reasonably, if not grandly appointed and there was a servant waiting to take an order that some wine should be fetched. As he went to carry out this instruction Pearce was sure he staggered which, given *Agamemnon* was at anchor on a relatively swell-free sea, was remarkable. Nelson obviously picked up on his expression, which caused him to speak very softly.

'My man Lepeé is a tad fond of sipping, I'm afraid. I chastise him but it does little good.'

As they sat down, Pearce was thinking that it was hard to imagine Nelson chastising anyone; it did not seem to be in his nature yet he must have done so many times in his naval career. You did not serve for over two decades and reach not only his rank, but also the appreciation of the likes of Sam Hood, without you had real ability, and the application of discipline was part of that.

'If I had a guinea,' Nelson added, 'for every time one of my officers has told me to dismiss him I would scarce need to worry about taking a prize.'

'I take it, sir, he has some attribute about which they do not know?'

'He saved my life, Mr Pearce, though I will allow that God's hand was in it as much as Lepeé, for I was near death with malaria on a land expedition in the Caribbean. He brought me downriver to safety and a restored health. I cannot just dismiss a man to whom I owe that.'

'I have friends like that, sir,' Pearce responded.

This was imparted with real feeling, for if he hardly knew Nelson the man had just gone up several notches in his estimation.

'And we must hang on to them, Mr Pearce, with all the grip we can muster.'

The wine decanter and two glasses arrived slowly in a far from straight line. The two officers sat in silence as the contents were poured and when that was unsteadily complete the man was kindly dismissed. When conversation did commence it began on general topics eventually settling on those twin naval stalwarts; previous battles and mutual acquaintances, which was fine until Nelson mentioned Ralph Barclay, referring to the conversation that they had engaged in off Tunis the previous year, in which Pearce had told him the story of his illegal impressment.

'Poor fellow lost an arm at Toulon. Does that not temper your grievance?'

Pearce was not to be put off by his host's obvious sympathy. 'No, sir, it does not, given it was an entirely illegal act, a fact I have been seeking to see him chastised for since the day it occurred.'

'Chastised?'

'I have an attorney looking into the matter.'

'Ah!' came the response, that and the taking of a quick sip of wine. 'I did know he was very short-handed at the outbreak of war.'

'Am I to gather, sir, that you approve?'

'Not entirely, but I can understand why he might be drawn into such an act.' Seeing a lack of agreement, Nelson continued quickly. 'You may not know that Barclay, like me, spent five years on the beach and I can tell you, Mr Pearce, there is not much more debilitating than spending that amount of time without a ship and on half pay. I think you might be astounded, and somewhat sympathetic given your parentage, to hear why I think this happened in my case.'

'Now, sir, it is my turn to be curious.'

'Surely it would not surprise you to know that I read some of your father's pamphlets?'

'No,' Pearce lied; it seemed to him very unlikely.

'I cannot say I agreed with the remedies he proposed, but I will say that Adam Pearce had the right of things in many areas.'

Nelson topped up his wine glass, but in such a way and with such a look on his face as to debar interruption.

'I was asked – tasked – really, to prepare a report on the state of the rural folk in my area of Norfolk and I spoke as I found. I saw poverty in the extreme, people living in a state of deep anxiety for fear that a bad harvest may bring them starvation. There was no meat on their table, indeed there were many hovels I visited for whom a table was a luxury.'

Nelson, not in any sense a tall man, seemed to shrink into his chair as he spoke and his chin was now close to his chest. 'I can only say that in speaking with honesty I did nothing for my prospects. I strongly advised some system of relief for the lowest of our brethren but that was not a message those who held the reins of power wanted to hear and they certainly did not want to tell that to the King, though I fear my view, perhaps even the whole report, must have been passed on.'

'And you think it caused you to be unemployed?'

'I cannot be certain and I have posed the question, albeit with some timidity, to Lord Hood, who as First Lord turned down my many written requests for a place. He will not say I was bypassed for that report, but it is wise to remember that he was and is a politician as well as a sailor.'

'Added to which he is a member of Pitt's government.'

'So you see, Mr Pearce, there is a certain amount of fellow-feeling in my assessment of this sorry tale for how are we to make our way in the world and prosper as naval officers without we have a ship and hands enough to crew it. If you tell me that Ralph Barclay stepped outside the strict bounds of the law to get men to crew his ship, after five years of want, I have to tell you that I do have some sympathy for him.'

'Will it be dinner for just one, Your Honour?' slurred Lepeé, who had slipped in while Nelson was talking.

'For two, Lepeé. Mr Pearce is off to Naples and he and I have much to discuss.'

CHAPTER FIFTEEN

Charlie Taverner seemed to have got himself in a right pickle. The flotilla midshipmen, a good thirty in number, had surrounded him and they were clearly not best pleased with whatever it was he had been saying to them. One, not young by any means but a burly fellow, had him by the scruff, while the rest were loud in their growling. Rufus, who had half entertained the idea of a repeat of his earlier encounter, had to detach himself from the group of overblown madams to whom he was talking and grab hold of Michael to come to the rescue.

'Say anything like that again, you swab, and we'll set you face down in the privy.'

'I is only passing on to you what I heard,' Charlie cried. 'I was having a quiet wet and along comes a whole tribe of bullocks, everyone an officer, who then sat down and began to drink like they hadn't seen water for a week. Well, I kept my head down with the likes of those coves around and by doing so I heard every word they said, not that it were hard, seeing as how they were braying loud.'

'Bullocks you say?'

'Redcoats to a man and 65th Foot, I gathered, 'cos they mentioned their regiment more'n once as the best in the whole army.'

'You,' Michael shouted, 'let him be or by the name of Jesus you'll feel my hand.'

When those facing Charlie turned to the sound of that call, their expressions as closed up as their fists and very ready to dispute, they had a moment's hesitation; O'Hagan was a sight to instil caution in any man. There was his sheer height and girth, as well as a face that was bright red – if they thought because of fury, Rufus reckoned it to be more to do with drink – and his great hams, with knuckles like walnuts, were raised up and fearsome.

Added to that, some of the seamen present, seeing there might be a chance to clout some of the mids with whom they sailed, jumped-up little bastards to their way of thinking, had moved to back Michael up, while to their rear the men the owner had sent out with clubs seemed ready to intervene if matters got out of hand. It was sufficient to give overall pause, but really it was the victim who took the heat out.

'Belay, Michael,' Charlie called, 'for these fine fellows have a right to hear what I learnt.'

'Fine fellows, my arse,' came a comment from behind O'Hagan.

'Happen you has the measure of it,' spoke up another, 'but it would be fair to hear what all the fuss is about.'

Charlie called, so he was now talking to the room, 'I was just telling this fellow here what the bullocks said about their Commodore Nelson, for it were not praise – far from it.'

That got a more extended growl, especially from the Agamemnons, proving that admiration for their captain was not confined to those who served abaft the mast.

'So let it out.'

'I would be obliged, good sir, if you could let go of my neckerchief.'

The atmosphere had changed so the senior-looking mid eased his grip on Charlie, who having been pinned against a wall, could sink a little so his feet were firmly planted again.

'Talk, man.'

'I will at that, Your Honour. They was saying that Nelson was a right nuisance at Calvi and the place would have fallen double quick if he had not kept poking his nose into matters about which he knew less than nowt.'

'Is that word for word?'

Charlie paused, and if Michael was too far gone to see it, Rufus was not. His mate was thinking on the wing and he had on his storytelling face; that cocked head and slight look of wonder, as if what he was relating was too far-fetched to be possible.

'Well, I don't want to be in the way of causin' trouble, but it were a mite more foul put than that. They was not kind about Captain Nelson's parentage, let me say, who could not be sure of a claim for any man or woman to have bred him. They reckoned him the spawn of some whore who had been found in the church doorway.'

That was not well received and Charlie spoke quickly lest the room was tempted to take it out on him. 'Nor were they mellow about his height, calling him a stunted dwarf and, it hurts me to say this, but they made out he was likely partial to his midshipmen, as much as they seemed to be partial to him. Said if he ever came to the Pensy Ambrose they would provide him with somewhere Italian to put his meat, for there was no shortage of bumboys in Leghorn.'

The anger was no growl now, but loud and continuous protests as Charlie added, his face darkening, 'Mind, they was of the opinion, and I nearly took issue with them for the way it were said, that all tars were alike in that respect.'

'What's this Pensy place?' called a voice.

'No notion, but I reckon it must be where they is billeted.' Charlie's face screwed up as if he was trying to remember. 'Yes, I reckon that to be the right of it. I had a mate called Ambrose so I recall the name, though it was said in the local fashion, with bits and bobs on the end.'

'I say these bullocks need to be minded of their manners,' said the mid who had collared Charlie, and that turned the growls to cheers, as well as shouts, filled with agreement and deadly threats.

Charlie was free now, and since every eye followed his assailant as he went to accost the man who ran the tavern, he was able to wink at Rufus without being observed. The conversation that followed with the owner, in a combination of stilted English and the local Tuscan, was not swift, but it must have been fruitful, because the midshipman was able to announce that he now had the location of a place called the Pensione d'Ambrosio with the added information that it was no more than a few streets distant.

'Now, I am minded, and I know my fellow mids will back me in this, to teach these bullocks a lesson and it would do us no harm to find out which of them can swim. You here who are Agamemnons, I leave it to you to decide if you will hear of your commander being so traduced or follow us to set the men who insulted him straight.'

The man closest to Rufus turned to ask what traduced meant;

the youngster was not able to tell him. 'But it can't be good mate.'

'So who's with me?'

That got a roar of approval as he led the way to the exit, followed by nearly everyone in the tavern, which brought a gloomy look to the swarthy face of the tavern keeper, who saw his profits for the night disappearing through the door. Michael, slightly bewildered, was swaying in the middle of a now near deserted floor when Charlie took his arm, calling to Rufus to grab the other.

'Come on, we best get to a boat an' back aboard *Larcher*. Last thing we want is to be still on land when the shit flies through the hawsehole.'

O'Hagan was not easy to move and both his friends kept a weather eye on his fists, for in times past they had seen them employed in the hostelry from which they took their soubriquet, and the notion of being on the receiving end was not one to savour. It was a struggle to get him through the door and out into the Italian night.

'Come along, Michael, keep your feet a'going. Remember John Pearce's orders.'

The curses that O'Hagan then heaped on that name were foul, insults that his friends would not repeat to the man at whom they were aimed. It was also a good thing he could not hear them either.

The meal John Pearce had consumed, if not spectacular, was pretty good, which proved that either Lepeé, or someone else in the pantry knew their stuff. He had already noted the quality of the wine and when he praised it he was treated to a sly smile and the information that it had been taken out of a prize ship he had taken and not declared as part of the ship's stores, as it should have been.

'One thing the French do well, Mr Pearce, is in the article of the grape.'

'I would be willing to drink to that, sir.'

'Then let us do so, but add that we must also confound them as our enemies.'

The table talk had ranged over a variety of subjects and with just two at the board it had flowed easily, Ralph Barclay notwithstanding, though the name did crop up on one occasion. Not that the host pressed: the case against the man was none of the commodore's doing and if he sought to mitigate Pearce's remarks it was not with passion enough to force a reaction.

Pearce was careful to make no mention of Hotham and his activities on Barclay's behalf – he did not feel he knew Nelson well enough to confide – though mention of the admiral's name produced a flash of distaste on Nelson's face; he was not a man who found it easy to disguise his feelings, which were quickly covered by unstinting praise for Samuel Hood, who was the best sailor and commanding admiral in the whole of the King's Navy.

'So you do not hold your five years on the beach against him?'

'No, Mr Pearce, he would have given me a ship if he could, but I do not ask any man to lay their head on the block for me. The people who stood in the way of my employment I like to think were not navy.'

Moving on, it was obvious Nelson hated the Revolution with a passion, born of his love of country and the stability of the English nation, added to which he blamed them fair and square for the loss of the American colonies. This being declaimed, Pearce was obliged to ask how he would have held on to them in the face of their intransigence, only to find his host short on a practical answer.

But given the vehemence of his opinion, it seemed best for Pearce not to come out, as had his father very vocally, in support of their claim to liberty.

Nelson was doing most of the talking, but it was not one-sided and he had the good grace to never raise an eyebrow at disagreement. His guest soon realised he was in the company of a committed warrior, a man keen to discuss battle tactics in a way that seemed to fly over his head, but he made what interjections he could, of a bellicose nature, which brought praise.

'I see you and I are of one mind there, Mr Pearce, but I wonder if we could move from shot and shell to your forthcoming mission?'

When Pearce nodded, it seemed to place some constraint on Nelson, who paused for several seconds before he continued.

'As well as the despatches I will give to you before you depart, I wonder if you would oblige me, as you did previously, by carrying some personal letters.'

'Of course.'

'There is one to Sir William Hamilton.' Nelson actually blushed then and his voice lost any assurance. 'I have written, too, another letter to his wife, Lady Hamilton.'

'Which I will happily deliver,' Pearce responded, failing to pick up on Nelson's discomfort.

'Without, I hope, troubling Sir William regarding its existence?'

That had Pearce pausing, but only for a brief period as he sought to fillet the bones out of what had just been said. Nelson wanted a letter delivered to a woman who was somewhat notorious in terms of gossip at home, without letting know her husband, who the same tittle-tattle had as a credulous old fool who had been ensnared by a beautiful Circe, which made him wonder at what might be the contents. On only a brief acquaintance he himself had seen that she was something of a temptress and was certainly attractive. Having thought that through, he was swift to conclude it was none of his concern.

'I will, of course, be happy to oblige, sir.'

'I hasten to add there is nothing untoward in this, Mr Pearce. It is merely that any man might object to another fellow communicating openly with his wife.'

But you wrote to her before, Pearce was thinking, and there were no instructions then requesting discretion, which begged the question of what had changed since? These thoughts had to be put aside, as Nelson was praising Emma Hamilton to the deckbeams.

'Lady Hamilton is as much an aid to our cause as is he. I swear when I asked for aid to support us at Toulon it was her intervention that caused it to be provided so speedily. When it comes to royal influence, she is the one to apply to, for she has the ear of the Queen.'

'A fact, sir, of which I was made aware when I met her.'

'And I am sure she made an equal impression on you, sir, as she did on me.'

Pearce remained silent, though still pondering on his host's now very apparent feelings of awkwardness; in Paris he had enjoyed conversations with the husband of his then mistress without experiencing the least awkwardness. Why would he not when the man's own mistress was in the same salon? How different was France from rural England, the society from which Nelson came, and Emily likewise; not London – it was as lax as any capital city would be about such relationships and Naples was even more so.

He was also thinking that Nelson, being in Leghorn and certain to go ashore, was bound to hear about Emily and him. Was this an opportunity to confide in a man who might be less quick to judge? After all, he seemingly held another man's wife in such high regard that he was cautious about her husband having knowledge of the depth of it?

It was a possible chance to counter any malicious tales Nelson was bound to hear, a chance to put the case for the triumph of love over duty. The chance came and then went; he had thought too long and he felt the moment to speak had passed again because Nelson was still praising.

'I have met them but once, though that was enough to have me esteem them both highly.' The emphasis was on the both. 'King George could not have a more accomplished representative in Naples, and Sir William would be the first person to tell you what a helpmeet she is even within the palace. The royal children are very fond of her.'

'I do not wish to allude to her reputation, sir—'

'Tripe, and uncooked at that,' Nelson snapped. 'Rumour of the most pernicious kind set against a lady those who speak of her have never met. You would struggle, sir, to find a kinder and more generous soul, who takes under her wing any of the waifs and strays who end up in Naples, for it is, as I am sure you are aware, a stop on the Grand Tour for those interested in classical Rome.'

'Sir William is certainly an avid collector.'

'He digs with gusto, that is true.' Nelson essayed another pause and a deep intake of breath. 'I am sure you found in him and his wife two people of a stock to make you proud. For the people who traduce them, well, I cannot tell you, Mr Pearce, how I abhor such talk.'

'It is not something of which I am fond, either, sir.'

'Naturally,' Nelson responded before reacting to a raised Pearce eyebrow. 'If I may make so bold, I have heard something of the same aimed at your person.'

He let that sink in, then took up again his refrain.

'And what do I find when I take the time to discover for myself what the truth is? I find an agreeable companion who, if he holds opinions with which I very much do not agree, has served as I once did before the mast and is, to my mind, a fellow of some presence and good conversation.'

'You flatter me, sir,' Pearce replied and he meant it; he also suspected he knew why.

Nelson grinned. 'There you go being modest again, Mr Pearce, which I have no hesitation in telling you will do you no good in the service. While I do not advocate the blowing of your own trumpet, it does no good to hide your light under a bushel.'

Shall I count the clichés, Pearce was wondering?

'I myself have ahead of me a notable destiny.' It was impossible not to react to such a statement and Pearce did not try; nor did it go unnoticed. 'Oh, I know it is not the done thing to talk in such a fashion, but I have had the certainty of that since I was relatively new to the navy and I had a dream that told me so.'

'You served before the mast, sir?' Pearce asked; he did not want to go to where Nelson was leading, being unsure if he could keep his face straight when presented with the outpourings of dreams, which to his mind tended to be claptrap whoever was talking. 'I find that odd.'

'Why so? I was sent on a voyage as a stripling, just after I took service with my Uncle Suckling. You may have heard of Captain Suckling, he was quite famous for a battle fought off Cape St Francis . . .'

'I am sorry to admit, sir, his name is not known to me.'

'Matters not, but my uncle sent me on a voyage aboard a merchant vessel, six months on the Triangular Passage in which I learnt to hand and reef if not to steer, to go aloft in foul weather and fair, to set and take in sail. More than that, Mr Pearce, I spent time with the kind of men I now command and I will tell you, sir, I find I understand them better than many of my fellows, which leads to fewer problems of discipline.'

'Which can only be a good thing.'

'I am no lover of the cat.'

Yet you can sympathise with Barclay who is your polar opposite; that thought had to be put aside as Nelson stood and went to his writing stand, returning with two sealed letters and an oilskin pouch.

'I entrust these to you, Mr Pearce. The pouch contains both your orders and Lord Hood's communication to Sir William, the others . . . well, we have already spoken of them.'

Since he remained standing Pearce had little choice but to do likewise.

'Once your mission is complete I wish you to join my squadron off the coast of Savoy – you will find the rendezvous with our man in Genoa. I intend to put you and *HMS Larcher* to close-inshore work, for we must find out what the Revolution is up to.'

'Sir.'

'So, until then, God speed. I expect you to sail at first light, given I am sure you are fully victualled. Forgive me if I do not see you to your boat, but I have a rate of paperwork to attend to, the downside, I must tell you, of the pennant Lord Hood granted me.'

* · *

The torch-bearing mob that descended on the Pensione d'Ambrosio were in no mood to talk, or even to wonder if there was anyone who needed to be spared from their wrath. The only admonishment that the man leading them had made, and this was to his fellow midshipman, was that they should avoid using their dirks, for if knives were drawn then more blood might be spilt than was wise.

To say they burst into the place was only partially true, given the entrance was too narrow, poured being a better description, and they laid about anyone found, be they servants or soldiers, which if it was unfair was the habit of a mob. The officers' servants sought to come to their aid and got a pounding for their efforts, while the men they attended to were likewise given a drubbing, barring their wounded Major Lipton, of course: no true Briton would assault a man with his arm in a sling.

Bruised and bleeding, the victims were noisily borne out of the smashed-open door to be carried to the harbour where, with a care that made sure they did not drown, and on run-up slings that men of the sea could produce in a trice, they were ducked repeatedly in the harbour until they lay in a dripping heap on the cobbles.

'And don't you go bad-mouthing our commodore again, or any other soul for that matter. If you do we won't haul you out but leave you to sink.'

The hired boat taking the Pelicans back to *HMS Larcher* had stopped well away from the quay and just as distant from their ship. They could see flaring torches and guess at what was taking place and it was enough to establish that matters had, in the case of John Pearce and the men who had insulted his lady, been settled.

'That was sharp, Charlie,' said Rufus softly.

'More'n one way to skin a cat, mate, but I have to say it was nip and tuck for a while who was going to get it.'

'You led them right up the garden.'

Their eyes fixed on the quay, they did not see the other boat being rowed beyond them towards the shore, so it came as a shock when they heard the voice of John Pearce calling to the pair sitting upright, just before he ordered his oarsmen to back to a stop.

'We's on our way back to *Larcher*, Capt'n,' Charlie shouted, he being quicker-witted than Rufus, while Michael could not take part: he was laid across a thwart and snoring. 'Michael is here with us and set for a sore head of the morning.'

The Pearce tone was mordant. 'Then I can take it you enjoyed your run ashore?'

'Had the time of our lives, Your Honour.'

'Well get some sleep, we weigh at first light. When Michael comes to, tell him to prepare my cabin to once more accommodate Mrs Barclay.'

'Aye, aye, sir.'

Then Pearce called to his boat crew. 'Give away, lads.'

CHAPTER SIXTEEN

Ralph Barclay had gone into a towering rage on finding the identity of the officer with whom his wife had sailed, as well as the proposed destination of the Mediterranean, information supplied to him by the Admiralty, that made even more galling when he was told there was no plan in place for *HMS Larcher* to return. Such was his passion it nearly brought on an apoplexy, one that alarmed his clerk-cum-secretary.

Cornelius Gherson's fear that his employer might do himself an injury was not based on any regard for his person, more it was a dread that should Barclay expire so he would be left not only without a job but also without a valuable source of income from his peculations. These he was able to carry out aboard *HMS Semele* and they were small, but they added to the stipend he was getting from Ommany and Druce for his advantageous – to them – way of scrutinising the use they made of their client's money. Gherson could read a book of complex accounts; Barclay could not.

They had rushed back to the offices of the prize agent to face an emollient Druce, who sought to calm his irate client and, once he had put a check on the more intemperate outbursts promising foul retribution on John Pearce, then did that which his duties required. He needed to find a solution that would solve Barclay's problems without causing the company of which he was a partner any of their own. The answer lay, as it had before, with Hodgeson.

While careful not to suggest anything conclusive, certainly nothing that would publicly shame Barclay, Druce had recommended that the thief taker be employed to find out how far this untoward relationship between John Pearce and his wife had gone. In short, was it, even if unlikely, innocent or had it strayed into areas that, while Druce never named them, were obvious to both parties.

'I am suggesting, Captain Barclay,' the prize agent put forward, 'that you need to be in possession of the facts before you can decide how to act.'

As a result, Hodgeson found himself once more in the New Forest enclave of Buckler's Hard, seeking out more information about the lady who had been observed on the deck of HMS *Larcher*. Not that he was having much in the way of luck, but local ignorance established one very obvious fact: Emily Barclay had not resided here at the Hard, there being no place in which she might have taken rooms. If you computed the time between her departing Nerot's Hotel and actually sailing away there was a gap, which implied she must have stayed somewhere.

Buckler's Hard was isolated and not surrounded by towns boasting decent hostelries, which narrowed matters down considerably. So starting at the most obvious place, which was

Lyndhurst, Hodgeson did that at which he was very experienced: he questioned those who would open up to him about who had stayed in such places.

This was never the owner: all they ever cared about was protecting their establishment against any hint of scandal that might affect future trade. But all coaching inns needed servants, lots of them, and some of the tasks were so menial, like emptying the night soil, it meant they were not filled with folk brimming with loyalty to the person who paid their meagre wage.

Indeed, often it was not a money payment but given in kind, in the form of a bed and food, so that such creatures were obliged to carry out other duties, such as sweeping away equine ordure or carrying bags in the hope of a tip, to fund a tankard of ale. The offer to buy for a bit of information was thus usually more than welcome.

'All servants talk, Mr Druce,' Hodgeson said, 'and the meaner their reward the more they are inclined to open up. If they did not, then the thief taker's job, which has got hard enough over the years, anyway, would become impossible.'

If Druce was nodding in agreement, he was also wondering at the nature of his own household. Was it secure, or as this man was implying, leaking like a sieve? Should he admonish his own servants to keep their tongues or would such an act imply to them there were secrets to sell? The notion that he might pay them better to ensure their loyalty did not enter into his ruminations.

'I worked my way down from Lyndhurst to the coast at Lymington and struck gold, though not with Mrs Barclay's name, nor that of John Pearce, but by a description of the pair. She was staying in the King's Head right enough, but under another name.'

'Which is?'

'Raynesford,' Hodgeson replied, with his employer noting that down. 'Both were registered under the same name and they occupied the same set of rooms.'

The sigh from Druce was audible and had him once more reflecting on the suitability of young women as wives to men old enough to know better.

'There is no doubt?'

'None, sir, for I cornered the owner and overcame his reluctance with threats.' Seeing the look of enquiry he added, 'It is easy to spread a rumour, Mr Druce, and the last thing the man who owned the King's Head needs is that his establishment should be known as a place for illicit trysts. Lymington is not London, sir, and such stories being abroad would ruin his trade.'

'So there is no doubt that there was lubricious activity?'

'No need to be a fly on the wall, Mr Druce, is there now? If two lovebirds share a bed then there is little doubt of what they get up to. Besides, proof of an act of adultery is not required for Captain Barclay's purposes, he merely has to show the evidence I have gathered for him to take any course of action he likes.'

'This is not a letter he is going to enjoy.'

'With respect, Mr Druce, if he has not made the connection by now, and understood what is going on between his wife and this John Pearce, he is living in a fool's paradise.'

'For all that is true, Hodgeson, it does not make dealing with the man any the more simple.'

Throughout the journey back to Torbay and now in his cabin aboard *HMS Semele*, Ralph Barclay had been gnawing on that very problem, for he had made what Hodgeson called 'the connection' all too readily. What neither Druce nor the investigator he had hired knew, was the other connection he had to Pearce, one that had nothing to do with his wife. They were certainly unaware of the man's attempts to get him into the dock on a charge of perjury.

The letter he had received from Admiral Hotham's clerk left him in no doubt that the situation was serious and if he praised the actions that had been taken on his behalf, it did not induce any feelings of security. His wife had threatened him with the same revelations as those being sought by the lawyer Pearce had engaged and, added to the worry of what that swine was doing with her, was concern at their present location. He had to assume their journey had been without mishap for there were people out there who could sink him without trace, most worryingly Toby Burns.

Gherson had watched him closely over the same period and if his expression betrayed nothing of his feelings, he was taking some pleasure in his employer's discomfort. Nor would he offer any verbal sympathy, for that would merely expose him to a blast of abuse, it being he who had undertaken to get hold of the copy of Barclay's court martial papers so they could be destroyed, a document which should never have existed in the first place.

That he had failed to do so was bad enough, yet Barclay had no idea how close Gherson had come to his own personal nemesis at the hands of one of London's most notorious villains, a slug called Jonathan Codge as well as the Bow Street Runners, this for the initiation of the burglary carried out on behalf of Barclay.

He had come close to being had up by the very same Runners, escaped by the merest fluke, then been forced to lie about the destruction of the document, claiming it had been destroyed by fire. When it transpired it was still in existence it had led to a blistering explosion of rage – his employer was prone to that – in which Gherson had been torn to shreds.

Part of Barclay's problem, as he filtered various courses of action through his mind, was the lack of anyone in whom to confide. Not much given, through a lifetime of experiences, to trusting his fellow humans in the first place, his present position as the captain of a seventy-four-gun ship of the line did not ease matters for it carried with it isolation.

None of his inferior officers were close enough to him to play the devil's advocate, and even if they had been he would not have suffered to engage them for the sheer loss of face such an encounter would entail. How could he command men who knew his inner turmoil? Nor was he – and he would, like all such people, deny the truth of the fact – open to taking advice, however sound or well intentioned.

As for his fellow captains, some of whom were under that same cloud with Lord Howe as he, talking to them risked the same end result as talking to his inferiors. Really there was only one person who he could use as a sounding board, and distasteful as he found it to give the role to his clerk, there was no choice.

Gherson's opening gambit posed the obvious question and it was done with a look of deep concern, one that belied the man's true feelings: he was enjoying himself. At one time he had harboured designs on Emily Barclay, for she was a tempting morsel. She would have said she rebuffed him; such was his vanity that Gherson thought of it as stupid self-denial based on her county morality. But in doing so she had crushed a vain man and created an enemy who was eager to pay her back for the way she had treated him.

'I am bound to ask, sir, what is the outcome you seek?' Getting no reply, which was what he had expected, he had the pleasure of laying out a set of equally unpleasant alternatives. 'Do you wish, as you have often stated, to force your wife back to the marital abode, or do you intend to cast her aside? In that case, how far do you want to take matters? For instance, though such a course would be horrendously difficult, would you aspire to seek a bill of divorce?'

There was a certain amount of goading in this; Gherson was not going to mention the very obvious solution to Barclay's dilemma and one, though it had never been openly stated, he knew his employer had considered. The captain of *HMS Semele* cared for only two things, his future in the navy and that he should not be made a laughing stock by the actions of others, and that was doubled in spades when it came to being exposed as a cuckold.

The response was slow to come, Barclay being patently uncomfortable. 'I have thought on all of these till my head spins, man, you know that.'

'Sir,' Gherson said with silky insincerity, 'I am as much at a stand myself, for I am, as you know, attached to you in a way that makes your wife's actions painful to me.'

Barclay wanted to yell at him then, he being not in the least degree fooled; he knew Gherson for what he was and he trusted him not at all. He was just as deceitful as Emily and his supposed loyalty was based on self-interest, which was at least something he could understand. But having him as a sounding board forced Barclay to hold in his anger, which allowed Gherson to continue.

'How do you act when someone has so utterly betrayed you and threatens to destroy every achievement for which have given your life? Mrs Barclay's actions do not only expose you to ridicule as her husband, but they also affect your stature as a senior post captain, the respect of your peers and certainly, in the case of Admiral Hotham, a superior who is in no doubt of your gifts?'

'By God, Gherson, if the truth ever gets out about my court martial he will be as damaged as me.'

'A fact of which, it would be safe to assume, the admiral is fully aware.' Gherson sighed then. 'It makes one wish for the gods of ancient times, who could strike people down with bolts of lightning.'

'I don't recall any gods, ancient or of our own time, ever coming to my aid. The trouble with you, Gherson, is that you have no idea of how I have had to struggle just to get to where I am. You have never been bullied in a mids berth, as I was, treated like a fool and openly insulted by senior lieutenants when I got my elevation. And even when I was made post those gods of whom you speak took away the one man who might have aided me and kept me in employment.'

'Lord Rodney.'

Gherson had replied by stating the obvious, this being a good way to mollify his master, though the temptation to respond by detailing the vicissitudes of his own life was tempting. His upbringing had been no bed of roses, either, with pious Huguenot parents who had chucked him out of his family home at a young age for nothing more than a few minor transgressions.

How would Barclay have coped in the rookeries and alleyways of London as a stray waif without a roof, a good-looking youth trying to make his way while avoiding all the traps into which such as he could fall, not all of which he managed to evade? A life of petty crime was full of danger but in the end it was those looks that brought salvation, that added to being supremely adept at numbers, added to the easy charm of a fellow who could lie without a twinge of conscience.

The regard of women had lifted Gherson out of paucity and he had targeted those who had a telling age difference with their spouse, added to which the man had to have some wealth, be in need of a numerate clerk and not too sharp at seeing exactly where his money was going. It was one such, Alderman Denby Carruthers, who, having realised his wife's infidelity, had hired thugs to throw him off London Bridge, only for Gherson to land alongside a passing boat carrying pressed men to be taken into the navy.

One of the men in that boat had been John Pearce, and if Gherson carried a grudge against Emily Barclay it was as nothing to the way he felt about that arrogant sod, and the fact that Emily Barclay had succumbed to him did not help. He would never admit, of course, to jealousy, but then he did not need to with a man who had provided him with enough reasons for hate without it.

'So far,' Barclay growled, when his clerk's silence had lasted too long, 'you have been very good at listing my difficulties. I do not hear a word of solution from your lips.'

Gherson's chin went to his chest, as if he was cogitating on a set of problems new to him. They were, of course, not that: he had spent nearly as much time thinking on the conundrum as had the captain and the conclusion he had come to was unassailable in argument. The answer could not be found here, while the threats were a thousand miles away. Nor could they be satisfactorily solved by any legal means he could think of and that left only the one option.

'I think, if you and Admiral Hotham could put your heads together, a workable solution would lead to a compound solution.'

'I don't know if you have noticed, Gherson, that such a thing is impossible. He's off Corsica and I am off Torbay.'

'It has always been my habit to treat one problem at a time.'

'Meaning?'

'Somehow, sir, you must get a posting to the Mediterranean and there you will be in a position to confront your demons in a way that might just provide an outcome that solves all your problems in one fell swoop. I can see no other manner in which to proceed.'

'Then that merely establishes, Gherson,' Barclay shouted, 'that you are a damned fool!'

That being as good as a dismissal, Gherson left the cabin, knowing he had planted a seed. That was what you had to do with the likes of Ralph Barclay, as he had with many of the other supposed men of success he had dealt with in his time. It made him wonder, for Barclay was not alone, how the Royal Navy enjoyed so much success when it was officered by people of such turgid reasoning.

His solution had not gone unacknowledged, but since Ralph Barclay had not thought of it himself he was damned if he was going to praise Gherson for saying it. The problem, once he had accepted the premise, was how to proceed in such a way as to gain the end he required. He could relinquish the command of HMS Semele at any time; God knows there were enough men of post rank who would be eager to take his place.

But that meant funding a trip out to the Mediterranean without a ship or any seeming purpose, which was no more desirable than giving up a command he had worked hard and schemed to get. If

214

he did relinquish *Semele*, how hard would it then be to get another ship and what effect would that have on his future in the service?

Survive long enough and he would get his flag, but it was no good being an admiral if you were without employment. The country was full of so-called 'yellow admirals', flag officers who held the rank but were either not trusted or lacked the influence to get any kind of posting. The notion of being one of those was anathema.

If sailors loved to talk of battle and prize money, they dreamt, whatever their present rank, of being a flag officer on a profitable station, the West or East Indies being at the pinnacle of the dream. Three years on either of those, with your inferior commanders bringing in prizes by the dozen! What followed were riches; you could purchase a country pile of real distinction with high gables, numerous rooms, stables full of horses and a coach house big enough to accommodate more than one carriage.

It would have surprised Ralph Barclay to know that Cornelius Gherson harboured the same vision. He knew who was above his employer on the captain's list and who would rise to a flag before him. Not that all would get there, disease or infirmity would take some and there was always room for an accident or two on a musket ball or cannon shot from the enemy, war being the best thing to thin ranks. This one with the Revolution looked as if it might go on for years.

If Barclay realised his ambition then his clerk, on whom he was dependant, as long as he stayed with the man, would likewise reach his. An admiral on station or in command of a fleet was presented with chances to line his pockets that were stupendous if properly handled and he saw himself as just the man to do the necessary peculating. It might not amount to a coach and four and a grand country residence, but it would mean independence, which was for Gherson craving enough.

'Sir?' Gherson asked, when Barclay called him back in.

'I need to write to the Duke of Portland.' That required Gherson to again hide a smile; clearly Barclay had thought on his proposal and seen the sense of it. 'It will have to be carefully worded, for he is an arrogant sod, and I will require you to hand-deliver it to him and him alone.'

'Am I presuming, sir, if I ask, that the contents might spell trouble for the present administration?'

'We may have to work on it to make it so, without it being too obvious. If the Duke is upset in any way he can cause us a great deal of nuisance.'

'Perhaps if I prepare a few drafts, sir, templates that you can consider?'

'Good idea, but it needs to be quick. God knows the French fleet may exit from Brest again and if they do we will be got out to engage them. Once we are at sea, or as long as they are seen as a present and immediate threat, nothing will get us posted elsewhere.'

'Might I suggest, sir, that you write a letter to Lord Howe, in which you allude to the way he missed the grain convoy.'

'He is as aware of that as anyone.'

'I would be inclined to say that you have, from your own resources, suppressed a pamphlet which questions the glory of his achievements and was due to be circulated widely.'

'No such pamphlet exists.'

God in Heaven, Gherson thought, how slow can this man be?

'I thought I might draw one up, to be included in the correspondence. It seems to me that if Lord Howe was amenable to you being shifted to the Mediterranean Fleet, it would be in our favour.'

Barclay was as aware as his clerk that he had missed a trick, so his response was, as was his habit, to be brusque. 'Then can I suggest you get on with it, man!'

CHAPTER SEVENTEEN

Letters travelling to and from the Mediterranean ran many risks and not just from foul weather. The Admiralty used postal packets to send fleet despatches on from England and vice versa. That such missives rarely contained anything approaching decisions of a strategic nature did not dent their value. In addition, packets carried everyday mail, the letters of sailors and soldiers penned to their loved ones. These could be a mine of information and that made the ships that carried them prime targets.

Given the route by which they travelled was a certainty, it was a miracle that more were not intercepted; but the ocean is vast and not every day is sunny and clear, especially in the Atlantic, so the privateers and the occasional roving vessels of the French state had to be lucky to even see one, never mind effect a capture.

In addition they were up against crews that virtually lived at sea and had a well-honed nose for risk, serving under captains of real ability, in command of craft designed for speed as well as heavy seas. Still, it was a long game and many a despatch would be sent by more than one boat to ensure its safe arrival.

The letters received by Lucknor, the London attorney acting for John Pearce, were replies to missives he had sent out months previously and it was an indication of the parlous state of Revolutionary naval warfare that they had made both journeys without encountering a hint of danger. The pair from Farmiloe and Digby answered the simple question he had posed; where were they on the night in late March the previous year in which Captain Barclay had gone out to press seamen?

Lucknor had been careful in his enquiry to underline that such a question posed no risk to them; all he asked for was a single sentence answer. Farmiloe confirmed he had been with Barclay and the young man was clearly bright enough to add no more to that, which indicated that he knew about the illegality, but being of the rank he was then and under orders, no blame could be laid at his door. Digby confirmed that on the night in question he had stayed aboard *HMS Brilliant* at Sheerness.

It was the third letter, the one from Toby Burns, that niggled Lucknor, in which the youngster implied that he could not be expected to remember where he had been on a night so far in the past. John Pearce had left with his lawyer, if not the whole transcript of Ralph Barclay's court martial, at least the bones of the testimony each person had given. That of Toby Burns stood out, given he could provide for that hearing a clear account of the very same night.

There was also a nagging question in regard to the composition of the communication; somehow, to a man with a nose trained to spot the way witnesses tended to dissemble, it smacked of a hand with more scholarship than that of a young and threatened midshipman. In short, it was too well assembled in the way it made its excuses. Yet the real problem was that it did nothing to advance his client's case by providing even a sliver of criminality upon which he could act.

Still, that very same fellow would be in the Mediterranean by now and he should be in a position to find out more than anyone based in London. All Lucknor could do was write to John Pearce and appraise him on the frustrations evident in the results of his enquiries. Once he had composed the letter, he was careful to immediately list the act in his ledger, adding to the growing bill, which made up the sum necessary to reward his work.

Was it necessary to send a statement of account to Alexander Davidson, Pearce's prize agent and the guarantor of the expenses? Looking at the accumulated sum Lucknor decided not: he was still just within the bounds of what his client had paid in advance.

Toby Burns was at a stand, with no idea what to do. If Admiral Hotham was polite to him, and he was in a distant sort of way, he was showing none of the obvious regard that had preceded his incarceration in Calvi, merely urging, on the rare occasions the midshipman could not get out of his way, that he prepare himself for a lieutenant's exam. Thus Toby lived in a perpetual state of limbo: was he about to be transferred to some dangerous duty? What had his high-ranking nemesis in mind for him? The one certainty in the young midshipman's mind was that there would be something and it would not be to his advantage.

Atmosphere aboard a ship of war, as it was in any closed community, had an acute nature that did not apply in normal surroundings. In a ship such as *HMS Britannia*, due to the nature of the flag officer, it was almost something you could touch. If Hotham was aware of how his moods permeated the vessel there was no doubt in anyone's mind that he would take pleasure from it. Right as of this moment there was a great deal for the man to be moody about.

The news that Lord Hood was going on leave and Hotham would succeed to the command had flown from ship to ship within no more than a day. It was almost as if the lower deck had a signalling system that transcended and was better than that of the fleet in which they served. Soon it was the subject of hushed speculation in the wardroom and the midshipmens' berth as well as the main-deck mess tables.

The frustrations of the last period of what Hotham saw as servitude were harder to bear than anything that had gone before. He could not wait for *Victory* to weigh and he saw it as typical of the departing C-in-C that he was vague about when his departure would be, his response to any guardedly put enquiry being that 'matters would be resolved when he was happy with the arrangements he must leave behind'.

Yet Hood could not just up anchor and depart without he included his successor in all the myriad problems that crossed his desk, so a boat set off from Hood's flagship with copies of the correspondence Old Sam had been engaged in with the various potentates who held power in the sea which the combined British and Spanish fleets sought to dominate. These were in numerous chests, and along with them, to answer any questions that arose, came the man who had aided Hood in all his activities, the executive officer and captain of the fleet.

Hotham, as he read of the latest exchanges between Hood and

his opposite number, Admiral Lángara, scoffed in a rather theatrical fashion, 'Lord Hood is excessively polite to our so-called Spanish "allies", Parker, given where they are stationed.'

After the debacle at Toulon, the Spaniards had retired to Minorca and were hardly, at that distance, in a position to readily engage the French and they showed no sign of being willing to put to sea to guard against the eventuality.

Besides such a concern, the suspicion was rampant, and not just in the mind of Hotham, that the Dons had not put in a full effort during the evacuation of Toulon. If they had worked hard to destroy the arsenal, they had been suspected of hampering the British efforts to get all the useable warships of the French navy out of the port before it fell.

This meant a goodly number of capital vessels, mainly those partly built, in need of repair, or just stripped of their masts and laid up in ordinary, had to be left behind to be remanned and made effective by those who took over the port. For the Spaniards it made sound strategic sense: a Royal Navy fleet twice its present size threatened their own position in a sea they saw as their preserve.

'I cannot say having them on my side makes me feel secure.'

If Hotham was expressing a forthright opinion it was one much shared by his officers as well as, to a man, the lower deck and even Parker would admit to reservations. Spain had been an enemy since before the Armada and had fought against Britain, usually in alliance with France, in numerous wars since; having them in support and as allies was strange indeed.

There was also the underlying truth, based on sheer greed, that when it came to an enemy vessel you wanted to capture, a Spanish Plate ship en route from the Americas was held to be the pinnacle of achievement, it being the way to instant wealth. This was a fact well attested to by the number of silver-laden galleons that had been taken in previous conflicts. How could anything of that nature be accomplished when they were fighting alongside you?

'I have to say, Parker, that if they are ever off my beam I will keep an eye open for slippage. Spain could change sides in a flash.'

'I grant they do not run their affairs as we would do in England, sir, but they are a monarchy and I think we can place some faith in their good intentions. After all, our joint enemy is dedicated to decapitating all monarchs.'

'Their sovereign is a feeble idiot. It is the Queen's lover, Godoy, who runs Spain.'

Parker would love to have said to Hotham, thank you for telling me something I already know only too damned well. But he kept his counsel; he too had a residual suspicion of the Dons for the very name and nature of the man just mentioned. The Bourbons of the present day were a sorry lot, nothing like, in stature and cunning, their predecessors of yesteryear; they were either feeble-minded as Hotham had said or too easily manipulated by court favourites, the latest of which was Manuel Godoy, rumoured to share the Queen's bed.

'I think, sir, we have to take the situation as we find it, which if you look at Lord Hood's correspondence you will see is the state of affairs with whomsoever you deal.'

Hotham went back to the pile and he had to look enthusiastic then; he did not want Parker reporting back to Hood that he found the task before him daunting, but it was. As well as fighting the warships of the Revolution, the Mediterranean Fleet was tasked to protect the vital and very lucrative trade that came from the East.

Failure to do so, leading to a steep rise in insurance rates on any of the routes that fed the wealth of the country, always led to questions in Parliament for the commercial interests were exceedingly powerful. Their disquiet then became bolts of disapproval sent down to the responsible commanders, and removal, if matters got out of hand, was not unknown.

Hood may have contained the main battle fleet, but the French had frigates and smaller warships roaming the Tyrrhenian Sea, the Adriatic and the Levantine trade route, with private ships as well, sailing under letters of marque, not that such official documents had to be granted. In short, any French trading ship that thought it a good idea to turn to licensed piracy, in place of their constrained natural function, was free to do so and that took no account of the corsairs of Barbary and Greece.

Before Hotham were letters to representatives of Britain who resided all over the inland sea, ambassadors in Naples and Istanbul, consuls or some kind of presence in every major trading port in Italy from Genoa round to Venice. Deys and beys dotted the shoreline from Algiers, through Cairo to the numerous entrepôts of the Levantine coast.

Then there were the Greek Islands and the Adriatic, which if nominally ruled by the Sultan and the Ottoman Empire seemed, from what could be read, to act as separate satrapies with scant control from the centre. Here, especially in the Adriatic and Peloponnese, Britain seemed to have very little leverage with the local pashas and a severe lack of knowledge of what was happening there, which, if it was not a pressing problem, would become one with French agents as active as those of their enemies.

'You will find,' Parker added, as Hotham alluded to this, 'that the government in Paris, if it can be so flattered by such a term, are adept at finding common cause with those who see opportunity in a disruption of the status quo, which is why Lord Hood has expended so much effort in keeping them neutral through a system of subsidies and threats. The last thing that will serve our purpose is that our enemies should be granted innumerable ports in which to shelter, places we dare not attack.'

'As well as being able to read, Admiral Parker, I have the wit to see where our problems lay.'

But not the grace, Parker thought, to say so in any way that could be called polite. He did not like Hotham, few people he knew did, but the man was well connected. The notion that he might make plain his distaste was therefore doubly unwise.

'I am here to assist you if you wish it, sir.'

The need for Hotham to acquaint himself seemed endless; as one chest was emptied and refilled another was opened yet there was, very obviously, one set of papers thinner than they should be, and that was the ones relating to correspondence between Samuel Hood and William Pitt, a deal of which, Hotham suspected, must relate to him and his actions. Such letters would not be flattering but there was nothing he could do about it, so he sought to put it out of his mind.

'Who is this Mehmet Pasha?' Hotham asked, lifting an especially thick pile of letters. 'Am I to judge by the amount of correspondence that he is a particular nuisance?'

'A Turkish governor, though one who pays no attention to the grand vizier in Istanbul. He controls the coast of Illyria and more vitally the Gulf of Ambracia. That is an ideal anchorage, with access to the deeper waters of the Med, in which any raiding vessel can take refuge, as long as they do not draw too much water under their keel. He is, as you have so rightly discerned, a singular menace.'

'We cannot check him through the Porte?'

'The writ of the Istanbul caliphate tends to run very low at the extremities of empire, and Mehmet Pasha ignores what he chooses to and obeys very little. A bloodthirsty cove, by all accounts, arbitrary with what he calls his "justice". The officer we sent to treat with him was of the opinion he was quite insane.'

'Naples?' Hotham replied after a long pause, indicating he had moved on, that followed by a pause as he read the latest communications. 'Sir William Hamilton is eager, I see, that we should place a squadron there.'

'He has a point. The narrows between Calabria and the coast of North Africa present an acute danger, added to which many of our merchant vessels en route to Gibraltar head for Naples and the Sicilian ports to trade, drop off passengers or take on water and stores, that being the only safe place at present to do so. It makes for a happy hunting ground for our enemies.'

That had the aspirant commander peering at another document, a copy, like many, of the items he had already perused. 'I see, Parker, by this last despatch, that Lord Hood was minded to oblige him.'

'Only if he can keep the French battle fleet at bay as well as in port and even then not until he knows what the Neapolitans could put to the task themselves. We are awaiting a reply to that query as of this moment.'

'Moment, Parker?'

'The answer we seek should be back with us in a week or so.'

'Then it is likely something I will have to decide upon, is it not?'

Parker knew what was being demanded of him, the date Hood

had set to up anchor, and he was not going to fall for it even if he knew it to be imminent. Yet he had been given a chance to rile Hotham and in a way that could not be laid at his door, a way to remind him that his command was going to be temporary.

'I am sure the C-in-C will advise on a course of action even if he departs before *HMS Larcher* rejoins.'

The name of the armed cutter produced a look that indicated that Parker had inflicted a wound, or so the captain of the fleet surmised and he felt a warm glow because of it. He was wrong: it was the thought of John Pearce that had made Hotham look as if he had just bitten a lemon.

Pearce was on deck and so was Emily Barclay, both enjoying fine weather and a breeze that, if warm, still cooled when set against the heat of the day. This created a mist that partially obscured the coastline along which they were sailing, the Bay of Gaeta. The shoreline was flat but just behind that hills rose, and if you peered, there were some high enough in the distance to be termed mountains.

If the panorama looked peaceful it was not; Pearce's orders had stated quite clearly that the routes in and out of Naples were dangerous. He also knew from casual conversations that further south, in the Straits of Messina, matters were even worse, it being a narrow stretch of water into which privateers, as they sought to snap up any merchant vessel that strayed into their path, could quickly dash and escape with like speed using the tidal flows.

Security indicated that these corsairs did not confine themselves to the narrows, given the amount of lucrative traffic that traversed the waters to the north and west of Sicily, so lookouts were set aloft to scan the horizon, though until now they had seen only one very obvious lumbering merchant ship and lots of tiny boats fishing the waters between the armed cutter and the shore.

Pearce, having mentioned corsairs to Emily, found it led on to Barbary pirates. He found himself relating to Emily the sad story of Ben Walker, one of the original Pelicans and a person of whom he rarely spoke; in the past he had gone no further than the name, even with her. Ben he described as the quiet one, a fellow who seemed to harbour some deep secret that he was unwilling to share, even with his fellow unfortunates, and even more gloomy was the truth that fate had not been kind to him.

Following on from the affair off Brittany, Ben had declined, like his fellow Pelicans, to take ship back home, staying aboard *HMS Brilliant*. Weeks later the frigate had got into an inconclusive scrap with an old-fashioned Algerine galley and the original story on Ben was that he had fallen overboard after the ship's mast on which he was working was hit by a cannonball.

He was last seen hanging on to a latticed hatch and floating, but there was no one who reckoned he could survive, that is until Pearce, in Algiers himself as part of a mission led by Nelson, had spotted Ben in a group of slaves engaged in loading a ship. Not only had this Pelican survived, he had obviously been plucked from the waves and kept alive to labour.

'I set out a plan to rescue him but that was blocked, the case being put to me that we could not endanger the whole relationship with the Dey of Algiers for the sake of one man.'

'I know you well enough to be aware that it likely haunts you.'

That was an easy assumption to make, given the low-spirited way her man had told his tale. And Emily was right for he felt it acutely; Pearce had never quite worked out at what point he seemed to accept responsibility for those with whom he had been pressed. Not all, for there were many more unfortunates dragged into Barclay's boats.

Most had been distant and then there was Cornelius Gherson, who he would have happily chucked overboard with his own hands. Yet accepted responsibility he had and Pearce felt it keenly if any of them were in trouble. His inability to rescue Ben Walker hurt.

He was just about to refer to the fact, and how deeply, when the cry came from the masthead, first naming one sail to larboard and then adding in quick succession two more, rigged like brigantines with no sign of any flag, which in itself brought on concern. Three such vessels sailing in company and without any form of identity presaged trouble.

At the shout Emily had, without prompting, ducked into their cabin and been replaced by Dorling. In the conversation that ensued it was reckoned the wind, which was a north-easterly, coming off the land, favoured *Larcher* and acted in the opposite manner to those vessels further out to sea. They were a fair distance off, thus the risk was slight, but it had to be accommodated.

'I don't want to set the whole ship by its ears. Even if they present a threat it will be a long time coming, probably even nightfall, before they can come up on us with this wind. Make sure Sam Kempshall has his cartridges filled and the flintlocks out and ready.'

'The cook?'

'Mr Bellam can keep his coppers lit. It will not aid us if we all go hungry to no purpose.'

There were other things that happened without Pearce saying anything, part preparations that good seamen made out of habit.

Thus the bosun, who went by the name of Birdy, was wont to check on certain parts of the rigging, as if he did not do so on a regular basis anyway. The gunner's brother, Brad Kempshall, would be looking to his plugs, tarred canvas and battens, to ensure that should they get into a spat he and his carpenter's mates had the means to stop any leaks caused by gunfire.

With all this taking place, albeit with no sense of haste, John Pearce was able to invite Emily back out to enjoy the sunshine, though all the while, up aloft, sharp eyes kept reporting the position of those three sails relative to their ship. There was no doubt they were closing, but at a rate so slow that, barring mishaps, HMS Larcher would raise the mountains of Ischia and the channel that led into the Bay of Naples without the need to fend them off.

As was habit once the sun went down and everyone had had their supper, there was amusement on the deck, with some singing: O'Hagan loved a ballad and others were keen on dancing, all done to mouth music for there was no fiddler aboard. Emily, too, would act the chanteuse, her voice high and sweet, as she would render to the crew the songs she had once sung at the side of her parents, siblings and cousins.

It was at times like these, under a star-filled sky on a warm night, that it was possible for John Pearce to feel he was part of a family.

CHAPTER EIGHTEEN

Nelson had quietly informed Pearce – in the unlikely event he did not know – that sailing into the capital and port of a major British ally imposed certain obligations on the captain of a King's ship. He was the representative of his sovereign, and while it was not the same as being aboard a ship of the line, where grandeur came naturally, so rare were such visits and so numerous were the numbers of English people residing in Naples, that *HMS Larcher* was bound to have a raft of folk wishing to visit. Perhaps even the Hamiltons would come aboard themselves.

So when the decks were scrubbed, it was with the kind of special care that would leave them, once dried, in a pristine state and the good Lord help anyone who stained them in the subsequent watch. Thus, when it came to blacking the cannon and chipping and painting the cannonballs, canvas had to be spread for security, while just outside the cabin Michael O'Hagan, who had proved a surprisingly dab hand at the job, was sponging and brushing the captain's best coat and hat while the owner sat in his shirtsleeves.

'Would it not be wiser to go about matters in a different order?' Emily asked. 'Surely it would be best to carry out the dirty tasks first, then scrub the deck.'

'Change the naval day, madam? Do you want to see me strung up from the yardarm?'

Pearce had reacted in mock horror, which made her laugh. The peeling sound had the men working in front of the pair looking up and smiling, and while their captain was doing likewise he was also thinking of what kind of reception he and she would get in the kingdom within whose waters he was about to anchor.

By repute Naples was a rather loose place but Pearce had to admit his knowledge of the kingdom was limited and no more than casual gossip. That being all he had to go on, it provided not much on which to base a theory, for if it had not been discussed, even Emily knew that he could not go sailing about the Mediterranean with her in tow.

He was a very junior officer and the service would not permit to him what it might turn a blind eye to in a senior post captain. Ralph Barclay had broken the regulation about sailing with wives and no one had checked him, it being one of those rules no one bothered to press home as long as it was conducted with discretion. Mistresses were another matter, and even admirals drew the line at a breech of that nature.

It did not give him any pleasure to think of Emily in those terms, but she was still another man's wife and he was putting off the moment, a potentially evil one to him, of the discussion they must have. Staying in Leghorn was out of the question, yet would

Naples serve any better? There was a strong national contingent resident there and a full-blown ambassadorial presence, while the wife of the incumbent was not so grand or free of taint that she could cast aspersions upon Emily Barclay.

The bosun broke into these ruminations, for Mr Bird had come to pass on a message. He was a tightly compact fellow, obviously strong and with a face, more so a nose, that looked as though it had been engaged in a few fist-filled encounters. O'Hagan reckoned him a tasty opponent, which from the Irishman was high praise. He also had a serious brow but that was easily overcome by a very winning smile and manner.

'Lookout sent down word, Your Honour, quiet like, that if you was to go to the prow the whole of the bay is now in clear view.'

'I fear to walk your pristine deck, Mr Bird.'

That got a grin. 'If you was to take off your shoes, ma'am, it would ease my mind.'

'And Mr Pearce?' Emily asked, with a mischievous look.

'Can hardly request the captain to walk in his stockings, can I?'

'Convention, Mr Bird, is a bore. Let me do that on your behalf. John, you must risk your best stockings.'

'You see, Mr Bird,' Pearce replied, as he slipped off his shoes, 'what little authority I have in my own cabin.'

'He's a smooth-talking bugger that Birdy,' opined Rufus Dommet, he and his mate Charlie being close enough to overhear the exchange. '"Ease my mind", for all love.'

'Don't let him hear you say it, Rufus, for he might fetch you a quiet clout and if he does your ears'll be ringing for a week.'

To say the Bay of Naples was astonishing was understatement. The great sweep, from the southern point of Sorrento all the way round to the promontory of Bàcoli was gifted with enough references all the way back to classical antiquity to mean its beauty should come as no surprise. Yet it did, for with the sun full up and distance enough to hide any flaws it provided a stunning panorama of the city, high buildings, church spires and the two castles, one of which dominated the port itself, the other, St Elmo, high above and menacing.

To the south, towering above and beyond the entire panorama lay the twin peaks of Vesuvius, seemingly so gentle, one top smoking as if it were in possession of a good pipe of tobacco, the other dormant. Yet it was still an object of some terror, for what it had done in the past was as much referred to as the city and the landscape over which it held fearful dominance. As they came closer in, the long frontage of the royal palace became the dominant feature in a bay now full of traffic.

Emily, standing in the prow, with her long hair blowing in the wind, was too much of an attraction for the Neapolitan males who caught sight of her. With an amused smile, Pearce noticed how tillers were put down and courses altered to bring the local fishermen and small trading ships across their path, so that those steering and manning them could blow her kisses and no doubt, for it was too much a dialect to comprehend, issue invitations to engage in any number of trysts.

The smell was the first thing that dented the image of Naples and the bay, and this to folk who were no strangers to urban stink. The city was in serious need of a downpour to clear away the accumulated filth of its teeming population, though in fairness that was a truth that could be applied to any busy port. Yet the climate here made the odour near to overpowering and it seemed to Pearce that perhaps that was what altered his lover's happy mood.

'What does it mean, coming here?'

His disposition changed as swiftly as her own. 'It cannot be worse than Leghorn.'

'What a recommendation – a lesser, perhaps, of two evils.'

'We have yet to land, yet to see what is possible.'

'And if it turns out to be possible, how often will a serving naval officer be at liberty to visit?'

With that remark Emily had hit the nail very firmly on the head. If it had never been openly stated she knew, as did he, that he was not rich, that the mere need for a source of income would constrain his freedom. Added to that he could be sent anywhere at the whim of anyone senior to him in the service.

Leghorn being a supply base for the fleet, his coming and going would have been fairly regular excepting the premise of being sent on a cruise. That would not hold here and the proof of the fact lay in *HMS Larcher* carrying despatches for an ambassador who, if Naples was visited by many a merchantman en route to London, rarely saw a British warship.

'Before I got married, John, I envisaged many months ashore parted from my spouse, perhaps even years, for it is not uncommon for a naval wife. Odd to think our union might have survived that way of living our life. My husband's mistake was to take me to sea with him and allow me an insight into his real character.'

'Emily.'

'But,' she added quickly, 'had that been the case I would have at least been surrounded by friends and family, so if I suffered, and I am sure I could have made a good fist of appearing to do so, it would have been in company. It must have occurred to you that I do not know a soul in Naples and if I stay here I will be faced with a burden of loneliness, for visits by you may not be just infrequent, they may be impossible.'

'I had hoped to see what was here before discussing this.'

She touched his hand, which was rare on deck; even if their relationship was no mystery, propriety could not be just set aside. 'Would it wound you if I say I could not bear to be parted from you in the same way as I once imagined.'

'We are on an adventure, Emily, and about to embark on a new part of that. Let us see what it brings.'

'On the wing as ever, John,' she replied, with a sad smile. 'But I will say if the stench is anything to go by it promises to be interesting.'

'Beggin' your pardon, sir, it is time for signalling.'

'Royal I suppose, Mr Dorling,' Pearce replied, pointing to the huge Bourbon standard that flew above the Palazzo Reale. 'If my father ever knew that I would one day salute a monarch, and there was an afterlife to which he did not subscribe, he would be looking for a bolt of lightning to aim at my head.'

'Twenty-one guns it is, Your Honour.'

The banging of the signal cannon soon followed, endlessly repeated, while a smaller number of guns replied from the formidable-looking fortress of St Elmo. A boat was sent out from the office of the harbour master to lead them to the point at which they could anchor.

Pearce and Emily went aft; it was time to be out of the way and for him to don his heavy blue coat and his hat. They would be under eyeglass scrutiny from the shore and by whom he had no idea. It would not do to appear as anything other than what he was in a telescope, the captain of a King's ship.

'I reckon he might jump ship, to be with his lady, brother – I know I would.'

Sam Kempshall advanced the opinion, gifted to his twin brother Brad, as he changed out of his working gear – he had been overseeing the blacking of the cannon – into clothing that might be more impressive to natives of a place he knew to be legendary for its ladies.

Never were two of that ilk so unalike: Sam the taller, with fine blond hair, Nordic blue eyes and broad shoulders, Brad the marginally less well built, and the possessor of dark hair and expressive brown eyes. They shared all the tribulations of normal siblings, great mates one minute and at each other's throat the next, Brad insisting that any dolt could fill powder cartridges but it took skill to work with wood. Sam was wont to respond that any idiot could shape a coffin and he might be tempted to do so and for one soul in particular.

'You'd jump ship, Sam, with Black Cath from Portsmouth Point, or any other brute that would part her legs.'

Sam was carefully tying his neckerchief, seeking to get it at just the right jaunty angle, using a very small scrap of mirror glass, which was held to be one of the most valuable possessions aboard ship and shared by all.

'Can't help if the ladies fall like ninepins, can I Brad, while you go mooning over some bit of flesh you'll never get on her back.'

'Ladies? Christ, you need a barber's probe down your prick after every encounter.'

That made Sam wince; it was a horror of which he had some experience and had him change the subject. 'Pearce is bound to gift us leave like he did at Leghorn?'

'Don't see why not,' Brad replied, edging his brother to one side so he could see his own reflection. 'Lord, we're a rate further off from Buckler's Hard than we were afore.'

'I hear the ladies of Naples are a fine bunch, dark in the skin and well shaped in the breast. I do like a big pair of—'

'Are you two going to be much longer at that looking glass?'

In making this demand, the cook cut off Sam's reference to prominent mammaries, which went with pursed lips and a telling gesture of cupped hands, this as the complaining voice kept up the abuse.

'You're worse than a couple of painted whores. If you don't get a move on we'll be at anchor and every bugger and his brother will be down below changing their rig.'

'Take more'n a looking glass to sort out your mug, Stevie Bellam, and the growing of another pin to boot.'

'Lack of leg don't signify when you're laying down, Sam, an' the one that matters is as it should be.'

You could feel the way coming off the ship even below decks and soon there came the rushed hiss of the anchor cable running through the hawsehole, as well as the commands that would back *Larcher* to render it taut. It was time for these warrants, not involved in the task, to get clear, for in minutes the 't'ween decks would be crowded with their shipmates, those tasked to row their captain ashore having precedence in the tidying line, for they had little time.

On deck their captain was waiting for them, fully accoutred. 'I will send out for you once I see how the land lies, Emily.'

She just nodded, which left him worrying as he made for the now lowered boat about the nature of her thoughts, that not eased as they crossed to the shore. His topsails having been in sight for half a day and his flags not much less, there was a man waiting for him on the main arch that led off the quay, as well as a fiacre to take them both to the residence of Ambassador Hamilton, which proved to be some distance away.

If it was inconvenient there were definite advantages to living outside the centre of Naples. Close to it was not the charming vision it had been out to sea; there was not a building that did not seem to be in some state of disrepair and many others looked close to collapse. Added to that the city was not just crowded, it heaved with humanity, so numerous were the inhabitants. They were noisy, too, leaving Pearce to wonder, as he had in Leghorn, why Italians exchanging pleasantries always sounded as if they were about to murder each other.

Some of the streets they passed through, not easily, such were the crowds, were open markets, with trestles heaving with the abundant produce of some of the most fertile earth in Europe. Vesuvius, which could be heard gently grumbling now, was a smoking threat that promised the kind of instant destruction recorded by Pliny the Elder. Yet it was also the source of fecund soil, which, with the sun and rain, had made this corner of Italy such an attractive place to reside for everyone, from Ancient Greeks to the present Bourbon monarchy and those who had come from Spain to support their standard. Two harvests were a commonplace if they had sufficient rain.

The man Sir William had sent to fetch him, despatched on sight of HMS Larcher preparing to anchor, spoke very little English, but the two had time to indulge in what that produced: a bit of French, as Latin-based as Italian, added to sign language and exaggerated gestures. It served to pass the time and if it could not be philosophical – such conversations never were – Pearce was assured that the weather was appallingly hot for the time of year. Having peaked in mid August it showed no sign of relenting and added was a fact that his nose told him: there had been no rain for weeks.

The Palazzo Sessa, home to Sir William and Lady Hamilton, lay at the apex of a steep climb. The horse pulling the fiacre struggled to easily overcome this incline, yet even if he felt for it he was unable, given his standing and his mission, to dismount and ease its burden, this while his Italian companion showed utter indifference.

The temperature dropped perceptibly as the conveyance entered the palace courtyard and it was welcome. Pearce, who was sweating, thought that by the time he got to meet the worthy he had come to see all the dandifying that had been done by him and Michael must be wasted. It was as well there was no sign of the man coming to meet him, so with a gesture to his guide he took time to remove his hat, mop his brow and open his waistcoat to allow his shirt to cool in the breeze coming off the shore he could not see, but was certainly nearby.

Aware of his needs the Italian took him inside the house portal to a gentle fountain spraying out water that felt ice cold in contrast to the air. Pearce, hat off, was enjoying, indeed revelling in the cooling spray on his face, when the voice made him spin round, the attempt he made to dry himself with the handkerchief he still held in his hand unsuccessful.

He thus came face to face, once more, with His Majesty's Ambassador to the Kingdom of Naples, this time with water dripping off his chin, his waistcoat undone and his hat in his hand. He saw before him a man for whom elegance clearly came easily. Hamilton was handsome, though not young, and dressed in fine linen clothing, as befitted the climate, while also he had a distinctly patrician air about him. It was not much of a stretch for his visitor, given his features, to imagine him in a toga, addressing the ancient Roman senate.

'Good day to you, Lieutenant Pearce, I see you have found the need to cool yourself.'

'I apologise for presenting myself thus, sir.'

'It is of no account. I myself take to the sea for the same purpose, for the heat of Naples is enough to kill a man. How my dear wife sustains her composure I do not know.'

Pearce reached into his pocket and produced his oilskin pouch. 'I bring another despatch from Lord Hood.'

'Excellent.'

'And a private communication from Captain Nelson.'

'Ah, the good fellow,' Hamilton replied in an absent-minded manner as he examined what Pearce had handed him.

I wonder, Pearce thought. Would you continue to see him in that light if you knew I also carried a letter to your wife of which he wishes you to remain ignorant?

'You must come indoors, where I have some iced sherbet waiting.'

With a soft arm Sir William ushered him into a doorway and up the staircase, this entirely lined by antique statuary interspersed with great urns full of flowers, their sides carved with classical motifs, the products of his host's digging efforts in Pompeii and Herculaneum.

The room he entered was as he recalled it: spacious and had that lovely smell of recently polished floors and furniture, mixed with the heady scent of fresh-cut flowers, while the windows that made up one side overlooked the Bay of Naples from the north, creating a view as beautiful as anything he had seen out at sea.

'May I be allowed to look upon it, sir?'

'Please do so, Lieutenant,' he replied, lifting and tinkling a bell.

Pearce had assumed that the bell ringing had been to summon a servant, and in part that was the case, for a man in livery entered with a tray bearing a jug and two stone cups. But it also brought into the room a woman of some beauty, with abundant raven-red hair and a figure that, even through her loose garments, was both full and becoming.

'Lady Emma, I'm sure you remember Lieutenant Pearce?'

'My dear Chevalier Hamilton, how could I forget such a handsome fellow?'

'Charmed, ma'am,' Pearce replied, with a low bow.

She had replied to her spouse in fluent French, at the same time coming close enough to Pearce for her hand to be kissed, sending forth a strong waft of the scent of lemons. Looking up, Pearce found himself staring into a pair of direct green eyes, which, added to the crooked smile, signalled a danger he had felt on their previous meeting.

Mind yourself, Pearce, he thought; we are in infested waters here.

CHAPTER NINETEEN

'Mr Dorling, I wonder if you would be so kind as to provide me with a boat?'

'You wish to go ashore, ma'am?'

'I do.'

That got a creased forehead; the master had no orders forbidding it nor did he have any to say it was permissible to oblige the captain's lady in such a request. As soon as her man had gone, Emily had requested the use of a telescope and had spent some time looking towards the shore, as well as the numerous merchant vessels in the harbour, noting especially those bearing British flags. No one, Dorling included, had evinced much surprise at this, Naples being a place of repute for the curious visitor; now he was wondering what she had been up to.

'Might I be allowed to point out that this city has a certain reputation for . . .'

'Being unsafe for unaccompanied ladies?' Dorling nodded. 'Is not every port like that?'

'This one be a mite worse than most.'

'Which is why I have asked Mr O'Hagan to accompany me.'

'Mr O'Hagan,' Dorling thought; since when was that Irish monster a Mr? He had no real choice but to accede: if there was a wigging to be issued for this let it be to her, not him.

The said Mr, having gone to fetch his footwear, was getting a proper grousing from two of his shipmates.

'Talk about falling on your feet, Michael; first you gets the cabin duty and how easy is that, then you get to go ashore when we is still stuck in the ship.'

'I was not the one to make it so, Charlie, it was John-boy.'

'Must be soft in the head if he sees you as a servant.'

'To be sure, he will be glad to hear you say that to him.'

'Which I will, when the chance presents.'

'There's now't for it, Charlie,' Rufus cut in. 'Michael was ever one up on us.'

'Well, it's not for the sharpness of his mind.'

'Was a time, Charlie Taverner, that you would have been bruised for saying that.'

Bravado was one of Charlie's traits and he was good at it, as he had to be in a previous fraught existence. He also knew the time was long gone when Michael would belt him for his cheek. Besides, the Irishman, when sober, could take as good a ribbing as the next man and not lose his temper. So what Charlie said next had all that in the mix.

'Happen, mate, you might not find that as easy goin' as you reckon.'

'Get me some coin,' Rufus hooted, 'I want a wager on that one.'

The voice from the companionway was brusque and there at the very top, glaring at them, was the face of Mr Bird. 'O'Hagan, the captain's lady is awaiting on you on deck. Taverner and Dommet, there's work to do so you best shift as well.'

'What a life!' said Charlie.

'I can think of worse, mate,' came the reply from Rufus, who was already climbing the stairway, Michael on his heels.

Emily was waiting and it was immediately obvious that she had gone to some trouble, wearing clothes that were more suitable for a special occasion than a mere expedition ashore – a cream-coloured dress and her best wide bonnet. Also, she was carrying the kind of bag in her hand that was very obvious and too big to be easily hidden.

'Keep an eye on that she is carrying, O'Hagan,' Dorling whispered. 'I have heard that when it comes to light fingers, Naples is the place of invention.'

'Jesus, why does she want a thing that size, anyway?'

'Best you ask her, you know her better than anyone, bar the captain hisself.'

That Michael declined to do, but once they were in the boat, the aim of his looks alerted Emily to his curiosity and that made her clutch the object closer, which was the wrong thing to do. Michael went from being interested to being questioning.

'Would you like me to take care of that bag, Mrs Barclay? Be safer in my mitt than your own.'

'No thank you, Michael, I can perfectly well take care of it.'

'Would I be permitted to ask the purpose?'

'Of going ashore?'

Such an obvious answer was mere prevarication, and if Michael might not have used such a word, she could see in his eyes that he knew what she was about until he just nodded and looked away; Emily had made him suspicious, which obliged her to remind herself that however kind and considerate he was to her, Michael was the best friend and supporter of John Pearce.

'I might as well tell you, Michael, for it will come out as soon as John—'

'The captain, ma'am,' Michael interrupted, indicating the men who were rowing.

'Yes. Well when he comes back aboard he will be told. I am going ashore to find a shipping agent and enquire as to the cost of a passage back to England. Since I do not intend to beg for the fare, I have fetched ashore everything I possess which has any value.'

That had Michael glaring at his shipmates, for each one wore an expression of shock or interest. Some exchanged looks that hinted at wonder about a subject he saw as none of their business. Good-humoured the Irishman might be, but no one mistook the message in his angry expression.

'I trust it does not trouble you to accompany me, Michael?'

'Captain would skin me if I let you go ashore on your own.'

Time spent with the Hamiltons allowed John Pearce to reaffirm his previous impression: that the ambassador's wife was an endemic flirt, with a habit of making statements that could be taken as double entendres, each one of which caused her to act as if she was shocked at either her own foolishness or her daring. Sir William found the whole thing amusing, which had his guest suspecting that for him it was part of the lady's charm: she was certainly not stuffy.

He and his papa had never moved in what could be called 'society' circles, but the marriage of the pair he was dining with had caused such a stir of gossip that it had permeated down to people who had no notion to care. Lady Hamilton was said to be, by the most malicious tongues, a one-time whore, albeit she had graced the salons of one of London's more elegant bagnios. She had at one time been the mistress of Sir William's nephew and it was humorously supposed she had been passed like a parcel to the uncle, first as a mistress, then as a wife.

King George, to whom Hamilton had been a childhood friend, was furious at the match and had only acceded to it taking place on a special request from the Queen of Naples, with whom the one-time Emma Lyons had become very intimate, a fact attested to by Nelson. On his last visit he had been in the audience as she performed her famous "Atitudes", rather risqué representations of women from classical antiquity, which somewhat underlined that reputation. Yet she clearly had the affection of her husband and Sir William was no fool, so was she the creature of rumour or something else entirely, this a run of thoughts interrupted by his host.

'You returned to Toulon when you left us last?'

'Yes, Sir William, and I took part in the evacuation, a terrible event, as I am sure you have heard.'

'Only from local sources who returned to Naples and they were less than flattering regarding the actions of Lord Hood.'

'They are much minded,' Lady Hamilton pronounced, 'to praise their own to the ceiling when it comes to evacuation.'

The absence of a reference to Toulon in that remark allowed for it to be misconstrued; it also allowed the hostess to pretend it had been an accident and make the sort of, 'did I really say that?' face, which had been used more than once. All it got from her husband was a quiet chortle. John Pearce, when the ambassador had returned his gaze to the food on his plate, got a direct and challenging stare. The silly woman look had disappeared.

He still had in his pocket Nelson's letter to her, not yet having been gifted a chance to pass it over. To do so meant they would need to be alone, which was not a situation to which he was looking forward. Indeed, so worrying was it that he was tempted to just whip it out at the table, hand it over and let the devil take the hindmost; he had no intention of getting into any kind of stew on behalf of an officer he barely knew, however much he was admired.

'Time will not permit us to talk of Toulon at present, Lieutenant, for I am due at the palace for the royal levee. So you will oblige me by dining with us tonight, which will afford us ample opportunity to talk.'

Politeness required the same response as he had made before. 'We are some way from my ship, sir, and in the dark—'

'Never mind that, I think you will recall that the Palazzo Sessa is not short of rooms with which to accommodate guests. If you need anything, like your linen freshened, you have only to ask Mrs Cadogan and it will be provided.'

'I feel I have been remiss, sir, in not enquiring about Lady Hamilton's mother.'

'Still with us, Lieutenant Pearce, and running our house with her usual efficiency, as remarkable a woman, in her own way, as her daughter.'

Michael O'Hagan had availed himself of a short naval hanger as well as a marlinspike, both prominent on his belt and, once she was out of the boat, he positioned himself on the side she carried her bag and it was as well he did given the attention she attracted. As soon as they landed on the crowded quayside the pair seemed to be surrounded by men, some of whom sought to touch Emily and had to be handed off by her escort.

There were dozens of street urchins too, filthy skin-and-bone children of both sexes, barefoot and in rags who Michael reckoned were intent on robbery, so that unbidden he took his charge's arm and once he had slipped his hand through made sure his grip was on the bag handle.

He kept an eye peeled, watching for a knife that would slit it open, not that he was allowed to keep it steady by the need to force a passage across a roadway that teemed with humanity and the loud exclamations of hucksters and traders. Emily was subjected to cries and gestures as they passed that even the person most ignorant of the Neapolitan dialect could see were full of vulgar sexual suggestions.

'We should have brought a raiding party ashore, Mrs Barclay, enough to keep these low scullies standing off.'

'We do not have far to go, Michael, just to that flag of St George, yonder.'

'Not a cross to cheer an Irishman.'

'But surely a place that will be inhabited by someone who speaks English.'

'You knew where we were headed?'

'I saw the flag from the deck, Michael, and I have high hopes it will be a trading house with links to home.'

'Get off, you little bugger,' Michael cried, as he saw a tiny hand trying to undo the clasp on Emily's bag, that followed by a sweep of his free hand and the sound of it landing on flesh. 'Beggin' your pardon, ma'am.'

'Compared to some of the lewdness being aimed at me from

the locals, Michael, that particular piece of blasphemy seems tame.'

As well as the flag flying above the door, there was a guard of sorts, who was not far off the girth and height of O'Hagan and he too was armed. Seeing that Emily was heading for the interior he was tasked to protect he stepped forward to drive back some of those importuning her.

With his help both she and Michael were ushered through the doorway, into a musty-smelling place, part warehouse and part a bureau, there being a pair of dry-stick-looking clerks standing at high desks, with quills in their hands. Behind them, all the way to the rafters, lay stacked goods waiting to be shipped.

'Sure, it's best I have no part in this, Mrs Barclay, John-boy would skin me if he thought I'd aided you.'

'If you wish to wait outside . . .'

'Just inside, out of the sun.'

Which he did, far enough away to render the conversation Emily had with one of the clerks as no more than a set of murmured exchanges. That it led to a conclusion Michael guessed for the subject of money was a trifle louder and he did hear clearly that payment in kind would not be readily accepted.

If the lady wanted a passage to England it would have to be paid for in hard coin and yes there were ships due to sail on the morrow. The conversation quieted again and glancing backwards Michael saw the clerk scribbling with his quill, then handing Emily a piece of paper; that in her hand, she rejoined him.

'I have the name of a Jewish merchant not far off who will give me cash for my valuables.'

'Would I be allowed to say I ain't happy about this?'

Michael O'Hagan had seen Emily Barclay determined before

and he knew well the look that she gave him, so she did not have to tell him that she would, if necessary, go on alone. With a sigh, he nodded and stood aside so she could exit.

'Oblige me, Mrs Barclay, by clutching that bag to your body. Something tells me I might need both hands free to get us to where you are going.'

John Pearce was sitting in a cool bedchamber half contemplating sending a note back to the ship to explain his continued absence. Yet that had its own complications, for he was well aware that if there was any chance of getting ashore his crew would be eager to partake of it and that was not a duty he was happy to leave entirely to his ship's master, so he put the notion aside; a day of waiting would not harm them and he could justify another in port without rising censure.

He was stripped to the waist and awaiting the return of his shirt, which had been taken from him to be washed and ironed on the instructions of Mrs Cadogan, as formidable a lady as he remembered from a very brief meeting. As soon as she left a servant had appeared with a tub of cool water, soap and a soft sponge, so that when his garment came back he had done everything bar shave, not really a concern since he had done so before departing the ship.

The lady who kept house for the Hamiltons was the very image of the housekeeper breed, squat of body with a mob cap and long dun-coloured dress, while at her hip she carried a set of keys so numerous it would not have disgraced Newgate Prison. Not imposing, she nevertheless had a look about her that would brook no nonsense and being the man he was, sociable by habit, John Pearce engaged her in conversation.

'I think I detected previously, Mrs Cadogan, that you are from the north-west area of England?'

That surprised her; she looked at him hard and her tone was not friendly, making it seem as if he had uncovered something. 'True enough, sir, as if it signifies.'

'I travelled a great deal, Mrs Cadogan, all over the country, in fact, and I pride myself on recognition of a person's native location. I have heard dialects so strong that a man from one part of the country would struggle to get a tankard of ale in another. Your accent has been modified, obviously, no doubt by living here in Naples.'

'You have an acute ear, sir.'

'I was fairly sure of it. In fact, I felt I had heard a trace of the same, fainter than yours, in Lady Hamilton.'

'Did you now?' she growled.

'I did not, I hope, say anything to offend you.'

An even deeper growl gave the lie to her response. 'No, sir, you did not. Now I am told you are staying for supper, so an hour before, Sir William's valet will come to shave you. In the meantime Lady Hamilton is about to take a walk in the chevalier's English Garden and asks if you be willing to keep her company.'

'Certainly,' Pearce replied, there being no real choice.

'The carriage will be outside presently.'

Emma Hamilton exited under a parasol and a large floppy bonnet to find John Pearce waiting to hand her into the open-topped carriage, the driver flicking his whip to move the horses as soon as they were both sat down. Once out of the courtyard the interior was exposed to the sun, which made the removal of that bonnet, and the laying of it on the seat, somewhat strange. But it did allow the light to play on her near mane of russet hair, which had obviously been combed to shine.

Once in the street the reason became obvious – the parasol was lifted high – for as they passed Pearce heard the cries of the locals hailing her as the Madonna, this accompanied by much papist crossing of head and breast, accolades which Lady Hamilton took with patrician grace and short thankful waves, not unlike a monarch expressing gratitude to her loyal subjects, that before she sent out a spray of small coins, causing her audience to scrabble for them.

'It has been thus ever since I first came to Naples, Lieutenant, they see in me the image of the Virgin, whom they reverence here, and call out to say so.'

It was as well she was looking away from him for that meant she did not see his arch response. Pearce also had to suppress any verbal rejoinder, which could only have been, given her reputation, to the inappropriate nature of such a tribute, added to the notion that the money was of superior import to her supposed image.

'It would do you no harm for you to raise your hat to the locals, Mr Pearce. A courtesy from a British officer will help cement our place in their hearts.'

'Do we have such a place, Lady Hamilton?'

That caused her to turn, her expression one of astonishment. 'Why yes, Sir William and I have worked assiduously to make it so.'

'I would have thought it of more import to be popular in the palace than in the streets.'

Her voice took on a harder quality. 'Rest assured, sir, we are, as I am sure I made plain to you before, held in high esteem there, too.'

Pearce could not avoid thinking of Nelson and nearly blurted out the depth of the man's regard, but it was a safer ploy, he felt, to change the subject entirely from both royalty and Nelsonian admiration. 'Your mother said we are going to the English Garden, which I must say is a name I find to be strange in such a place as this.'

'It has been created by my husband, Mr Pearce, as a gift to His Majesty King Ferdinand. It is not unusual to find him walking there of an early evening, poor man.'

'Poor?'

'He is dull in the wits, a simpleton who has only two pursuits in life and neither of them having anything to do with ruling his kingdom. That he leaves to the Queen.'

'And they are?'

The green eyes fixed him and there was a trace of amusement at the very edges of her lips.

'The chase, at which he is as wild as the beasts he hunts, Lieutenant, and copulation, at which he is relentless and quite lacking in discrimination, which is why I asked that you should accompany me. I hope I do not shock you?'

'You need protection from the King?' Pearce replied, refusing to be drawn.

'Only in the nature of having company, sir, which serves to contain his more outré habits. His Majesty, if he comes across a lone female, and this has happened to me, is wont to expose himself and I do assure you he is massively endowed and naturally priapic, so it is quite alarming even to a woman of experience.'

Pearce was wondering where this was leading, so he changed the subject once more. 'I do hope I did not upset your mother.'

'In what way?'

'I identified that she came from the north-west of England, which has a particular mode of speech.'

'She does, so it would hardly be likely to cause offence.'

'I think it was when I referred to a trace in your own voice of the same.'

'Ah' was all she said, this as the carriage passed under an arch and into an open area, gravelled and home to scores of like conveyances.

'Here we are, sir, at Sir William's garden, which, as you can see, is very popular.'

Looking around Pearce observed the very same trees he might have seen at home: pines, elms, an oak that was well on the way to maturity, hazel and bushes and shrubs clearly imported from England, all arranged to provide cool walkways and paths down which to promenade. His hostess had to be handed down and as she made the ground she smiled at him.

'We shall walk, Lieutenant Pearce, and perhaps take a seat in one of the arbours Sir William has created, where it will be cool.'

'Delighted,' he replied, even if he was far from it.

'And as we walk, Mr Pearce, do not fear to take my arm, for it is a comfort to a lady to have the aid of a man in pleasant pursuits.'

That had him remarking on the trees, to avoid any mistake of interpretation. What followed was a passage of greetings and nods as he and Emma Hamilton passed several groups, including couples, engaged in the same pursuit of taking the cooler evening air, with she giving him quiet asides as to the connections of those they had just passed. Such and such were lovers of long-standing, that fellow has several mistresses, the lady with him being only one. There was only one pair she identified as being wed and when he referred to the singularity of that she laughed.

'Fidelity is in short supply in this part of the world, Lieutenant Pearce. Now, here is a spot of which I am fond, where we will be hidden from the common gaze and where we can take a seat.'

With that she led him into a shaded arbour that had a small Doric temple at its heart, of the kind he had seen at Versailles; so much for an English garden, though it had to be admitted they were common in those too. The seat was marble and once Lady Hamilton had seated herself and arranged her dress she invited him to join her by patting the spot by her side.

'This gives me a perfect opportunity to give to you this letter,' Pearce said, pulling the missive from his pocket. 'It is a private communication from Commodore Nelson.'

John Pearce had no idea if this lady had in mind what he feared. What he did know was that in presenting Nelson's letter, he had entirely removed the possibility that it might be seduction.

CHAPTER TWENTY

O'Hagan was sure that Emily Barclay had gone as far as to actually book a passage; at the house of the Jewish moneylender he had waited outside, so had no idea of what she had offered for cash and how much she had received. Again, at the trading house the conversation had been so *sotto voce* as to render him no more than a part witness, though the word 'Palermo' was mentioned several times, not that it made any sense to him.

In the boat and rowing out to *HMS Larcher* she said nothing, but had an air about her that pointed to a clear notion of what was to follow, this confirmed when, back aboard, she called him into the tiny cabin where the Irishman found her packing her chest.

'As you can see, Michael, I have elected to leave the ship.'

'And the man who commands it.'

If Emily replied with a yes, it had no force in it and she turned enough away to avoid him seeing her face, her reply then continuing in a voice cracked with emotion. 'I feel I do not have a choice.'

'Sure, it's not for me to pronounce on the way other folks live their lives.'

The eyes that turned on him then were, as he had suspected, damp. 'Yet I am not the only one who holds him in deep affection.'

'When a man does what John-boy has on my behalf, it would be unnatural not to care. Same goes for Rufus and Charlie.'

'It is more than that, Michael.'

'There's truth there.'

'I will go home to England, and if God wills it, then John will return to me there. I will need this shipped over to the merchant vessel on which I am to take passage. She is called the *Sandown Castle* and is anchored just off the Castel dell'Ovo, which is that large fort on the seafront.'

'Now?'

'Shortly, for she is to weigh at dawn.'

'Do you not intend to wait until John-boy comes back on board?'

She produced a wan smile. 'A coward would not.'

'I know you too well to think of you in that manner.'

'I will wait and I am sure when John comes back he will urge me to stay in Naples, insisting it will only be of short duration, and we both know how persuasive he can be. The fact that my chest is gone will strengthen my resolve to resist his blandishments, and it is for the best.'

Her voice quickened, as if she feared he might act in argument as a Pearce surrogate.

'I can only hamper him! He may loathe the King's Navy with every fibre of his being, Michael, but it is an occupation and one of the few open to a man of his talents. How can he pursue that with the constant thought in the back of his mind that I might not be happy, indeed might not be safe from opprobrium, as was the case in Leghorn? And what, if he does not derive a living from the navy, will he do?'

Michael's mind went back to the day off Leghorn when Pearce had handed him some coin, whereas before he would have handed over his purse and trusted Michael not to be greedy. That was as good a way of saying he needed to be careful with his money; this from a man who, as long as he had some, had previously been indifferent.

If he was not privy to every detail of the standing of his friend – John Pearce played such things close – Michael knew it was not strong. There was prize money from the taking of the *Valmy*, but that was locked up in a dispute between the two captains who had been involved in its capture, this while Pearce applied likewise through the court for a bigger share than he had been so far allotted, that of a midshipman instead of an able seaman.

If he had been flush on their last trip to the Vendée it had been because he had government money to spend, and there was half a hint the man who had gifted it to him was not happy with the way for which it had been accounted, so perhaps he was burdened there, so all that could be said as truth was his credit was good. Michael O'Hagan had been poor enough in his own life, and flush as well, to know how quickly a man could go from one to the other.

'He will worry about how you are going to see to your needs, Mrs Barclay.'

In the name, which she had come to detest, lay one solution: she still had evidence that could put her husband in the dock, enough to extract from him the means to live in comfort if not luxury, though to say so to John Pearce was to make him livid. That being really none of Michael's business, though his concern was warming, she gave a reply that she knew would mollify him, the same one she had prepared for the man she was leaving.

'I know that John has a good line of credit from Mr Davidson, his prize agent, and he has his naval pay. I am sure he will not object to me drawing on those. If you want no part of shifting my chest, I will ask of Mr Dorling.'

'Which, as the saints know, is a good way to put the poor man in a tight spot.'

Seeing that to be as good as acquiescence Emily thanked Michael heartily, though she resisted the temptation to do what she really wanted and kiss him on the cheek.

The production of Nelson's letter had put paid to any attempt at dalliance contemplated by Emma Hamilton. Not that Pearce had been sure it was her intention; perhaps what had taken place, the coming into the cool arbour, had been genuine or at the very worst just another manifestation of her desire – almost a need – to flirt. Yet when he sat down he ensured a decent space between them.

'You did not see fit to give this to me when we first met?'

'Your husband was present.'

That made her frown. 'And what difference would that make?'

'Commodore Nelson was most insistent that it should be passed to you without Sir William knowing.'

The way she burst out laughing was so unladylike that it had Pearce warming to her, for if he had found her a troubling companion, that lack of stuffiness he had noticed on first encounter was something to be admired, it being so very un-English. Love Emily as he might, she would never have referred to the King's endowment in the same manner as this lady, for it did not just border on vulgarity, it so readily surpassed it.

'The poor man, he is so very smitten.'

The silent thought was obvious for he had seen the commodore mooning over a rather florid opera singer. *And not just by you, milady!*

'Commodore, you say?' Pearce nodded. 'Captain Nelson came to Naples for three days, in which we entertained him as we must, while we collectively sought supplies for the effort at Toulon. Sir William was most unusually taken with him, and that on their very first meeting. Claimed him to be a new Sir Francis Drake, so acute was his perception of what was needed to defeat France.'

'And you, Lady Hamilton?'

'I liked him, but I found the way he sought to engage my eye when he thought no one was looking a trifle tiresome.'

Pearce could not resist it. 'You do not approve of admiration?'

That had those green eyes narrow. 'Am I being teased, sir?'

'Only slightly.'

'You intrigue me, Lieutenant,' she said with some force, as she waved Nelson's letter. 'You will readily understand that you are not the sole naval officer to visit us; indeed, over the years there have been many. *Au fond* they tend to be gauche fellows – awkward, in fact, and not at home in domestic surroundings.'

'Is the Palazzo Sessa such a thing?'

'Oh, it is grand, that I will admit, but I feel it would not matter if it was an English farmhouse. I am inclined to think that the men who officer the King's Navy are only at home on their ships, for once ashore they turn into blushing boobies who seem to possess two left feet, added to the inability to speak without a stammer.'

'A ship's deck is no place in which to refine your manners or your conversation.'

'A fact, I am sure, but one that does not apply to you.'

'Am I in receipt of a compliment or a slight?'

Pearce's smile took the sting out of that question and Lady Hamilton responded with another peal of laughter. 'There you are, Lieutenant, quite able to hold your own, though sailors at least are famed for skill at that.'

The double meaning of that had her putting her hand to her mouth in mock horror, which dented the rising opinion Pearce had of her. Determined not to let her get away with what was pure mischief, he decided not to be outdone.

'We have less need of that than the King of Naples, it seems.'

'Sir!' she exclaimed, pretending to be shocked.

'Me even less,' Pearce added, 'being as I am heavily committed to a certain lady.'

'You have a lover?'

'I do and she has a husband.'

There was calculation in letting that out: this woman could be a help to Emily in what was a strange city and she would surely not demure, given her previous allusion to the common lack of fidelity, to their present estate, this confirmed by what followed.

'I think, in being so open about it, Mr Pearce, you would not find yourself out of place in the society of Naples.' That said, she stood and proffered her arm. 'Time we went back to Sir William, don't you think?'

Unbeknown to Emily Barclay, fretting aboard *HMS Larcher* as the day faded into night, her lover was having a fine if simple dinner with the Hamiltons and, as requested, he gave Sir William a first-hand account of the debacle at Toulon, not forgetting to add that if the government at home had chosen to support Lord Hood, instead of sending off an expedition to the Caribbean, the British and their allies might hold the port still.

'For the place could only be held with a strong commitment of troops.'

'Never underestimate the power of the sugar lobby, Mr Pearce. They have the ear of the men in power for they have deep pockets. Added to that, King George frets that having lost America, he might also lose the likes of Jamaica.'

'To the Jonathans?'

Sir William smiled. 'To anyone, the French included, but that does not preclude the fledgling democracy.'

'Unlikely sir, I know little of the new United States but I am aware they have no navy.'

'They don't have much of anything, from what I hear, and since we banned them trading with the Caribbean colonies it is rumoured they are on their uppers, which has my old friend dreaming that they might be recovered one day.'

'You were a friend of King George I recall.'

'While I recall telling you what a rakehell he was, Mr Pearce, never out of some bedchamber or other and forever setting the poor watchmen by their ears. And drink, you never saw the like.'

'And him being so famously upright now.'

'Upright and half mad,' Lady Hamilton snapped. 'Talking to trees and the like.'

It was impossible not to hear the voice of his dead father then, railing against a system that allowed a man to rule who could not talk sense, with the alternative an heir universally held to be an utter fool. The state paid to keep them in luxury while the common folk lived on the edge of starvation.

'Perhaps you know, Sir William, for I do not, if he is fully recovered?'

'No, George Rex will not speak with me any more, he has become such a pious booby. We discussed on your last visit how he denies to his sons that in which he indulged himself and thus ensures the one fate that awaits all rulers.' The question was on the face of his guest. 'That is that the man designated to succeed them should hold them in contempt. It has been thus since ancient times.'

That was only worth a nod and a sip of wine.

'I am a student of the classical age, Mr Pearce.'

'For which you are justly famous, sir, as are your finds.'

That got the old man glowing and he was off on the ruins of Pompeii and Herculaneum, where he went frequently to dig. 'Though scraping would be a better description, sir, for the ruins are delicate. Not the structures, so much, as the art to be found on the walls and the objects that must be gently prised from the thick bed of lava.'

'You must show the lieutenant your latest finds, husband.'

'Only if he would care to see them.'

'I would be honoured, sir.'

Emma suppressed a yawn. 'Then you will forgive me leaving you gentlemen to that.'

'My dear,' Sir William replied, solicitously. 'You are not fatigued.'

'No, but I have had a private letter from Commodore Nelson, discretely delivered by Lieutenant Pearce. He has been given a pennant of that rank you know . . .'

'I do, my love, he told me in the letter he sent to me.'

Pearce was watching them both, seeking to discern if the news of the private letter to his wife caused Sir William any anxiety, but there was none.

'I dare say,' Sir William continued, with a wry smile, 'he sent you his undying affection once more?'

'Suffice to say,' his wife responded, in what Pearce took to be an intimate jest, 'his ardour seems to have moved to a higher plane, so much so that he fears for you to be privy to it.'

'How little he really knows me, my dear.'

'True and it is yours to read if you so desire.'

'I would not dream of doing so, unless it is your wish.'

'Let us see what he has to say,' Emma replied with an indulgent smile, before turning to Pearce. 'Lieutenant, I bid you good night and if I do not see you of the morning I wish you bon voyage.'

Both men were on their feet as she stood, Pearce bowing. Her husband spoke as she left the room and Pearce was not sure she was out of earshot.

'My wife was quite taken with Nelson, which surprised me, for much as I admire his acuity when it comes to a strategy in fighting the French, I do not see him as a cooing swain of the type to tug at the heart of a woman of experience.'

'You do not object that he chooses on this occasion to write to your wife without your knowledge?'

'Good Lord No!' He seemed shocked by the question, though Pearce thought that a touch exaggerated. 'What gentleman could possibly object to another man finding his wife attractive, and who, Lieutenant, would want to live with such a creature? I have known men, friends even, who have seen fit to tie themselves to ladies not of unsurpassing comeliness to avoid anxiety and never seen the sense of it, jealousy being such a tedious emotion. Now, bring your wine and prepare to be entertained, for I will show you that the ancients had no such concerns.'

The chamber into which the ambassador led Pearce was packed with virtu of the kind that enthralled the learned of London and filled the houses of rich men returning from their Grand Tour, most of which he had seen on his previous visit, only then his guide had been an unshockable Emma Hamilton, though there were some new additions. The main collection consisted of white marble statuary showing nude studies of both sexes, noble busts of both gods and mere mortals, as well as salvers, platters, plates and drinking vessels, some gold, many more fired clay, all of which were decorated with complex motifs.

Some were pastoral scenes, shepherds or flower-gathering maidens, but most were the exact opposite and were so lewd in their artwork, showing every kind of sexual variation, that Pearce found himself engaged in the same conversation he had shared with Sir William's wife, including, without being specific about the reasons, of his sojourn in Paris. As before he alluded to the kind of drawing he had seen displayed under the colonnades of the Palais Royale in Paris, home to the Duc d'Orléans, jealous cousin to King Louis and held by many to be the pornographer-in-chief.

Many had been salacious representations of Marie Antoinette, accusing her in graphic detail of a Sapphic love for her favourite, the Princess de Lamballe, but the denigration was not confined to that either in stories or art. The Queen was seen in congress with priests, demons and a multitude of animals, none of which, from what the Pearces, père et fils, could gather, having any relation to truth.

Whatever their real purpose, they had done much to undermine the rule of her husband, which suited d'Orleans.

'Crude by comparison, Mr Pearce, bad art and designed merely to shock.'

'These Roman artefacts were not?'

'Look at the quality of what is before you.'

'It is certainly superior to what I observed in Paris, but one cannot help wonder at such open representation.'

'I do not think the ancients thought as we do. They saw life for what it was, not what some of our more sober Puritans would have us believe. The good folk of Naples are not much more reticent, though they do draw the line at some things.'

Sir William produced the kind of lopsided grin men use to share a confidence. 'There is a sculpture in the bowels of the royal palace, dug up from what was a large garden in Pompeii, that shows the great god Pan copulating with a she-goat. Few are allowed to gaze upon it lest it corrupt their minds and tempt them to paganism. I am one of those who have been lucky enough to do so.'

'I'm not sure I would rush to emulate that luck.'

'It is the finest thing, sir, if earthy in the extreme. My dear wife fumes at being banned from viewing it herself.'

'I am aware that Lady Hamilton is familiar with your personal collection and does not find it shocking?'

'Of course not, for if my dear wife has one quality that I esteem it is her lack of hypocrisy.'

'Which is a gift I too admire.'

'Do you admire Emma, Lieutenant?'

Careful Pearce; you cannot say yes or no. 'Not in the way your question implies, sir.'

'She tends to collect admirers.'

'Let us say that I value her charm.'

Sir William was examining a large vase not far off his own height, one he had already shown proudly to Pearce as one of the high points of his finds, which depicted a rather detailed orgy involving numerous couplings. Added to that he had a certain wistful look on his face as he spoke.

'Time to retire, I think. You will find my replies to Lord Hood waiting for you in the morning, Lieutenant. Good night.'

Pearce had trouble getting to sleep, for the Palazzo Sessa was not a quiet establishment; there was the noise of servants finishing their daily tasks, walls and floors that seemed to creek endlessly and after the day he had just had there was a residual suspicion that his privacy might not be respected.

But sleep came eventually and it was deep enough to last until he was woken by the first light of morning. He was up and ready to exit the palazzo quickly, and as promised there were return despatches waiting for him as well as two letters addressed to Commodore Nelson, one in a spidery hand and smelling of lemons he assumed to be that of Lady Hamilton.

He could not fault the ambassador for care; the same fiacre that had brought him the day before was waiting by the gate to take him back, a more pleasant journey in the cool of the morning. On the quay he bespoke a local boat to take him out to his ship, idly noting that several vessels had weighed with the dawn and were now well out to sea.

Aboard *HMS Larcher* they jumped to it when they saw him approach and he was piped aboard with all ceremony, though when he smiled he wondered why no one would catch his eye, and that slight confusion was multiplied by a large factor when he entered his cabin. He was standing, not believing what he was seeing, when Michael entered behind him to tell him what had occurred in his absence. John Pearce was back on deck as soon as he finished, yelling like a banshee.

'Mr Dorling, all hands to weigh immediately and set me a course for Palermo.'

CHAPTER TWENTY-ONE

Hodgeson the thief taker was still in pursuit of Cornelius Gherson, though without the same level of attention he had given to finding Emily Barclay, this for the very simple reason that the man who engaged him had, in every conversation they had shared, put more emphasis on the lady than the man. If there was a hint of doubt in Hodgeson's mind as to the seriousness of this particular task it was no more than that until he met a possible source of good information.

It mattered not that he was a fellow so low in character that the sewer rats of London would avoid his company; it was necessary to stoop to discover and Jonathan Codge inhabited a world that knew the likes of Hodgeson only too well. Usually its denizens took good care to avoid him and his ilk, for they lived outside the law, yet when he entered the grimy and dim basement tavern where Codge held court no one made a quick exit, for to do so would only arouse suspicion.

The man being sought was at his usual table and was, as always – and this was a mystery to any person of sense – surrounded by a small coterie of acolytes who seemed to hang on his every word, and there was no shortage of those. Codge had an opinion on everything as well as a particular fondness for singing his own praises. Needless to say, he was a man never to be found in the wrong.

'I've come to see you, Codge,' Hodgeson said softly, standing over him, though far enough back to avoid appearing intimidating.

Codge did not look up as he replied. 'Happen I don't want to see you.'

'Never known you blink at a chance to make money.'

The mention of potential profit had Codge's drinking companions sit forward eagerly – only the man himself did not move – and Hodgeson threw a raking glance which told him that he did not know their faces. Such a fact came as no surprise, for to be a follower of Codge was to risk being the one to take the fall for his actions – many had gone that route – yet there never seemed to be a shortage of fools willing to fill the places of those that had already been betrayed. This was just his latest batch of dupes.

Codge spun up and out of his bench seat and nodded to Hodgeson, who followed him to another part of the tavern, a place so small and crowded that they were barely out of earshot or elbow space. Those in occupation of the required spot shifted at a growl, for Codge was not a man to lightly cross, being a big and handy bully as well as free with his fists. What followed had to be carried out in whispers, with their heads close together.

'I am on the lookout for a cove called Cornelius Gherson.'

'What makes you think I might know of him?'

'I learnt long ago that if you want to know what's afoot in the rookeries there is only one person to ask and that's you.'

The statement was not true, but it never did any harm to flatter to excess this particular villain, who had no idea that such a thing as excess in that line existed.

'What is he wanted for?'

'Do I take it you know him?'

'Never said that, did I?'

'It's a private enquiry, nothing to do with the law, which is why it pays.'

'If I did know of him, or could find out, I wouldn't want to do anything that might drop an innocent into the pit, so knowing of the purpose . . .'

Hodgeson had established something long ago when talking to the likes of this man: there was as much in what they did not say as the words employed. Even if he could not be certain, he had a strong feeling that Codge knew Gherson and might even know his whereabouts. Given he would sell his own mother for a tankard of flat beer the notion that he might protect anyone was close to a joke.

'Happen you could put the word out, Codge; folk will tell you things they would keep close with others.'

'For half a guinea?' That was steep, but Hodgeson nodded. 'With maybe a whole one or more for the wherefore?'

The thief taker did not respond to that; it never would do to commit too early to a payment. 'I can give you a description.'

When that was provided something strange happened, especially with a man who kept everything so close; it was said of him that the left hand never knew what the right hand was about and certainly none of the scallywags he shared ale with ever knew the whole tale of anything in which he involved them, this so he could ditch them to the Runners if his crimes went awry. Yet as Hodgeson provided the details he had been given by Edward Druce, Codge snorted in a way that indicated he was trying not to laugh. It was brief and soon controlled, but it was evident and troubling.

'I'll ask about. Don't know the fellow at all, but by that likeness he should be easy to spot, that is if he is in my bailiwick.'

Hodgeson was thinking how wrong that was – there was no end of folk like that in London – but he said nothing. The two heads had parted slightly and even in the dim light the thief taker could see that the look on his face, especially his eyes, was far from right, it was too opaque. Nor was he convinced by the tone of Codge's voice. He was obliged to the half guinea and that he handed over, unconcerned, for it was prize agent money not his own, but as he gave instructions as to where any news should be sent he was troubled.

Once he had left those feelings would have multiplied had he heard what was said. When Codge was back at his usual table he launched into a discussion on the best way to make a profit out of a hunt for a felon: to tell the thief taker where to find him, or to tell the quarry he was being sought and charge him for silence?

In the long walk back to the Strand Hodgeson had much time to think, this when he was not eyeing up the coves that loitered in doorways and on street corners with no apparent purpose, to see if he recognised any of them, making sure as well that no light fingers got too close to the pockets of his coat.

In his game there was no code of honour but there was a need to be on guard, for it was not unknown for a man in pursuit of a lawbreaker to fall foul of that very same regulator himself, and right of this moment Hodgeson was not comfortable.

There had been reservations about the hunt for Emily Barclay, a feeling that her husband, who was a choleric individual, might, when and if Hodgeson found her, act in a manner to cause more trouble than peace. Indeed, he might inflict physical harm on the lady and that extended to the notion, at the very edge of Hodgeson's concerns, that he might do murder.

In laying out this fact to Edward Druce there had been a modicum of compassion for Mrs Barclay, yet there was as much concern for himself, for what man knew, when blame was being apportioned for a crime, who would be caught up in its tangles?

If his thoughts on this Gherson fellow were not of the same order they were manifest. Disquiet was not a feeling he enjoyed and there was only one place he could lay that to rest, even if, in the process, he might find himself out of employment. His last thought, as he entered the offices of Ommany and Druce, was that it would be wise to get his bill to date settled before he sought clarity.

'I believe I have found this Gherson fellow, Mr Druce.'

When it came to hiding his feelings, Codge might be rated the past master, but Edward Druce was a novice. The blood quite literally drained from his face and when he replied his voice was croaked.

'Where?'

'That is, as yet, unknown to me, but I have found a fellow who

274

knows him well and is sure he can lead me to him in days, if not hours.'

The silence that followed confirmed all of Hodgeson's misgivings. There was no joy in his employer's face, quite the reverse and Druce had begun to fidget, which to a thief taker of many years' experience was a sure sign of a fellow preparing to lie. Time to lay out his cards.

'Question is, Mr Druce, do you really want him found?'

'What makes you say that man?' The sharp tone was bluster and very obviously so.

'Would you be kind enough, sir, to describe his appearance to me once more.'

Another long and telling pause followed. 'Am I to understand it does not tally with what your informant says?'

God, Hodgeson thought, you might be good at making money, Mr Druce, but don't you ever go outside the law for there's only one place you will end up and that is with a noose round your neck.

'Black hair, you said, swarthy complexion, ugly to look at and maybe a touch of the tar brush . . .'

'Yes, well.'

Hodgeson merely opened his hands in silent enquiry and it was several seconds until Druce spoke again.

'There are certain things I am not at liberty to tell you.'

'Which brings me back to my first question, sir: do you want him found?'

Druce was fidgeting again, hands opening and closing, then the fingers of one drumming on the desk, this while the man opposite employed silence, the proven tool of interrogation.

'Mr Hodgeson,' Druce said finally, 'I am wondering how much faith I can place in you?'

'You are paying me, sir, I am therefore yours to instruct.'

'It may not be that simple.'

'I've been plying my trade for many a year, sir, and I will tell you that not every act I have performed has been on the strict side of the law, not that I will tell you the circumstances, you understand. But I have one rule and that is the man who pays is the person for whom I act, though I will never put myself at risk of the hand of the law on my own collar, even for a stipend.'

'I find myself in a bind.'

'Then I might just be the man to ease it.'

It came out in dribs, drabs and many a stutter, about the relative with a wife half his age who had been cuckolded by said Gherson and was so incensed he wanted the man dealt with. How he, Druce, had been engaged to find the miscreant.

'Why you, sir?'

The prize agent was reluctant to answer that, but obviously concluded his story would not hold water if he did not. 'I have contacts with the Impress Service and provided him with assistance before.'

'A rough bunch indeed, sir.'

Druce replied with real haste. 'Not that I knew the nature of his intentions when I sent them to him. I thought the aim was a sound beating, which, given the way Gherson had both compromised the lady of the house and stolen money, was not too harsh a punishment.'

'And they went beyond that?'

Hodgeson listened to the tale of Gherson being thrown off London Bridge into a raging torrent that should have drowned and mutilated him – Druce was relieved it had not and had been angry when told. The man had not only survived but surfaced again and had obviously thwarted the same relative once more. He was now open in his desire to have the man found and taken care of. If he had tried to kill him once, there could be no doubt of his purpose now.

When Druce told him that Gherson was clerk to Captain Ralph Barclay, it took all of Hodgeson's self-control to keep a straight face, this while he wondered at what kind of web he was in. He listened in silence as his employer insisted that Gherson was a valuable go-between and that it would not aid the firm if any harm came to him, quite apart from any reluctance to become involved in an act of violence.

'You have not named this relative, sir.' Druce made to speak, no doubt to say that he would never do so, but a held-up hand saved him the trouble. 'Nor will I ask for that unless I find it necessary. What I ask now is what is needed?'

'I cannot be seen to be idle. You do not know my . . . relative, but he is a man of a forceful nature and does not lack for both wealth and position – enough, should I be seen to cross him, to cause difficulties both personally and professionally.'

'So, you need to keep him thinking that you, or in this case myself, are working flat out to find Gherson?'

'Yes, but I am at a loss to know how that might be done.'

'Gherson, I take it, is with Captain Barclay?' Druce did not want to acknowledge that, but he had to. 'And where is the officer?'

'Torbay, where he commands a seventy-four, part of the Channel Fleet. He was recently part of that on the Glorious First.'

'A valuable client, then?'

'Very!'

Druce had replied with a force that indicated how much Ralph Barclay had coming from the recent battle, yet it was obvious this false arrangement had been created before Lord Howe's great victory, therefore the man had been of high value before.

'So, how does one go about this, Hodgeson?'

'That's easy, Mr Druce, a sighting here, a sighting there, wild goose chases all over the place and regular reports of possibilities and disappointments. Time, perhaps, to cool the passions of the man who wants Gherson's blood.'

'Perhaps,' Druce said, without much conviction.

It was only later, nursing a tankard of ale in a nearby tavern called the Pelican, while ruminating on the conversation, that Hodgeson arrived at a certain conclusion. If Barclay was a valuable client, then Gherson must stand higher in that regard with Ommany and Druce, or why risk anything to protect him?

Which must mean the fellow as a source of extra and not strictly above-board income to the agency. Once a thief always a thief, but one to be cosseted if he was acting for the right person and that thought, seen through to a conclusion, made the kind of sense Hodgeson felt he needed. He was not the type to put the squeeze on anyone but he was keen to gather nuggets of information that might protect him and that was one to savour.

The other thought he had in the Pelican was a warm one: he had just engaged himself for maybe a year of paid employment, which caused him to raise his tankard to his lips and utter a toast to Cornelius Gherson who would, with his active assistance, never be found.

* * *

Gherson entered the great cabin of *HMS Semele*, staggering slightly as he crossed to the man seated at the desk; there had been a full gale out in the Channel and though Torbay was protected from the prevailing westerlies, the residual swell made the ship rise and fall too much for a man with poor sea legs.

'A reply from Lord Howe, sir.'

Ralph Barclay took it eagerly, tore open the seal and began to read, the contents soon having him chortling. 'I will wager the old sod took no pleasure in having this penned for him. He thanks me for my prompt action over the pamphlet, which is the opposite of the truth, I'm sure, and goes on to say that if he can be of service to me I only have to ask.'

Barclay then looked up at Gherson, his face creased with bewilderment. 'It's almost as if he has already discerned my intentions.'

There was no mystery there for his clerk, even if Ralph Barclay had never said openly what those were. His wife was in the Mediterranean and so was the scoundrel who had stolen her away. So that was where his employer wanted to be and Gherson quite favoured the notion too, it being a warm and generally benign station whereas the Channel, as had just been proven, was cold, wet and stormy.

There would be no independent cruising on this station either, which was the route to profit; the fleet would stay in Torbay and only go to sea if the French emerged, and having just been trounced two months previously that might be a long time in coming. Then there was the chance of confounding John Pearce, who would scarce expect the husband of his lover to turn up in the same waters. All in all, to a man to whom mischief came naturally, it promised to be interesting.

'Would I be allowed to say, sir, that in matters of protecting his back, Lord Howe will be no fool.'

'Aye! No doubt he saw bits of paper flooding the nation questioning his fitness to command, as well as demanding the real facts of his victory.'

Ralph Barclay lapsed into silence then as he conjured up an image of the doddery sixty-eight-year-old fuming as he sat in a tub of hot spring water seeking to ease his bones, for he was in full agreement with Gherson. Black Dick knew the pamphlet Gherson had produced was a threat – it had been intended as that – and Barclay was sure he would have heard by now the motion for several of his captains to demand a court to clear their names of the accusations of tardiness. That was something he would not welcome either, for it could not but tarnish the glory of his recent triumph.

'Somehow he must be made aware of the mention I made of the grain convoy and the way he was being humbugged in my log.'

His clerk saw right away what his captain was driving at: if others were furious at Lord Howe, they did not have what Barclay possessed, which was written and timely information of his possible error of judgement. If that came out at a court martial it would carry massively more weight than mere pique at being passed over for a medal or recognition. Knowing that was possible, any man in his right mind would move to head it off.

'Might I suggest a letter to the Duke of Portland, sir?'

'Saying?'

'I would suggest the tone should be a desire not to embarrass the government of which he is a part. Perhaps a reference to the impossibility of serving under a commanding admiral who clearly has little faith in your abilities.'

'And he might reply that I should give up my command.'

'God forbid that, sir.'

'Dammed right, Gherson.'

'A reference to the time the vessels of the Mediterranean Fleet have been on station might prompt a thought that some are in need of replacement.'

If Ralph Barclay looked hard at his clerk then it was for effect; he was not surprised that the man had drawn the correct conclusions for, if he was as untrustworthy as a weasel, Gherson did not lack for low cunning. That he was engaged in minor peculations was also known, but Barclay accepted that; as long as it did not get out of hand, it could be tolerated and any replacement might steal even more.

'It's too obvious. You don't know the man as do I. Insufferably arrogant would be the best description, so anything too pointed, anything that hints at manipulation, will only get his back up.'

'Then you must make plain your desire to serve your country, added to questions about Lord Howe's ability to act, given he is not even with his fleet, but taking the waters in Bath, which is unendurable to a man who craves to be at the enemy.'

'Leaving Portland to draw his own conclusions?'

'Precisely, sir.'

Ralph Barclay's face darkened then as a host of thoughts filled his mind, none of them in the least bit pleasant, for he saw himself as a laughing stock. His wife gallivanting about the Mediterranean in the company of a man not her husband was not a thing that would go unremarked. For a man to whom reputation was everything it was a blow almost beyond comprehension that such a state of affairs should come to pass and when he spoke his tone of voice reflected the fact.

'As long as I can get to that bastard Pearce, Gherson! I swear I will see him strung up by his thumbs for the disgrace he has visited on me.'

CHAPTER TWENTY-TWO

No one aboard *HMS Larcher* had any doubt about the need to get to sea in a hurry; they had seen the captain's lady over the side at the first sign of daylight and with some regrets, for she was popular and would be missed. Only the destination raised a question and that in the minds of the few who knew what and where Palermo was, as well as where it lay.

The knowledge of that destination port had only come about by luck; Michael had found out, by the merest fluke, when delivering Mrs Barclay and her sea chest to the *Sandown Castle*. The man welcoming her aboard, the captain he assumed, had loudly referred to the fact that with a good wind they would raise Palermo in a day and night, and once they had seen landed the passengers they were carrying, would up anchor and set course for a happy return to home shores.

The goodbye had been awkward for both the Irishman and his charge, for there could be none of the intimacy of close friends or relatives parting. All she could do was quietly thank him for not seeking to persuade her to wait for the missing John Pearce, which Emily might well have done had she not already paid for her passage and in doing so pledged most of her money.

Michael did what was expected of him, he knuckled his forehead, added a polite wish for a good journey and made to get back into his boat. Only in his eyes could Emily discern his true feelings, which were of sadness. He was also dreading his friend coming back aboard, for he would not take the news with much grace, a supposition proved to be only too correct; if blame was not spoken of, it was, Michael could see, in the accuser's expression.

'It be a courtesy to let the harbour master know of our leaving, sir.'

That got Dorling a glare. 'Bugger the harbour master – if he has eyes he will be well able to see.'

The reply that followed, another question, was put with some trepidation. 'Courtesy signals, Your Honour?'

'If I observe a man not hauling on rope or canvas to get as much speed on this tub as possible I will see the cat out of the bag for the first time in this commission.'

'Didn't need to go calling our barky a tub,' whispered one of the carpenter's mates to Brad Kempshall.

'He's in a rare passion and entitled to be. He don't mean it.'

'Better not,' came the reply, 'or he'll need more'n a cat to keep the peace.'

It was hard to tell, looking around the busy deck, how many shared that sentiment; like all tars the men of *Larcher* had a pride in their ship. Such a feeling was a commonplace in the navy and in the merchant service as well, for the vessel in which these men sailed was their home as well as their employ, and being a superstitious bunch, anything that implied it was less than the best was seen as tempting an unfeeling providence.

Pearce was like a showground flea, jumping about, seeking to aid men going about their tasks and generally being held to hinder more than help, added to which, for a man who usually addressed them with regard to their feelings, his shouting and bawling was causing them to avoid his eye. When he got in the way of the plucking up of the anchor, it fell to the only two common seamen aboard who knew him well enough to moan and to tell him to shift.

'You ain't helping, Capt'n,' Charlie growled, giving Pearce a look that was close to a flogging offence.

Rufus was gentler in his rebuke. 'Not unknown for a man to lose his leg if it gets caught in an anchor cable, Your Honour.'

It was that exaggerated courtesy from these two that stopped John Pearce from his bellowing interference, though he glared at them to let his Pelicans know that they had overstepped the mark. But that was all he did, before he went back to the tight space between the binnacle and the wheel that was his own preserve, there to fret uselessly as he saw the anchor fished and catted, then the first raised canvas catch the wind.

No one watching him could sense how much he was berating himself; he had stayed off the ship to indulge Sir William Hamilton and in the process had allowed Emily a chance to act on her own instincts, which he was sure he could have dissuaded her from had he been present. Now he had to catch this *Sandown Castle*, which should not be too difficult, her being a merchantman, and then persuade her to come back on board *Larcher*.

'Michael,' he said, having taken a deep breath to calm himself, 'join me in the cabin, if you please.'

The Irishman knew what was coming and was sure he had no answers that would satisfy the man posing the questions. Yet he did have the advantage that he would not need to seek to avoid a repeat of what Emily Barclay had said to him; they knew each other too well. For once, it was a conversation of a private nature conducted without reserve; John Pearce did not care if anyone heard, but he would have been gratified to observe, if he had been in a position to do so, that no one tried.

'Mrs Barclay sees herself stuck in Naples and never seeing you, John-boy, and all alone as well, which I take leave to say I can see is not a happy prospect.'

'I was in the process of seeking to ameliorate that.'

'If you're not going to talk in English I can make out, maybe I should talk in the Erse.'

'I was trying to find her some form of companionship, so that if she stayed in Naples she would have company.'

It was the drop of the eyes that alerted O'Hagan to the doubtful nature of that response and he was on to it quick. 'How so?'

John Pearce was not comfortable lying – not that he was incapable – and especially to those he considered friends, so the temptation to gild what had been a passing thought and turn it into a conversation sounded false in his ears; judging by the look Michael was giving him it was even less convincing to him.

'Who is this Lady Hamilton?'

Pearce could see the doubts growing as he described her – it had been a mistake to start by saying she was a famous beauty and a one-time courtesan – as well as what had happened to elevate her to her present position as the wife of the British Ambassador. The more he described her the lower he could see he was sinking in his friend's opinion, until finally Michael let fly his suspicions.

'I have high hopes that you kept your breeches buttoned, John-boy?'

'What do you take me for?'

'Wouldn't be the first time your prick had got you into hot water, as Rufus, Charlie and I know to our cost.'

That brought Pearce to the blush; his three companions had been sent to sea while he was dallying in London with a society lady who saw a newly minted hero and a handsome cove just made lieutenant as a fitting bedpost trophy. It had lasted but a few days but they had been vital to the Pelicans.

'That was in the past,' Pearce protested. 'My intention was to introduce Lady Hamilton to Emily and ask her to take her under her wing.'

'And this she agreed to?'

The reply was as angry as it needed to be to cover for embarrassment. 'I never got the chance to ask.'

'Can I say that Mrs Barclay took herself off out of concern for you?'

'Then she has utterly failed in her purpose, Michael. But as a friend, can I ask you to tell me everything she said to you, for if I am going to change her mind I will need all the force I can muster?'

Back on deck, as he ran over what had been said in his cabin, Pearce found he could not fault Emily's logic even if he was dismayed at her actions, for she had spoken naught but the plain truth. He had seen too much of the world to think of it as a place of compassion; life was, for most, as the philosopher Hobbes had said, nasty, brutish and short and nothing was as unforgiving as penury, which led to another conclusion: what was he fit for if not where he was now?

In travelling with his father there had been the vague allusion to the day he might need to think of an occupation – perhaps the law would serve, if the money could be found to article John to a solicitor – but circumstances had assured that, if he had been parentally tutored in Latin, Greek and the Classics, no conclusion was ever arrived at.

It was not something to discuss when sleeping in a barn for the night or, as was sometimes possible in high summer, under the stars. When he was enrolled in a school, the two were, for short periods, apart. Tomorrow was always a new town and a new audience needing to be told that they were being trodden on by authority and men who became rich on the back of their labours, a message sometimes well received, at others the response being sods of turf and worse. Even when still in one place, and that was rare, there had always been the fact that Adam Pearce would eventually move on.

By the time it became a more pressing matter, with a son approaching manhood, Adam and John Pearce were locked up in the Fleet Prison for the parental jibes at the government and the monarchy, trumped-up accusations certainly, but that did not deter the men in power from applying them. The gap between release and the flight to Paris was too short to even contemplate what might become of the younger of the pair.

Here he was on the deck of a ship, by what had to be seen to be a pure fluke, in command. That was a station he could happily occupy, though he found such things as the Sunday service trying, sticking to a reading of the Articles of War, but would it last? There had to be real doubt about that.

The circumstances that had got him his present position were unlikely to prevail for ever, more probable was that he would become an officer aboard a ship commanded by another – it had to be admitted perhaps a proper seaman like Henry Digby who had earned his rank. That could be tolerated but it was a shot of a long nature.

He had sailed with Digby to La Rochelle and the man had been good to him, seen that he was struggling and provided much help with the rudiments of seamanship and navigation; it would be wishing for the moon with anyone else and he would, no doubt, find himself exposed as unfit for his rank under another commander. So, should he leave the navy and should he tell Emily of his determination to do so as soon as he had delivered *Larcher* back to the fleet?

How was he to live at ease with a married woman? The notion of it being a sin did not feature with him but it would with Emily. Many times he had thought of telling her of his vague plan to use the evidence against her husband to force him into seeking a bill of divorce. Such a thing was horrendous in its expense and complexity and was only possible by the passage of a parliamentary statute annulling the Barclay marriage.

Ralph Barclay was, if not rich, well off and might see it as a proper use of his money to lay it out for the protection of his own reputation, but what would that expose Emily to? Leghorn would be as nothing to the opprobrium that would be heaped on her in England by a society that lived off hypocrisy.

This took his mind back to Naples and the conversation he had had with Lady Hamilton in that arbour. Could he make something of himself there – he was not without enterprise – and live openly with Emily in a place where, if the ambassadress were right, no one would turn a hair?

John Pearce was a man who found it easy, sometimes too easy, to feel sanguine. He was also prone, once he had settled on a course of action, to see it as natural and obvious. *HMS Larcher* would overhaul that lubberly merchant ship and he would go aboard and make his case to her.

'Deck there, sail ho, dead ahead.'

They had to wait for what seemed an age until the lookout added that it was square-rigged and even longer to identify it, by its broad beam and steep tumblehome, as a merchant vessel.

'We'll know if it's *Sandown Castle* within two bells, Your Honour, and overhaul her before the sun starts to dip.'

'Thank you, Mr Dorling, and can I say, if I was short with you this morning, I apologise.'

'Two more sail, on deck – two-masted, ten points off the larboard beam.'

Pearce had his coat off anyway, it being too hot to wear, so in a flash he had grabbed a telescope and made for the shrouds, his actions in climbing and the pace at which he achieved it getting approving nods from a crew proud to have a man in command who did not see it as beneath his pride to act so or to apologise, which had been overheard.

The man aloft moved so his captain could get a purchase on the crosstrees and begin to employ his eyeglass, then there followed that natural hiatus until certain matters became clear. The two ships spotted had their prows aimed in the same direction as him, towards *Sandown Castle*, albeit they were closer, which naturally raised the spectre as to their purpose, and they were, from what he could make out, brigantines. Were they the same vessels he had seen on the way to Naples, for it was a common vessel in these waters? It was highly possible since they flew no flag that he could see.

As the hulls became visible on the swell it was possible to make out their gun ports, five a side and very likely there would be bow and stern chasers too, though that did nothing to indicate their calibre. The next thing to calculate was, if they were hostile, how quickly were they closing on what might be their quarry, and then what effect the sighting of *HMS Larcher* would have on their intentions.

Had the captain of Emily's vessel spotted them, merchant vessels, with their crews the bare minimum in numbers, being notoriously slack in that department? From what he could discern, and it was far from positive, *Sandown Castle* was sailing easy. There was a fair amount of canvas aloft but not the suit of sails that would indicate they saw danger and needed to press on; that at least he could change.

'Deck there, get one of the cannon loaded with powder and fire it off.'

He was half talking to himself as well as the lookout when he said, 'If the sight of three unknown vessels in his wake does not get him spurring on, then nothing will.'

The sound of the booming cannon was faint but unmistakable and Captain Fleming, florid of face from having consumed a fair amount of wine, lifted his head slowly to register it. His guests, passengers being entertained to luncheon, looked at him if not with alarm, certainly with curiosity, and seeing it as his duty to ensure that nothing troubled them, he spoke soothingly.

'Nothing to concern ourselves with, I am sure.'

Only Emily understood, she being the sole fellow national aboard. The rest were either Sicilian or Neapolitan, people who sailed the route between the two main cities of the kingdom for a variety of reasons and by whatever means presented itself. Their looks of incomprehension were total; it would not be too much of a stretch to say that being from the part of the world in which they lived they would probably struggle with Italian.

'Does anyone speak French?'

Emily asked the question in that language and one elderly fellow responded. That allowed her to pass on the captain's message and the interlocutor spoke of it in some local dialect, not that it served for everyone. Soon the table was a babble of unintelligible shouting, for being natives of region, no conversation could be carried out in any other fashion. That was still pertaining when the first mate, to whom everyone had been introduced, entered and whispered in his captain's ear.

'I fear I must go on deck, Miss Raynesford, there are some ships in our wake and they require identification. I would ask that you pass that message on to your fellow passengers, as you have been good enough to just do, but I would also request that you do so in such a fashion as to reassure them it is again nothing for which they need to be concerned.'

'Of course,' Emily replied, wondering why he had made such a point, her expression bringing out the explanation, delivered with humorous gravity. 'You see how excitable as a race they are, Miss. Let us not stimulate their passions any more than need be.'

* * *

Pearce was back on deck questioning Michael O'Hagan, who had not been paying enough attention when he went aboard to tell Pearce the number of guns carried on *Sandown Castle*, only that he had noticed some, certainly two, their calibre being unknown. But there had to be more, given any ship sailing the waters between England and the Levant needed to be able to protect itself from small-boat raiders even in peacetime. They could never carry enough to ward off a warship and licensed privateers – letters of marque – were an ever-present danger at times of conflict.

Pearce looked over the starboard rail, having articulated that very point. 'I think our friends yonder are of a different hue to the odd felucca, Michael. They are not the kind of ships to bear cargo, from what I can see, and I would not like to state without equivocation that we can outsail them.'

'If I'm going to keep serving you, I am going to need some schooling. For the love of Christ speak plain.'

'Deck there, ship dead ahead is raising more sail.'

Pearce looked up at the flag streaming out towards the prow, for the wind was near dead astern, wondering if the man in command of the merchantman could see it. Perhaps he was thinking he had three ships in pursuit.

'It might all be innocent, of course,' he murmured. 'This has to be a well-worn and busy route.'

'But?'

'Aloft, are they closing quicker than us?'

'They are, Your Honour, but not by much.'

Having observed them that did not come as a surprise, but what was required now was a touch of trigonometry.

'Mr Dorling, I need a calculation on that, just in case they are hostile. I need to know how long our merchant friend must look to his own defences before we can come to his aid.'

His master nodded, took what he needed and made for the shrouds. He did not give Pearce the look he might, for which his captain was grateful: the reckoning that a man who had been brought up in the navy from midshipman to command, would have done the sums himself.

'Pass the word to clear for action, though Mr Bellam can keep his coppers boiling for a while yet. Mr Kempshall, I will have another blast of powder, which will perhaps let our merchant friend know that at least one of the vessels in his wake is a comrade.'

'Odds, John-boy,' O'Hagan whispered, not that he needed to with the noise of the ship being prepared for battle, 'them being two?'

'Depends on the captain of what I reckon to be the ship carrying Emily. If he can fight, the case is equal. If not, it will be a hot engagement.'

Many too overheard that; but there was not even a look that indicated it was not a fight they needed to get into.

CHAPTER TWENTY-THREE

Noon allowed Pearce to establish his position and to then calculate, with his master, how much sailing time, if the wind held true, the merchantman would need to raise the harbour of Palermo. The best guess, and luck would play a part, was at or near first light, which meant she would be required to fend off an attack, there being no alternative. *Larcher* being dead astern made it impossible to calculate what kind of fight the British ship could put up, so how long that could last was a mystery.

Dorling had calculated there would be a decent gap and some hours of daylight between the brigantines closing and *Larcher* coming up; thus it was necessary to work on the assumption that she might suffer some damage and worse, could be boarded, which would be a stymie. Even holding them off, *Sandown*'s captain would be fighting against two vessels if not better armed than him, certainly with cannon more competently handled.

The man had everything set that he could and had eased off his course somewhat, yawing and jibbing to let the wind play better on his sails and that was the only thing of interest for a long time. As usual at sea, there was the feeling of standing still and no certainty, either, of what was unfolding; it was perfectly possible that what Pearce saw as potential threats, much as he doubted it for the lack of identifying flags, might be on an entirely innocent voyage of their own.

'Seems to me, Your Honour, they are the same we saw two days past.'

This information came from the man who had just been relieved from his duties aloft and Pearce did not trouble to ask him how certain he was; if he had been that he would have said so. All he could do was advance the time of the crew's dinner so that should they get into a battle they would at least do so with contented bellies.

Yet there was one fact he wanted to make clear, which involved calling both watches to assemble in front of the binnacle before they, with a few exceptions, were allowed to get to where their tables would have been; with the ship cleared for fighting they would have to eat sitting on the deck.

'We may have got to where we are for one purpose, which I know all of you can guess. But I must tell you that from what I can see around us I would close with the *Sandown Castle* regardless of any personal interest. She is a British trading vessel and therefore entitled to our protection, and what is closing on her stern means, if they are hostile, we must act as if we are where we are by pure accident.'

The faces before him, assembled in a fashion that only pertained on Sundays, looked different from those on the sanctified days. There was no piety in their expressions – many, like Michael O'Hagan, said their own prayers while he read out the Articles of War – and no fear of the laws of the navy he read out on those occasions, which promised much punishment for numerous offences. They were looking belligerent now, as if trying to tell their captain they were with him.

'The task is to get that merchant ship into a safe harbour and if needs must we will suffer to gain her the time. But as soon as I feel we have given her the space to achieve that I doubt the action, should there be one, will continue. The odds are too great so be prepared to run and get out of our ship a speed we have never previously achieved, for I fear we will need it.'

If he sounded full of certainty John Pearce, once he had sent them below, was far from that; he knew there was no disgrace, even in such a fighting fellowship as the Royal Navy, to shy away from an obviously unwinnable battle. It was never acceptable to just sacrifice your ship for what could be seen as personal glory, and stories he had heard of courts martial told of a number of commanders roundly condemned for doing so.

This might be that very kind of occasion and though he cared not for the risk to himself if he declined the action or pursued it, he had more of a concern for those who might suffer if it did come to a fight. This obliged him to gnaw over his reasons for proceeding, given the outcome, even if *Sandown Castle* turned out to be a terrier, was on the very cusp of uncertainty. Would he really have continued without the love of his life being in danger?

The die had not yet been irrevocably cast, so he had the luxury of considering possible outcomes and the varying factors needing to be assessed. It was moot if the armament of his potential enemies were much greater in calibre than his own; it was the number that counted and there he was on the losing side of the ledger, for he only had eight cannon to set against their twenty combined. What he would not give for a couple of carronades!

Having accepted that, it was not all in the other vessel's favour. *HMS Larcher* was of a design, fore-and-aft rigged, with that damn great bowsprit close to half again her own length, that made her more manoeuvrable than a brigantine and certainly more so than a full square-rigger; added to that he had a fine and fully worked-up crew.

Yet some of that advantage in manoeuvre disappeared when in combat. It was dangerous to have a full suit of headsails set when guns were going off. Added to that area of canvas, the risk of setting it alight himself notwithstanding, the rigging and bowsprit that supported it represented a target to anyone seeking to disable him. There was the chance, his vessel being a large version of the designated rating, to raise some square sails if he had to come up into the wind, but to do that as well as fight was asking for a lot from his men.

'Activity on deck, Your Honour,' came the cry from the poor soul aloft who would have to wait for his victuals and probably consume them cold. 'Looks to me as if they are clearing away their guns.'

Given their twin masts were in plain view from the deck, Pearce put a telescope of his own on them and that allowed him to see something which made his heart near stop and fixed his determination to proceed. He did not need the man aloft to tell him that flags had broken out on both mastheads, nor that they were black with four white crescents surrounding a two bladed sword. That was the pennant of North African pirates and the thought that Emily might fall into such hands meant he would see every man aboard *Larcher* dead rather than let that happen.

'Damn me, where is the navy when you need them?' Captain Fleming demanded, to no one in particular; the only person on the poop with him being his first mate. 'And why was I told that ships such as these were paid our English gold to stay in port?'

Behind him his crew were working to clear the decks of hen coops, barrels, spare hatch covers and untidy coils of rope, for a merchant vessel was not navy and a clear deck was far from a prerequisite. They would have to load the cannon soon, a half-dozen pieces, twenty-eight pounders that were likely to be of a heavier metal than his trio of pursuers. Not that size would avail him of much, for he had a crew ill trained to employ them.

They would have to be prepared, loaded then run up against the ports, and when it came to firing them off it was one side or the other, for they would need to be immediately reloaded and he lacked the crew numbers to service both. Fleming had already calculated that nightfall would not save him and anyway, with a wind coming in a few points off due north it would be a clear night with both starlight and a moon to contend with.

'Captain, forgive me for troubling you, but your guests are being made anxious by the activity.'

'Miss Raynesford,' Fleming replied, raising his hat as he wondered by what right she thought she could just ascend to his poop without permission. 'You should not be here, it is not your place.'

His tone, which unknown to her was partly brought on by worry, caused some irritation and a sharp response.

'I do not recall when booking my passage being told there were parts of the ship barred to me, and I would point out to you that I have many times had the freedom of King's ships.' Seeing that left an explanatory gap, she added, 'I am betrothed to a naval officer.'

The lie about betrothal seemed to come easily, but Emily was wondering if she was blushing for it. Just then *Larcher* fired off another blast of black powder, which distracted Fleming and his first mate, then had his passenger asking the purpose.

'I do not know, Miss, only that it has happened more than once. If it is a demand to heave to, it is one I intend to ignore.'

Emily had moved from the top of the steps to the taffrail and looked out, her hand shading her eyes, in the process ignoring a hiss of disapproval from Fleming. She did not recognise the vessel, never having seen *Larcher* bow-on and in full sail. Besides, with all its canvas set and stiffly drawing, the hull was well hidden. A swift turn of the head showed to her the other pair, somewhat closer even to an untrained eye, and being off the larboard quarter their flags were just visible, if mysterious to her.

'Do you know of these fellows, Captain?'

'They are nothing with which you need concern yourself.'

'Then why, pray, are your crew unloosing the cannon?'

'A precaution, no more,' he lied, for those black flags were no more a mystery to him than any other sailor who traversed these seas: they signalled murder for adult men and hell for the women and young boys.

'Captain Fleming, if I am in some danger I would be better off if I knew, and that, I would suggest, might apply to the rest of your passengers.'

'You want them running around like headless chickens. Panic will not aid us.'

If it was not a shout, Emily's response was close to one. 'Panic will not aid what?'

It was the first mate who noticed that this female passenger was able to stand without a handhold on a rising and falling deck, which was singular: most could barely take a step without a stumble and he whispered this fact in his superior's ear, which changed the angry look on Fleming's face. That countenance was typical of the breed: full weather-beaten cheeks, a purplish nose that attested to his drinking habit and a voice that betrayed his origins as a West Countryman.

'We have three vessels in our wake, and we are unsure of their purpose. On such a busy route as this, sailing in company is not unknown, but from what I can observe none of the vessels is of a size to be a bearer of cargo. Certainly the fellow firing off blank shot is way too small.'

Still at the taffrail Emily looked aft, and far from reassured – she had the impression Fleming was seeking to evade the truth – she mentally reversed what she had seen many times from the deck of *HMS Larcher*, acres of arched canvas, which led to an obvious conclusion.

Emily imparted what she suspected as softly as the wind would allow. 'One of them may be in search of me, sir.'

About to ask why, Fleming stopped himself; a beautiful young woman such as she, in flight, had to have as cause a crisis of the heart. 'Look closely and see if you can name her for me.'

'Would I be allowed your telescope, sir?'

'It is not an easy instrument to employ.'

'For a novice, sir, which I am not.'

Taking it from Fleming, Emily put it to her eye and swiftly

adjusted it, lifting it a fraction to examine what she could see of the vessel that interested her from prow to the top of its single mast, as well as the indistinct countenance of the man who sat in the crosstrees. It was his shape more than the face, that and the billowing linen he was wearing, too white to be the garment of a mere sailor.

'I think you will find, sir, that the vessel you have indicated is an armed cutter named *HMS Larcher* and the man in command is a Lieutenant John Pearce.'

'In pursuit of you, Miss Raynesford?'

'I expect so.'

Fleming smiled, for he had a chance to tease her and if she thought it inappropriate she had no idea just how seriously so it was; he was still unwilling to impart how much trouble they might be in.

'Then should I heave to?'

'No!'

The boom of another cannon split the air but this time there was no smoke from the fellow who had just been named. This time it came from one of the brigantines and it was not merely powder, it was a ranging round shot which if it fell well into their wake, told the man who had ordered it fired just how long it would be before he could strike home to cause damage.

'Damnation,' Fleming shouted, shaking a useless fist.

'What does that tell you, Captain?' Emily asked.

'It indicates that we are in some difficulty, which I had hoped was not the case. Now, if you would be so good as to go below, the deck is not going to be the place for a lady for some time to come.'

As she obeyed, she failed to hear what Fleming added in talking to his first mate. 'Have a pistol loaded and set aside. If what is coming goes badly, Miss Raynesford should be offered the option of not succumbing to a life of carnal slavery.'

'And the rest of our passengers?'

'They are not from our country and thus we cannot concern ourselves as we would for one of our own. Now let us get at least one side of our cannon loaded, for I have to find a way to confound the ease with which those sods reckon to take us.'

'Fell well short,' said Charlie Taverner, who had a good pair of eyes and had seen the plume of water sent up by that ranging shot. 'Sod'll need to do better than that.'

'So will we by the looks of it, Charlie.'

'A'feart, Rufus?'

'Ain't human not to be,' came the reply, as the freckled youngster looked aloft to where his captain had placed himself. 'What is it about Pearce that he gets into so many scrapes and against high odds?'

'Sups with the devil, most like.'

'Get away, Charlie.'

They were stood over a grinding wheel, with all the ship's swords in barrels at their side, one half full of those now razor-edged, the other holding those yet to be sharpened. Elsewhere, muskets and pistols were being primed, loaded and their hammers carefully closed, to be put in racks under the hammock nettings in which they would rest secure and not go off by misadventure.

Aloft, Pearce had likewise seen the shot and discerned its purpose, the landing of which told him more than Dorling's trigonometry calculations about how much time he would have between the pirates ranging alongside *Sandown Castle* and he getting close enough to employ his own cannon. It was not a thought to make him sanguine.

Against that, these brigantines would have seen his flag and would know he was hostile to them, so he had to reckon they were banking on one of two things for success: him deciding the odds were too great or their carrying the merchantman before he could intervene. Having had his glass trained on the stern of the ship, he had seen the female figure on the poop and even if it was not certain, he was sure in his own mind it was Emily.

His thighs were aching from being sat in such an unfamiliar position, pains that the men who normally occupied the spot were no doubt immune to. Shifting did little good, providing only a few seconds of less discomfort, and in truth he was not doing any good up here other than occupying his own mind.

Down below all was ready, the fires for the coppers now doused and one of the ship's boats loaded with what livestock they carried within the ship – the chickens in their coop, a pig and a small calf that Bellam had bought in Leghorn, as well as the ship's goat, all ready to be put over the side and out of harm's way. When the first shot was fired the line holding it to the ship would be cast off.

'Mr Dorling,' he shouted, 'I doubt those fellows yonder think us friends, but let us emulate them and give them a waterspout to look at. It may alter their thinking.'

Pearce resisted the temptation to pun and term it a long shot; this was no time for levity. The gun was fired, sending forward on the wind another billowing cloud of black smoke, the smell of which rose to hit the captain's nostrils. He watched the ball, fired high, land well short, which meant an impressive plume of water, or, he could not help but think, a signal to a potential enemy that he was a dolt.

Pearce nearly slipped off the pole on which he was sat – only his leg hooked round a yard prevented it – as he saw the *Sandown Castle* suddenly yaw in a more telling way than previously, to present its side to the approaching brigantines. One by one it fired its cannon, sending up spouts of water alongside the leading adversary, a signal that the merchantman had heavier ordnance and intended to use it now the target was within their range.

Obviously the man had his crew on the sheets for they were hauled hard before the smoke cleared and the yards, which had swung loose, were pulled back to take the wind, the canvas billowing out as the way came back on to the vessel. If he had lost time by the manoeuvre, the man in charge had told those seeking to overhaul him of his intention to fight.

'Perhaps you are a terrier after all, sir.'

The way the pair of brigantines checked their speed was the next surprise, which left John Pearce puzzled as to why. They had the ability to manoeuvre in a way denied to a broad-beamed merchant vessel and the option of ranging along two sides, which the *Sandown Castle* would struggle to reply to, given it would take seven or eight men to reload each of her cannon and they would not be either as numerous or as nimble as the navy with swabbing and ramming.

'They fear for their hulls,' he said to himself, that being the only conclusion he could draw. 'And maybe their masts.'

The more he gnawed on that the more sense it made: if a British fleet with a secure base and local ports to go to had that as a problem, how much more so a vessel without a nearby haven into which they could sail, for if they were, as their flag claimed, from

Barbary, there was not an anchorage capable of providing repair that would welcome them within a hundred miles.

He felt better, for the odds had evened if not tipped; the nature of the contest had changed and he knew he must send to them the impression that he would sacrifice his ship to protect his fellow countryman, for he was sure they would not. Tucking the telescope into a loop of rope set there for the purpose, Pearce grabbed a backstay and, hand over hand, slid down to the deck.

'Mr Dorling, we will maintain our present suit of sails until we have loosed off our first broadside.'

'Am I allowed to say there is risk in that, sir.'

'Never fear to say to me that I am wrong, Mr Dorling, for the whole ship's company is well aware of how often that is the case.'

Every man who could see their captain was gifted a wide grin, which cheered them: if John Pearce was up for the fight and in that mood, things must be on the up.

'I intend to visit some surprises on yonder fellows; that, Mr Dorling, will be the first.'

CHAPTER TWENTY-FOUR

The entire nature of the potential fight had changed; the brigantines were splitting up, but doing so at a slower rate of sailing than hitherto. Watching them, Pearce could work out the tactic, which would be to come within long range of the *Sandown*'s cannon and get them to loose off a salvo.

The man working out how to proceed was no fool: he knew what kind of crew such a vessel carried, could analyse their proficiency, and while one vessel took a risk the other could seek to get closer on the other beam. The action would be reversed until an opening came in which one could get alongside and board.

If either could get men on to the deck of the merchantman and overcome resistance the cannon then became the weapon of the corsairs, which threw all the advantage their way, for they would have three sets of ordnance to employ against *HMS Larcher*, added to which the heavier-calibre cannon, worked by men who better knew their trade, would mean suicide for any attempt at rescue. If the odds had shifted they still looked unfavourable.

Unbeknown to John Pearce he had a soulmate in Captain Fleming. The man had been at sea since he was a toddler, his father having been a merchant captain and uxorious enough to wish to sail in the company of his wife, as well as his numerous children. If he was wont to bluster a bit, and had a questionable sense of humour, he could see what needed to be done to preserve his vessel: Fleming knew that if he did not somehow combine with the approaching armed cutter he was in danger of being taken.

As soon as the corsairs split up he spun his wheel to get across the wake of the one to his south-east, taking advantage of his square rig and greater area of canvas to try and steal his wind, but he was not content with that. His cannon boomed once more and if the firing lacked accuracy it did not suffer for effect; the brigantine he was challenging put down her own helm very sharply to widen the gap.

His consort on the other beam thought this to be a chance and aimed his prow for the side of *Sandown Castle*, but Fleming's precaution of loading all his cannon meant that those on his starboard side were ready as soon as the ports were open and the weapons were run out. The enemy found himself closing at a rate that would make anything that hit him serious, but his only way to avoid that was to let fly his own sheets, so he came to a near halt before seeking to get his cannon to bear.

The exchange left both vessels wreathed in smoke out of which came the red spouts of angry flame. The corsair hit home and even through the haze Pearce could see wood flying, deadly splinters that would slice into any flesh it encountered, to either wound, maim or kill. What he could not see was that down below, as she had done in the past, Emily Barclay had cleared a space and had raided Fleming's chests for the means to deal with wounds, this while her fellow passengers cowered in various places pleading with God to save them.

A swift swing of his telescope showed Pearce that one of the merchant guns had hit a sail, leaving a great hole in the canvas, this as the captain of that vessel shifted his own wheel to get clear. It was a moment of crisis: if the second pirate ship could get alongside his quarry *Sandown* was doomed.

What saved her was that sail plan again, for it took nearly all of its opponent's wind, more and more the closer he sought to close, and that allowed time for the men on the merchantman to reload. If it was not more than five minutes, it seemed like a Creation age from the deck of *Larcher*, where they aimed to get off two salvoes in much less than two minutes. Of necessity, the aim was wild, more designed to scare off than to wound.

'How long, Mr Dorling?'

'There's hardly a grain of sand left in the glass, Your Honour, and we'll be in range.'

Time, Pearce thought, to pick his own target. The obvious one and closest to him was the vessel on the larboard beam of *Sandown*, but the fellow to starboard was struggling with his wind and if Pearce could get to him with that in his favour then all the advantage lay with him. It was a chance to change the odds entirely in his favour and so not to be missed.

'Set me on the starboard beam.'

'Aye, aye, sir,' Dorling said, as he eased the wheel to comply.

It was immediately obvious that the other corsair was not going to stand by and see his consort suffer, for he got his foremast yards round to draw on that same wind and get, if not in the path of the armed cutter, certainly into a position to inflict damage, which had Pearce wondering if his notion of keeping set a full suit of canvas was going to turn out to be a mistake.

'Mr Bird, I want those larboard cannon aimed as far forward as is possible. We must strike that fellow yonder before he strikes us.'

How different it was aboard this to something more generously proportioned, like a ship of the line. There the captain would have half a dozen officers standing by on batteries of cannon waiting to open fire, to then follow that with speedy salvoes and firing at will. Here he had a man who carried out a whole host of other duties when not fighting, but had to step into this breach in action. He would only do that which he was told; Pearce controlled every gun as well as its timing.

The rammers were under the trunnions within seconds, levering them until the side of the muzzles rested against the edge of the open port, this while his enemy came on. Pearce knew that he would soon have to put down his own helm so that his guns could bear and it was a case of who would judge it right first. On this occasion the captain of *HMS Larcher*, wanting to badly wound, waited a fraction too long.

The brigantine began its turn early and because of that beat Pearce to the advantage; the enemy guns spoke first, only a few seconds before those of the armed cutter, for sure, but that was significant, for it was enemy cannon imposing confusion before those of *Larcher* could do likewise. His man had wisely loaded his cannon with chain shot, no doubt intended to wound *Sandown*

Castle but equally, if not even more deadly against a vessel that had its full suit of sails still set.

Larcher's headsails were ripped to shreds, with blocks falling and ropes flying everywhere as they were either split by chain shot or came under too much increase in strain to hold. It was only by good luck that the bowsprit, vital to sail an armed cutter, was left unwounded. If it was a plus that *Larcher* had taken great chunks out of the enemy scantlings, it was poor recompense for the loss of speed that had been inflicted.

The choice to quickly reload had been taken away from Pearce – he needed that flapping canvas out of the way and some replacement to the upper headsails to give him steerage way, and in this he found out just how proficient was the crew he commanded. While some reloaded, albeit slower than they would normally, others rushed to retie lines and ropes and to get attached those sails that were still of use; sad to say, others were dragging wounded men to the companionway.

'Gunners, aim for the hull.'

With his enemy still closing it was now a race to reload that Pearce reckoned he must lose, only to find that endless training now paid a dividend. If he did not beat his man to the punch they fired simultaneously, and the wedges having been knocked out from under his muzzles, the shot, at what was a much closer range, slammed into the enemy hull.

One *Larcher* ball went clean through the forward part just above the waterline, which on a fast-sailing vessel was dangerous, and luckily his enemy failed to capitalise on his earlier success. If it was only a subconscious thought, Pearce was again reckoning that training would tell. Under fire his men would carry out their tasks by habit; men less well honed would rush their reloading and even more so the way they aimed.

HMS Larcher had not completely lost way but her ability to both sail and manoeuvre was badly compromised, and even if he could count some success, Pearce still had two enemies to fight and the other one was heading to catch him between two fires, ignoring *Sandown Castle* on the very wise principle that if they could see off this warship then the merchantman must easily fall.

He did not have the advantage in any area other than the speed of his gunnery, which left Pearce no choice but to invite his enemies into a slogging match of exchanged cannonballs and chain shot. His aim was to so scare them that, if he had guessed right, they would sheer off for fear of sustaining wounds beyond repair. There was no standing around like a statue now; if it was a small deck he traversed it all, kicking out of the way fallen blocks and bits of rigging and wood to encourage his men.

His voice became hoarse from shouting as he ordered those seeking to effect emergency repairs to belay and man the cannon on both sides. One battery had yet to be fired and that he saved for the second brigantine, not that he had the choice now to spin and engage his original opponent.

He was calling for those supplying the guns to emulate his enemies and get up from below some bar shot so he could scythe the enemy rigging in the way they had done to him. With what he was sure he had, superior skill, he would be able to alternate firing at hull and rigging so his enemies would not know what next to expect.

With a brigantine on either beam now, what followed was murderous and it was only after several salvoes that he realised he had, if not taken the initiative, evened matters up: his cannon were being loaded at near twice the speed of his enemies and his shot, with more studious aiming, was striking home with more effect. The hulls of both brigantines were holed and their rigging had suffered, albeit not to the measure of his own.

Yet in the cacophony of noise and the billowing acrid smoke, Pearce also knew how his vessel was suffering; it could not be otherwise and he was losing men, which if a bloody-minded captain would not have taken into consideration, Pearce could not countenance. Also, he suspected that if anything major went, like his main and only mast, he would be at the mercy of his enemies. Yet he had a friend: *Sandown Castle* had come about and was labouring to come to his aid against the wind, which presented a solution to what was fast becoming a fight he could not win.

'Mr Dorling, we need some sail set and we must get way on the ship. You see to that and I will take the wheel.'

It was with admiration, and also with much ducking as shots were aimed in his direction, that he watched Dorling, and the man was not alone, go about his duties as if there was no battle taking place. From his vantage point he could see Charlie and Rufus plying one gun, with Michael O'Hagan on another, all black from head to foot now but toiling away. His master soon had men knotting and splicing, a feat under fire and one not without casualties, but soon they had canvas rigged which would bear a load of wind.

As he began to pull out of the zone of deadly danger his opponents were forced to react, for their prows were facing counter to that of *Larcher* and they were now making a desperate attempt to swing round to close and trap him by fouling what rigging he had assembled; if that was a worry it meant the firing of cannon had dropped away.

The armed cutter was moving like a tub, but it was progressing and Pearce aimed the prow then lashed off the wheel, before running to the side and plucking out a musket, shouting that anyone idle should do likewise. Taking an aim he suspected to be useless – the short Sea Service Brown Bess was notoriously inaccurate – he tried to shoot the man on the wheel on the nearest enemy deck, this to disrupt what he was being ordered to do.

It failed completely: the bowsprits were round and aiming for *Larcher* amidships, though the brigantines had practically nothing in the line of cannon they could bring to bear, and what guns Pearce had that were still firing began to take chunks out of the enemy bows.

'Arm yourselves with axes,' he shouted to one group. 'If they foul our rigging, get us clear.'

He grabbed one of the swords his Pelicans had been sharpening and set himself to use it, only then realising that his activities had opened the wound inflicted by Lipton. That, apart from an odd twinge, was an injury he had forgotten. He was bleeding again but that did not signify in such a contest; had he stopped to look he would have seen that half his crew had some kind of wound and it had to be the case that some of them, taken below, had succumbed to much worse.

Larcher was so very nearly pinned, only just escaping the trap, but now Pearce had two vessels on his stern, which exposed him to their broadsides. It was hunger for the trophy that saved him, for both men in command wanted to see their cannonballs run the length of his ship, the best way to kill and the sure way to disable an enemy.

They got in each other's way, which led to a panicked effort to back off and avoid them snagging their own rigging. This meant that very few cannon actually fired and nothing hit anything vital, except a ball that, with a loud clang, caught a muzzle and ricocheted off into the sea. Pearce was back on the wheel, shouting through a rasping throat to people seeking to still effect repairs, willing his vessel to go faster by pushing at the wheel, so desperate was he.

And there before him was *Sandown Castle*, inching towards *Larcher* at no greater speed. He could see the man on the forepeak, the captain by his braided coat, urging him on and he needed no encouragement. Pearce did not see the block that broke his arm, how could he since it fell from above, sliced from its place by round shot, gunfire which had recommenced. Perhaps if he had not had such a firm grip on the spoke of the wheel it would have done less harm.

The weight of the triple block took him to the deck and he only knew the bone was gone when he sought to put his weight upon that arm, his scream of pain loud enough to carry over the mayhem all around. The blackened face that appeared above him was welcome indeed, as was the Irish accent, Michael aiding him to his feet.

'Get Mr Dorling on the wheel, we must come alongside *Sandown Castle*.'

'Take it easy, John-boy, you're hurt.'

'Tell them to lash us off to their side and if they wish to do so fire through our rigging, but to avoid the mast.'

Michael was heading him for the companionway, which would take them below, but Pearce steadied his feet, dug them in and refused to budge. Looking down at his useless arm Pearce actually shouted at his friend.

'Get me a line and lash this bastard to my body, then stay by my side, for I will need you.'

'What in the name of Jesus do you intend?'

'To win, Michael, what else?'

Dorling was by his side now. 'Orders, Captain?'

'Get us tied to that dammed merchantman, then get everyone aboard with all the weapons they can bear. We are going to invite these swine to board and, by Harry, if they do it will be a bloody deck that we drive them off.'

Without orders, the likes of Charlie and Rufus had got grappling irons ready and as soon as they were close enough these were cast to hook the side of *Sandown Castle* and men hauled heartily to bring the two vessels together, which they did with a horrible crunch. Lines came down from the higher deck and like something from a fairground show the men of the armed cutter swarmed up onto the deck of the merchantman, having thrown up every weapon they could before they left.

Michael O'Hagan lifted his friend bodily and so high that he could be taken by the armpits and hauled onto his companion deck. This was not without agony, and Pearce bit his lip so hard it bled; better that than he should bleat. It took a moment for Pearce to contain his pain, this when he stood holding onto a hammock netting, but he still saw himself in command and he was not prepared to relinquish that responsibility.

'If they board you cannot fight, John-boy.'

'Put a weapon in my left hand.'

'Christ in heaven, the number of times I have wanted to do this.'

It was not the complete Pelican punch, but it was enough to floor John Pearce, who never saw the attempt to board, missed the fight on the deck that saw the corsair soundly beaten and forced to withdraw, did not hear the jeers of his crew and that of *Sandown Castle*. When he woke his arm was in splints and he was being administered to by Emily. He had no idea that half the night had passed and if those same enemies were trailing the ship, which was towing *HMS Larcher* now, they were not seeking to close.

'You are a hard man to leave, John Pearce.'

'Then,' he replied, 'would it not be best to cease to try?'

'A conversation, my love, for the time we are safe in harbour.'

'I cannot see myself parted from you, Emily, and I have a notion—'

'Enough!' she commanded. 'Put it aside for now.'

The ships that entered Palermo harbour the next day, at noon, looked a sorry sight, none more so than *HMS Larcher*, much damaged and her rigging in tatters. Worse was the butcher's bill, with ten of his crew dead, while the lazaretto held two dozen more with wounds of various severity. John Pearce, ambulant if weak, was depressed by his examination of both and said so.

'Some of my men have perished and many more bear wounds. I will have to explain this somehow, Emily, which I feel I could do with Lord Hood, who would see that if I suffered harm I saved a British merchant vessel.'

'Surely you will not be censured?'

'If Hotham has taken command, I will struggle to avoid it.'

'This is no time to fret on that, John. There is only one thing I fret on, and you know only too well what that is, so damn Sir William Hotham.'

* * *

In San Fiorenzo Bay, the heart of that admiral lifted as he saw the topsails of *HMS Victory* finally disappear. He was now in command of the Mediterranean Fleet and Hood could whistle to confound him. He had many avenues he wished to explore and he was sure that in time he would find a way to bring the French fleet to battle and inflict on them a resounding defeat, one that would assure him a place in the peerage of England. Yet there were other matters equally pressing and so he called in his clerk.

'Toomey, fetch me the correspondence relating to that Pasha fellow in old Illyria, Mehmet I seem to recall is his name. A capricious fellow and murderous too, I am told. I have a feeling there are one or two coves to whom I feel the need to introduce him.'

To discover more great books and to
place an order visit our website at
www.allisonandbusby.com

Don't forget to sign up to our free newsletter at
www.allisonandbusby.com/newsletter
for latest releases, events and exclusive offers

 Allison & Busby Books
 @AllisonandBusby

You can also call us on
020 7580 1080
for orders, queries
and reading recommendations